CW01551647

A PLAY FOR LOVE

THE SCOTTISH BILLIONAIRES

M. S. PARKER

BELMONTE PUBLISHING, LLC

Copyright © 2023 Belmonte Publishing LLC

Published by Belmonte Publishing LLC

READING ORDER

.

ONE

LONDON

"THANK YOU," THE DIRECTOR SHOUTED, WAVING HIS hand and gesturing for me to stop singing. I let out a long breath and stepped off the majestic stage at the famous old Broadway theater. The creak of the floorboards beneath my feet reminded me of the countless performers who had stood in my place, hoping for their big break. Auditioning for the national tour of Les Misérables was a dream come true, and the jitters building inside me all day faded away as I sensed the room's energy change. It felt like I had nailed it. The director's smile and the casting crew's excited chatter confirmed it.

My best friend, Gin, had been by my side throughout all the grueling hours of preparation and stood there with a beaming grin on her face.

"London, girl, you killed it out there!" she said, pulling me into a tight hug.

"Thanks, Gin," I said, a huge grin spreading across my face. "I couldn't have done it without you."

"Shoot, you didn't need me," she replied, waving a dismissive hand. "You were slaying it all on your own. I could tell from the way you were belting out 'On My Own' during rehearsals that you were going to knock their socks off."

The director sauntered over with a wide grin on his face, extending his hand to me. "Wonderful audition, London. You really brought Éponine to life on stage. We were all blown away."

I felt my heart skip a beat as a small, excited squeal escaped my lips. "Thank you so much! I worked really hard on this."

He chuckled, shaking my hand firmly. "Trust me, it shows. We'll be in touch soon to let you know if you got the part, but for now, I just wanted to share how impressed we all were with your audition."

It was impossible not to beam with pride at his words. It was a surreal moment, and I was grateful for the recognition.

After gathering my belongings, Gin and I exited the theater, basking in the afterglow of my audition. The energy of Broadway buzzed around us, the sound of car horns and people chatting filling the air. I took a deep breath, trying to process everything that had just happened.

"Girl, that was amazing!" Gin exclaimed, linking her arm with mine. "I knew you had it in you."

I smiled, feeling a warm rush of gratitude for her support. "Thanks, Gin. You're the best."

With a specific target in mind, we walked along the crowded street, the thrum of excitement building with every step. Finally, we arrived at our destination - a cozy pub with warm lighting and vintage posters of past Broadway shows adorning the walls. The place was packed with fellow actors and theater fans, all chattering excitedly about the upcoming shows.

We found a cozy spot at a small pub table and took a seat, the dim lighting and vintage posters creating the perfect ambiance for our post-audition celebration. I ordered us each a cold pint of beer and we clinked our glasses together before taking a long sip.

"Cheers to a successful audition!" Gin said, grinning from ear to ear.

I laughed. "Cheers to surviving the nerves and belting out Éponine's heart-wrenching ballads without completely breaking down."

Gin raised her glass. "To that!"

As we sipped our beers, we chatted about the upcoming tour and what it would be like to travel the country performing on legendary stages. Gin and I had known each other for years and studied theater together at Boston University. Even though Gin never had the same aspirations as me to make it on Broadway, she still took on minor roles in off-Broadway shows and was always my biggest supporter. I truly loved her for that.

As we chatted and sipped our beers, two tall, good-looking guys came over with charming smiles. One of them said, "Hey, excuse me, we couldn't help but notice you two. We're actors too, just like you."

I raised an eyebrow. "Oh really? And what gave us away?"

The first guy flashed a grin. "Come on, you both look like you were born to be on stage. The theater world would miss out on two stunning ladies if you weren't actors."

Gin rolled her eyes. "Smooth talker. So, what show are you guys in?"

The second guy spoke up, "We're actually in 'Hamilton.'"

"Wow, impressive," I said, trying to sound nonchalant.

"But sorry guys, it's girls' night tonight. Maybe we'll run into each other again sometime."

The first guy persisted, "Aw, come on. Let us buy you a round of drinks."

Gin chuckled. "Thanks, but we're good."

The guys shrugged and walked away. I couldn't help but steal a glance at the first guy, noticing his charming smile and good looks. It had been a very long time since I'd been on a date.

"Well, that was unexpected," I said, turning to Gin with a grin.

"Being in the theater world, you never know who you'll run into," she replied.

I clinked my glass with hers. "But tonight, it's just us girls."

Gin laughed. "Agreed."

"I can't believe you're going to be in Les Mis!" Gin exclaimed, overflowing with excitement.

I grinned, taking a swig of my beer. "I know, right? But let's not count our chickens before they hatch," I said.

"Please," Gin rolled her eyes. "You nailed it. The director and his team were all over you. You've got this."

My stomach grumbled loudly, and I rubbed it sheepishly. "Speaking of nailing things, I'm starving. Let's order some food."

After flagging down the waitress and placing our order, we chatted about the show's potential and what it would be like to tour. Gin was already making plans to visit me wherever the show took me.

"You're going to be a star, London," she said, raising her glass. "I can feel it."

As soon as our food arrived, the tantalizing aroma of crispy chicken tenders and fries filled the air, making our stomachs grumble even louder. We eagerly dug in, savoring each bite with relish. In between mouthfuls, we chatted and giggled, enjoying the moment and the unbreakable bond of our friendship. It was in these simple moments, surrounded by good food and splendid company, that I knew I was exactly where I was meant to be.

An hour later, after finishing our meal, I let out a content sigh, feeling satisfied and relaxed. "I hate to say it, but I'm beat. I'm ready to head home," I said with a stretch.

"What? No way, we can't call it a night yet," Gin protested, pouting.

"I know, but my bed is calling my name," I replied with a smile. "I promise we'll have another girls' night soon."

"Come on, just one more drink or we can go clubbing. It'll be fun!" Gin begged, her eyes shining.

"I appreciate the offer, but I'm not as young as I used to be. I need my beauty sleep," I said with a chuckle.

"Oh, come on. You're always so responsible. Live a little! Let your hair down! Dance the night away!" Gin said, trying to persuade me.

"Thanks, but I need to save my energy for the tour."

"Fine, but don't come crying to me when you're old and gray, regretting not going clubbing when you had the chance," Gin said, pretending to pout.

"I'll live vicariously through your Instagram stories," I replied with a grin.

Gin laughed and gave me a hug. "Okay, I'll let you off the hook this time. But we're going out next time, no excuses."

"Deal," I replied.

While Gin stayed, I said goodbye and headed home, feeling pumped and ready for the tour. The thought of traveling the country, performing on legendary stages, and working with top-notch actors and crew was exhilarating. It would be hard work and long hours but being part of such a famous production would make it all worth it. I was eager for what was to come and the memories that awaited me.

With a smile on my face and a bounce in my step, I walked home, ready for anything.

———

THE SOUND of my phone ringing, the piercing noise cutting through my headache, woke me. The bright sunlight shining through my curtains and the city smells coming in through my open window reminded me of the previous night's celebration. I felt the familiar ache of a hangover as I groggily picked up the phone and saw Gin's name flash on the screen. I answered, trying to sound upbeat, "Hey, what's up?"

"London, I have some bad news," Gin said, her voice heavy with disappointment.

My heart sank. "What happened?" I asked, already dreading the answer.

"I went to the club last night and ran into the director of Les Misérables' boyfriend. He told me they're going with someone else for the role. Some Hollywood big shot's grand-daughter got it just because of her connections," Gin explained, sounding angry on my behalf.

I couldn't believe what I was hearing. It felt like a punch to the gut. I had given it my all and felt so sure that the part was mine. I was angry, frustrated and completely heartbroken.

"This is such bullshit," I said, feeling the tears flow. "Why do things always have to be so unfair?"

"I know, I know," Gin said, trying to offer some comfort.

"It sucks, but don't let this get you down. You're too talented to let one setback define you."

"But it's not just one setback," I said, my voice cracking. "It is constant rejection and disappointment. How much more can I take?"

"You're a fighter, London. You'll get through this," Gin said, her voice full of encouragement.

As we said our goodbyes, I lay in my bed, staring at the ceiling, feeling defeated, hungover, and wondering what could have been, the bitter taste of rejection still in my mouth.

TWO
SPENCER

As the curtain came down on my hit show's performance in London's West End, I felt a rush of excitement. The crowd erupted into applause, with cries of "Bravo!" and "Encore!" ringing through the theater. I took a deep breath, soaking up the energy of the space and feeling grateful for the journey that led to this moment. Despite the long nights and endless rehearsals, it had all been worth it.

But it was bittersweet. After a year of sold-out shows and critical success, it was time for a break. The theater needed renovations, so we were going on a six-month hiatus.

I should have been delighted, but a nagging sense of uncertainty lingered in the back of my mind. I had made plans with a director to set up another show during the hiatus, but those plans had fallen through. It wasn't the first time this director had backed out on me, and once again, I was disappointed. But I refused to let it dampen the celebratory atmosphere of the night.

The reverberating sound from the applause was ringing in my ears. The energy of the theater still buzzed around me, and I looked around, taking it all in for one last time.

This was it.

This was why I became a theater producer. It wasn't for the money or fame. I wanted to create art. My goal was for people to associate the name Spencer York with productions that evoked emotions like joy, tears, and entertainment. Despite not having formal training in acting, set design, or music, I had a clear vision in my head and the resources to bring it to fruition.

I had come a long way since my early days as a producer, when I was still finding my footing and trying to establish myself in the industry. It certainly hadn't been easy, but I never let go of my dream to create meaningful and impactful theater. And now, here I was in one of the most prestigious theaters in London, surrounded by a cast and crew who had become like family to me.

As the applause faded and the audience headed for the exits, I made my way backstage to congratulate everybody on a brilliant performance. The excitement was palpable, with actors milling around, the scent of stage makeup and hairspray in the air, and the sounds of chatter and laughter all around. I loved every bit, and the energy of the theater was fueling my passion for the craft.

I always prided myself on being hands on with the cast and crew, taking the time to know each of them by name. I loved working with them and helping them grow as performers.

I greeted everyone, shaking hands and even hugging some. As I made my way to the dressing rooms, I came to the lead, Anjelika Pym, a talented and fresh-faced actress who made her debut in my show. Her performance had been nothing short of magnificent.

"Anjelika, my dear," I said, congratulating her as I leaned in to kiss her cheeks. "You were breathtaking tonight. I have a feeling you'll shine even brighter when you're back on stage in the renovated theater."

"Merci, Spencer," Anjelika replied with a smile, her French accent becoming more pronounced now that she was out of character. "You always know how to make a girl feel special."

I noticed a plane ticket peeking out of her purse on the dressing table. "Ah, the life of a traveling performer," I grinned. "I bet you'll be sipping café au lait and indulging in croissants every morning in Paris for the next few months? It sounds a lot more appealing than the traditional English breakfast of a greasy fry-up and a cup of lukewarm tea."

"You know me too well, Spencer," Anjelika laughed, her eyes sparkling. "I've been counting down the days until I can see my family again. It's been way too long."

With her stunning beauty and undeniable talent, Anjelika left most men mesmerized, including me. Her sparkling eyes and charming smile were a constant temptation, but I knew that acting on these feelings would be unprofessional and could harm my relationship with her and the rest of the cast.

But, oh boy, it was difficult to resist her charm. The way her costume accentuated her curves, and her accent emphasized her words. It was all incredibly tempting.

For this reason, I kept the conversation light and centered on the future, discussing plans for the upcoming hiatus and our shared excitement for returning to the renovated theater in six months.

As the place emptied, I took in the lingering energy before leaving. The costumes and sets were being packed away, the lights were dimmed, and the stage crew was wrapping up for the last time. Props were scattered, and the floor was littered with confetti, creating a beautiful mess.

As I stepped out the door, the crisp November air hit my face, sending shivers down my spine. The sky was dark, lit only by streetlamps and passing cars. The chill seeped through my coat, and I pulled it tighter around me, as the familiar scent of London, a mix of damp earth and diesel, enveloped me.

I was halfway to my car when my phone rang, and I checked the caller ID. The number wasn't familiar, but I answered it anyway.

"Spencer, how are you?"

"Stan?" I said, recognizing the voice on the other end. Stan Longley, a New Yorker in his mid-forties, came to London a few years ago to check out the scene. We had become friends and kept in touch, but him calling me out of the blue on a Saturday night was unexpected. "I'm well," I said. "Everything okay?"

"It sure is," he said with a chuckle. "Tonight was your last night before your show goes on hiatus, right?"

"Yes," I replied, surprised that he knew.

"Any plans for the next couple of months?"

My curiosity piqued, I asked, "Are you suggesting a holiday to New York?"

"Not exactly," Stan said. "I was wondering if you'd be interested in bringing your show to Broadway."

I was momentarily stunned. "You're serious?"

"Absolutely, Spencer. How about it? Are you ready to take on Broadway?"

"I-I don't know what to say," I stammered, my mind racing with the possibilities. "A Broadway production? That's a dream come true."

"Let's make it a reality, shall we?" Stan said, his voice full of excitement. "We can talk more about it tomorrow."

As I ended my conversation with Stan, I pocketed the

phone in disbelief. Broadway. The mere thought of it was overwhelming. A grin spread across my face as I felt a rush of excitement course through my body. This was definitely a cause for celebration, so instead of heading for my car, I quickened my pace towards the pub down the street, my mind racing with the possibilities.

Getting my show on the West End had been phenomenal, but Broadway was the ultimate dream. The mecca of theater, it was where the greats had made their mark. It was thrilling to think that we would perform my show on the same stage as theirs.

With determination in my step, I pushed open the door to the pub and made my way to the bar. I was ready to raise a pint to Broadway and the journey ahead. This was just the start, and I couldn't wait to see where it would lead me.

THREE
LONDON

On the bustling streets of Manhattan, I walked arm-in-arm with my three closest friends as the crisp air nipped at my cheeks. The city was alive with holiday energy, twinkling lights illuminating the streets, and the scent of roasting chestnuts and gingerbread filling the air. My friends and I made our way through the crowds of Black Friday shoppers, surrounded by the sounds of chatter and the rustling of shopping bags.

I'd just returned to New York from my brother's wedding in San Ramon, California, and I was more than ready for a change of fortune. It had been two months since my unsuccessful audition for the role of Éponine in Les Misérables, and things had just kept sliding downhill from there.

I had auditioned for half a dozen roles of varying sizes, both on and off Broadway, and only got two call backs. Unfortunately, I didn't get either of those roles.

"Did anything wild and exciting happen at Eoin's wedding?" Gin asked, mischief dancing in her hazel eyes.

Mercedes, the eldest in our group, turned to me with a wicked grin. "Please tell me you got laid."

"London isn't like you, Mercedes," Rocio, the only guy in our group, interjected with a friendly nudge. "She keeps her love life on the down-low."

I felt heat flood my cheeks. "I didn't get laid. Not that it would be anyone's business if I did."

"See?" Rocio grinned. "Like I said. She doesn't broadcast."

"But something happened," Gin pressed, her wheat-colored curls falling into her face.

I hesitated for a moment before finally sighing. "It's not that big of a deal," I said, my friends already leaning in.

"It might not be," Gin said, "but that doesn't mean it's not a story worth hearing."

"Fine, fine," I said, rolling my eyes and feeling embarrassed. "I jumped into the fountain with my sister."

"You what?!" Mercedes gasped, her eyes wide with shock and her voice filled with disbelief.

"I know," I said, holding up my hands in surrender. "It was a dumb idea, but I was feeling a little...tipsy."

"Tipsy? You must have been drunk," Gin said, her laughter echoing in the street.

"Yeah, yeah," I said, feeling sheepish. "I was hot, and it looked inviting."

"I bet you looked like a mermaid in that fountain," Rocio said.

"A very drunk mermaid," Mercedes added, still laughing.

"Hey, at least I made a splash," I joked, joining in on the laughter.

"You definitely did that," Gin said. "But let's try to keep you out of the fountains today, okay?"

"Definitely," I said. "Now, let's go find some deals before all the good stuff is gone."

"Ooh, look at those!" Mercedes pointed excitedly at a display case of sparkling crystal unicorns. "I want one!"

"You do realize that the point of Christmas shopping is to buy things for other people, right?" Rocio teased, raising an eyebrow.

She grinned at him. "Then you buy it for me."

Mercedes linked her arm with Rocio's and led him inside the store while Gin lingered with me. We browsed through a rack of silk scarves, each picking one up and examining it closely. I ran my fingers over the soft material, trying to decide if my sister-in-law would like the plum-colored one or the one with the pink roses.

"You seem like something else is bothering you," Gin said, catching my eye.

I shook my head, trying to brush it off. "It's nothing."

But Gin could tell there was more to it. "You'll get something soon," she reassured me, giving my arm a squeeze.

"Maybe," I replied, feeling a wave of discouragement wash over me.

"London, listen to me," Gin said, her tone firm. "You are an incredible actress, and you have the drive and passion to make it in this industry. You've already accomplished so much, and you have so much more to offer. Don't let one setback bring you down. You will get another opportunity, and when you do, you'll knock it out of the park."

"But what if I don't?" I asked, feeling a lump form in my throat.

"Then you'll try again, and again, and again. Failure is not the opposite of success, it's a part of it. Every successful person has failed countless times. It's how you learn, grow, and become better. And you, London, will become better. You'll get that next role, and it'll be even better than the last one. And one day, you'll be standing on that stage, accepting an award, and you'll look back at this moment and realize that it was just a minor setback in your incredible journey."

Gin could always give me a renewed sense of determination and confidence. "Thanks Gin, I needed that," I said, giving her a grateful smile.

"Anytime," she replied, giving me a hug. "Now, let's go buy some unicorns and take over Broadway!"

We laughed and headed back to join Mercedes and Rocio, ready to tackle the rest of our shopping head-on.

"I HAVE the perfect guy for you," Mercedes declared, a twinkle in her eye as we made our way to the checkout.

"Oh no, not another one of your blind dates," I groaned, already imagining the worst.

"Hey, what's that supposed to mean?" Mercedes feigned offense, but her laughter gave her away.

As we stepped out into the snowy morning, I explained, "Let's just acknowledge that your track record with men is, shall we say, less than impressive."

Mercedes shrugged, her red hair bouncing with the movement. "I beg to differ. I'm a matchmaking pro."

"Hardly," I grinned. "Remember that guy you set me up with who called his mom from the restaurant to ask what he should order for dinner? Yeah, that's what I mean."

Mercedes shrugged nonchalantly. "I thought you'd appreciate a guy who was close with his mother."

"There's close, and then there's his mom still setting out

his clothes for him every morning," I pointed out with a laugh.

"Alright, alright. You got me there," Mercedes conceded with a grin. "But please, give me one more chance. I promise, this guy is different."

I hesitated, "I don't know, Mercedes. Right now, I'm focusing on my career."

"And what's wrong with having a little fun on the side? It'll help you relax before those auditions," Mercedes said with a sly smile.

I shook my head, "I don't just sleep with anyone, Mercedes. I need to have a connection with the person, not just physical attraction."

"I understand that," Mercedes said with a nod. "And I truly believe you'll have that connection with this guy."

I raised an eyebrow skeptically.

"Just one date," Mercedes begged, grabbing my arm and leaning in. "Please let me set it up."

I sighed. "You will not let up until I agree, will you?"

"Nope," she grinned.

"Fine, you win," I said, giving in to Mercedes' pleading. "But just one date, and if he's not the one, that's it. No more dates."

Mercedes let out a triumphant whoop and broke into a celebratory jig, causing a crowd of Black Friday shoppers to stop and stare in amazement.

"Just be prepared," Gin warned with a chuckle. "If this guy turns out to be a catch, Mercedes will never let you live it down."

I wasn't worried.

"Come on," Rocio said, taking Mercedes' hand. "We've got sixteen more stores to hit before we call it a day."

"Sixteen?!" Gin exclaimed in shock. "I didn't sign up for that!"

Rocio grinned mischievously. "We never set a limit for the day."

"We should have," Gin grumbled, but her tone was playful.

"Maybe you and I can slip away for some hot chocolate while Mercedes and Rocio take on a few stores on their own," I suggested, winking at Gin.

"Hot chocolate and Christmas cookies?" Gin's face lit up with excitement. "Now you're talking."

As we walked down the crowded sidewalk, the conversation shifted from my love life to our shopping plan, and I breathed a sigh of relief. I'd go on the date, and who knows, maybe I'd find someone I'd like. Not for a relationship, but maybe for some hot, sweaty fun.

What was the worst that could happen?

FOUR
SPENCER

Mandatory family dinners were a staple of my upbringing as a member of the York family. Although they were not a weekly occurrence, attendance was expected when a dinner invitation was extended. As my sisters and I grew up and moved out of the family home, the tradition continued, though less often.

Tonight marked the first family dinner in three months, and everyone was in attendance, including my grandmother, Opal Johnston York Masters. She always emphasized her connections to powerful families by introducing herself with all three of her surnames. At seventy-nine, she stood tall at nearly six feet and was slender, yet strong. She could easily outpace people half her age.

Upon entering, she immediately focused on my father and remarked, "I see you've been cheating on your diet again, Raynard. Perhaps I should have a word with your cook."

I noticed my eldest sister, Fleur, tense up at grandmother's words, and I understood her discomfort. After the birth of her third child, Fleur had struggled to regain her pre-

pregnancy figure, and grandmother's cold, blue gaze missed no opportunity to point out any extra pounds she saw on any of us. She had had five children herself and had always returned to her regular clothing within a couple of weeks.

"Are you without your husband this evening?" Grandmother questioned Fleur, her gaze flicking down to Harrison and Matthew, who stood in front of their mother, unnaturally still for ten- and seven-year-old boys.

"Parker is taking Jane to the bathroom," Fleur replied with a forced smile. "They'll be right down."

Grandmother sniffed and moved down the line to my twin sister, Anne.

"You cut your hair again," Grandmother remarked. "If it were any shorter, you could be mistaken for your brother." Her ability to express her displeasure with both of us with a single comment impressed me.

"It's easier to take care of it this way, Grandmother," Anne replied with a polite smile that didn't quite reach her dark blue eyes. "My work keeps me pretty busy."

Grandmother's face contorted into a scowl, making her dissatisfaction clear. "All that social media silliness is interfering with your ability to fulfill your duties to the family." Grandmother raised an eyebrow. "I take it you haven't found a suitable man to settle down with yet."

Anne's smile stiffened. "No, Grandmother. I haven't had the time for dating."

"Anne's been helping me with my charity. We received recognition from his majesty this past week," my mother, Eloise DeBois York, said in a neutral tone, but the pride was clear in her voice.

Grandmother made a sound that showed she couldn't find anything lacking in the information. That alone was an accomplishment.

"And what about you, Spencer?" Grandmother stopped in front of me. "Do you have anything to report?"

I suppressed the urge to shrug and shove my hands in my pockets. "There's interest in my show from Broadway."

Grandmother's expression remained unchanged. "Is that so? We'll talk about this later."

The tone in her voice was ominous, and a sense of dread fell over me.

Grandmother's attention turned to my younger sister, Gabriella, who had been waiting patiently for her turn. Gabriella was the youngest adult in the family, six years younger than Anne and me. Her hair was a luxurious, dark brown that flowed down her shoulders in soft waves, like a waterfall of chocolate, contrasting with her fair skin. Her eyes were the same brilliant blue as mine, shining like sapphires against her delicate features.

"I assume you're still studying?" Grandmother asked Gabriella.

"Yes, I am," Gabriella answered calmly. "And I'm doing very well. I'm at the top of my class."

"I sure hope you're not planning to follow in Anne's footsteps for not carrying on the family name?" Grandmother asked with a wry smile.

The sound of quick footsteps echoing down the stairs cut off Gabriella's response. We all knew who was coming.

My older sister's husband, Parker Linden, must have caught Jane as she reached the bottom of the stairs, because he appeared a minute later, holding a happy little girl. His already-red face darkened when he saw Grandmother's disapproving expression.

"Hello, Grandmother," Parker greeted her.

As expected, Grandmother ignored Parker and took my father's arm. "Let's go have dinner, shall we?"

The rest of us followed as they headed towards the dining room.

"Is your show really going to be on Broadway?" Gabriella whispered, her voice full of excitement as she and I walked at the back of the group.

"Maybe," I said, trying to sound nonchalant. "I got a call from an old chum in America who wants me to come to New York."

"Oh my gosh, that's fantastic!" Gabriella said, squeezing my arm.

Although Gabriella wasn't particularly interested in the theater, she's always been my biggest supporter, just as I was for her.

As we settled at the dining room table, the children were taken to the kitchen by the housekeeper, Mrs. Reynolds, following Grandmother's outdated belief that children should dine separately.

We chatted politely over the meal, but after finishing the main course, Grandmother focused her attention on me.

"Spencer, I've decided that you will accompany your father to all events that require his presence this year," Grandmother declared. "It's time to prepare you for your position as head of the family one day."

I could feel the tension building in my chest, knowing this would not go well. I braced myself to speak my mind.

"I'm sorry, Grandmother, but I won't be able to do that," I said, trying to keep my voice calm.

The room fell silent, and I could feel the pressure of everyone's eyes on me.

"And why, may I ask, would that be the case?" Grandmother's voice was icy, and I could see her frustration clearly on her face.

"I'm leaving for New York next week, and I don't know how long I'll be gone," I replied.

Grandmother's eyes narrowed, and I sensed her disapproval radiating towards me. "You're thirty years old, Spencer York. It's time for you to take on the responsibilities of your family name."

It was the type of statement that made me feel like I was back in boarding school, being scolded by the headmaster.

"I'm not neglecting my responsibilities, Grandmother," I said, struggling to keep my voice level. "I've already made plans with a friend from New York about my show. The Broadway possibility I mentioned earlier."

Grandmother shook her head and pursed her lips, then turned to my father. "Raynard."

"Spencer," my father said, "couldn't you put that off until sometime later in the year?"

I was all too familiar with the conciliatory tone in my father's voice. It was the one he used whenever he was caught between his mother and the rest of the family. I never questioned his love for any of us, but Grandmother was a force to be reckoned with.

"Unfortunately, I can't," I said truthfully. "I have a short hiatus from the West End show while the theater is being remodeled. If I want to put together a Broadway production, now is my only chance."

"You cannot simply run off to America on a whim," Grandmother said.

I knew better than to tell her it wasn't a whim. To her, my work in the theater was nothing more than a hobby, similar to members of the royal family who played polo or did dressage. She saw the value of the arts—or at least claimed she did—but in her mind; it wasn't a place for a York to be seriously involved.

I knew, however, what would speak to her.

"I gave my word," I said. "I told my friend I would go to New York to meet with him and the Shubert Foundation. They're a well-respected organization and everything is already set in place. It would look bad on the family if I backed out."

Grandmother's face twisted in annoyance, her lips forming a thin line, before she spoke. "I guess you have to go then," she said, her irritation clear in her voice. "But leaving this week is not an option. I've arranged for you to meet Elisabet Wellington this Friday evening," she added.

I clenched my jaw and tried not to show my annoyance on my face. Fortunately, I was well-practiced in hiding my emotions. Either people in families like mine learned to control their expressions or they got swept away by the avarice of the upper class.

"Thank you, Grandmother, but I'm not interested in dating Elisabet Wellington," I said.

I was familiar with the name, but I hadn't met the woman. I didn't need to, though. She wasn't the first person Grandmother had tried to set me up with in the past few years. Whatever else Elisabet was, I had little doubt she came from a wealthy, aristocratic family and was likely to inherit most or all of her family's wealth, if she hadn't already.

"I understand that a man doesn't need to worry about his biological clock as a woman does," Grandmother said, giving Anne a pointed look. "But that doesn't mean you can delay finding a suitable wife."

"I can find my own dates, Grandmother," I said, giving her my most charming and professional smile, the one that had always gotten me what I wanted from whoever I was trying to win over. Except Grandmother was immune to my charms and always had been.

"I said a suitable wife," she replied, her tone dismissive. "The women you associate with are not from high-bred families."

She meant they weren't born into wealthy, noble families like ours. The only reason Grandmother had approved of my parents' relationship was because my mother had distant ties to French nobility.

"We already had this conversation before you went to university," Grandmother continued. "Your parents have allowed your theater interest to continue for much longer than I would have, but you've all three assured me you understand your responsibilities."

"I do," I said, my tone firm.

"Then you'll meet with Elisabet," Grandmother said, her tone leaving no room for further discussion.

Shit.

"Are we talking about Elisabet Wellington?" Anne asked from her seat across from me. "I think we went to school together."

"Yes," Grandmother said, her tone dismissive. "Of course you did."

She said it as-if there were only one school in the country for aristocratic young women.

Anne frowned. "It can't possibly be the woman I'm thinking of. Daughter of Arthur and Margaret Wellington?"

"Yes, those are her parents," Grandmother said, her tone becoming impatient. "Please get to the point, Anne, and stop being tedious."

"Elisabet is a lesbian," Anne said matter-of-factly.

Grandmother stiffened. "That can't be. They assured me she would fulfill her responsibilities."

"Well, we wouldn't want to risk infidelity with another woman," Anne shrugged. "Just imagine the scandal." She finished her wine, and we all watched her, waiting to hear what she would say next. "Her parents barely kept her expulsion from school under wraps."

"She came home to care for her sick mother," Grandmother said, her tone defensive.

"That was the official story," Anne agreed, "but they caught Elisabet in a compromising situation with one of the school's maids. The maid was fired, and they asked Elisabet to leave."

"That's impossible," Grandmother said, her tone skeptical. "We would have heard about something like that."

"Not if the Wellingtons paid everyone involved to keep quiet," Anne countered, her tone matter-of-fact.

"Then how do you know?" Gabriella asked, her tone one of curiosity.

"I saw them together," Anne said. "It wasn't my secret to share, but now the situation has changed. I wouldn't want our family to be involved in an arrangement that could lead to embarrassment."

Grandmother's lips formed a tight line, as if she'd tasted something unpleasant. "Alright. I'll inform the Wellingtons that Spencer won't be meeting with their daughter, as he'll be out of the country."

Grandmother's disappointment was as clear as a bell. Of course, she wouldn't breathe a word of the scandal to anyone, not even to the Wellingtons. It was all about maintaining appearances, and heaven forbid anyone found out that she had made a mistake due to not having all the facts. The thought made me quietly amused, but I kept a straight face, not wanting to make the situation worse.

"When you return home, Spencer, I will arrange a more

suitable match for you," Grandmother said firmly. "I expect you to show her the proper respect and attention."

I simply nodded and gave my sister a grateful look. Grandmother hadn't given up, but I'd at least been given a reprieve.

Sometimes, I hated my life. The burden of upholding the York family's reputation and legacy was overwhelming, but the idea of marrying someone I didn't love just for the sake of tradition and reputation was unbearable to me.

FIVE
LONDON

I WAS BOILING WITH ANGER, MY MIND FILLED WITH thoughts of all the creative ways I could get revenge on Mercedes for setting me up on a date with the most disgusting man I had ever met.

Howie Durtz, who worked in A&R at Manhattan Records, was her brilliant idea to end my dating drought. On the surface, he was undeniably attractive, with his golden hair and dark, intriguing eyes. He even had the connections to get us into one of the city's most elite clubs. But as soon as he spoke, it became clear that his good looks were the only impressive thing about him. His immaturity and arrogance were palpable, and I failed to understand how Mercedes could have spent time with him without realizing his true nature.

"...then I told him that if he had been more of a man, his wife wouldn't have begged me all night to bang her." Howie laughed, an obnoxious bray, from across the small cocktail table. He downed his fourth shot of tequila and barely stifled a belch.

"Do you always talk about sex with other women on a

date?" I kept my tone calm, but my crossed arms and lack of a smile should have given him a sign of my mood.

"Oh, come on," Howie said. "It's not like I fucked her. The woman was a dog."

"You're kinda missing the point." I unfolded my arms long enough to snag my margarita and take a drink.

"It was just a fucking story. Geez." Howie shook his head. "Lighten up."

I was still trying to figure out how in the world to respond to *those* particular statements when he excused himself for the second time this evening. As soon as he was out of sight, I pulled my phone out of my purse and furiously typed a message to Mercedes.

Don't tell me you didn't know the guy's a dick?

I was livid as I thought about the massive jerk she had set me up with. A patronizing douche who had no qualms about bragging about his conquests. There were so many better things I could have been doing on my Saturday night, like seeing a show at one of the off-Broadway theaters and making new contacts. With only a few weeks left until Christmas, I wanted to audition as much as possible. Networking was the key to finding new casting opportunities.

My phone chimed with a message from Mercedes.

He's hot. And well-endowed, I've heard.

My anger rose again. I scowled at my phone and typed out a response:

He's obnoxious and a loser.

I hit send and waited for her reply. Three dots appeared on my screen, and then her message came through.

He fucks like a champ.

I couldn't believe the audacity of my friend, and I

muttered "What the hell?" under my breath. I typed out another message,

You had sex with him, and I'm supposed to be sloppy seconds? I don't even want to know the answer to that.

I added a glaring emoticon before sending the message.

As I slipped my phone into my purse, I noticed Howie approaching. He dropped into his chair and signaled for the waitress to bring him another drink, gesturing to my half-empty glass. "You better hurry and catch up," he said with a smirk.

I forced a tight smile and replied, "I'm good, thanks."

"So, where were we?" He sniffed and brushed the back of his hand against his nose, his eyes gleaming with a hint of lust. "Right, we were talking about work. You're an actress, huh? Theater, I assume. You don't do any other acting?" He wiggled his eyebrows suggestively and sniffed again. This time, when he brushed his nose, I saw a streak of blood on his hand.

He looked down and laughed, a cruel, guttural sound. "Oops."

He grabbed a napkin and wiped off the blood, tossing the wadded-up paper onto the table without a second thought. The smell of cheap cologne and something else, something sour and acrid, hung heavy in the air.

"That's disgusting," I whispered, feeling repulsion crawl up my spine.

"Sorry," he grinned, and now I saw what I had missed before. There was a small smudge of white powder just under one nostril. Combined with the blood, it was a fairly obvious conclusion that this guy was going to the bathroom to snort coke.

"Now, you're an actress, but you haven't made it big

yet." He reached across the table to grab my hand. "Maybe I can help with that."

I pulled my hand back, my heart racing. "No, thank you."

"Come on, a little private movie starring you and me," he leered, his breath hot and foul on my face. "In the right hands, it can do wonders for a person's career."

I couldn't take it any longer. I had to get out of the restaurant and away from Howie. He made my skin crawl, and his suggestion to make a sextape with me was the last straw.

"Listen, buddy," I said, trying to keep the sarcasm out of my voice. "I don't need your help or your so-called private movie. I'm leaving." My chair was making a loud noise as I stood up. "And don't try to stop me."

But Howie wasn't done. He reached out and grabbed my wrist, his grip tight. "Come on, don't be like that. You know you want to stay and have a little fun."

I jerked my arm away from him, anger flowing through me. "You're disgusting. I want nothing to do with you."

He laughed, a cruel sound. "You'll regret this, sweetheart. You'll see that you're throwing away a golden opportunity."

But I wasn't listening. I threw a couple of bills on the table to cover my drink, spun around and marched toward the exit, my heart pounding in my chest.

As I burst through the doors of the club and stepped into the cool night air, the feeling of anger still lingered.

The wind was bitterly cold, and I tightened my coat around me, hunching my shoulders as I walked down the sidewalk, keeping my head down. There were no taxis in front of the club. I didn't think Howie would come after me, but I would not take any risks. I would find a cab further down the street.

I had made it almost a block when it started to rain. Not a nice, warm rain. No, this was a nasty, sleety rain that froze everything it touched and soaked through the fabric in seconds. And not a single taxi in sight.

Dammit.

I turned and saw a warm light shining through a large plate-glass window. George's Pub. That would be a good place to call a car.

I hurried and ducked inside, as I closed my eyes in relief at the warm air that surrounded me.

And then someone sprayed something all over me.

SIX

SPENCER

"What do you think of New York so far?" Stan Longley spread his arms wide, as if to encompass the entire city. "A day is hardly enough time to see everything we offer, but it's a good start, isn't it?"

After arriving in New York only yesterday, Stan appeared early this morning at my hotel, insisting on giving me a tour of his city.

"It's quite the sight," I said, watching the neon lights of Times Square flicker and glow, casting a colorful aura over the bustling crowds of people. The sounds of honking cars and chatter filled the evening air as we walked down the crowded sidewalk. The busy energy of the city was invigorating but also overwhelming for me, who had just arrived from London the day before and was still feeling jet-lagged. "But I should let you know I went to Columbia University, so this isn't my first time in the city."

"Oh, I see. You're a seasoned New Yorker then," Stan said with a chuckle. "Well, I hope I could show you something new today."

"Oh, yes," I said with a grin. "I have to admit, it has

changed little since I lived here. It's still as busy and vibrant as ever."

"Yes, that's the beauty of New York," Stan said with a twinkle in his eye, a hint of nostalgia in his voice. "The city is always changing, always evolving, but it remains the same at its core."

"It certainly does," I agreed.

"Well, I hope you're thirsty," Stan said, leading the way down a side street. "I know just the place. A little British pub I like to frequent. They serve a perfect pint of Guinness."

"Ah, the nectar of the gods," I replied with a grin. "I can hardly wait."

As we walked down the street, it started raining, but our spirits were lifted when we saw the cozy British pub. Its warm yellow light illuminated the street, and I could hear laughter and clinking glasses even from outside. Stan declared, "Perfect timing. This is just the spot to help ease your jet lag," as he held the door open for me to enter.

We stepped inside and were greeted by the scent of wood polish and hops. The sound of a musician playing traditional British folk music added to the warm ambiance, making me feel a sense of familiarity and comfort, despite it being my first time in the pub.

"I might just make it until midnight after all," I said as we settled at a high table and ordered food and drinks. A minute later, two pints of Guinness were placed in front of us.

"Here's to a productive trip, Stan," I said, raising my beer in a toast. "Cheers!"

"Cheers, Spencer," Stan replied, clinking his glass against mine.

"Tastes just like home," I quipped with a grin, taking a

sip. "I might have to stay here permanently now I know they serve a good pint."

"I'll keep you well-stocked," Stan laughed. "But don't get too comfortable. We've got a big day coming up. I've set up a meeting with the theater owner Monday morning."

"Monday morning?" I chuckled, trying to hide my excitement. "I'm not exactly a morning person, you know."

"Don't worry, it's not until 10 am," Stan smirked. "Plenty of time for a leisurely breakfast."

"Ah, 10 am, the civilized hour for a meeting," I grinned. "As long as there's coffee involved, I'm good."

"Coffee? I thought you were more of a tea person," Stan chuckled. "I'll make sure there's a pot waiting for you. But first, let's enjoy the rest of the evening and raise a glass to our hopefully upcoming success on Broadway."

"Cheers to that!" I raised my glass. "Here's making Broadway history together."

Stan leaned back and glanced around the pub. "You know, the pub owners are from Liverpool," he said. "They came here about fifteen years ago."

"I have high hopes for their fish and chips then," I said as the server returned with our food. "They better have malt vinegar for the chips."

"I'll never understand why you Brits like malt vinegar on fries," Stan grinned.

"It's called chips, not fries," I chuckled and reached for the salt, only to spill half of it.

"Oops, just made a little mess," I said, wiping the salt off the table with a napkin.

"Better throw some salt over your shoulder," Stan grinned. "Don't want anything jinxing the show."

I rolled my eyes and chuckled, playing along as I picked up the salt shaker and tossed some over my shoulder.

"Wrong shoulder," Stan smirked.

"What?" I asked, trying to hide my annoyance.

"You threw it over your right shoulder," he explained, chuckling. "You have to do it over your left. The devil sits on the left shoulder."

"Bloody hell, Stan." I shook my head in mock frustration.

"What can I say? That's the rule," he shrugged.

I picked up the salt shaker again, but this time, I applied too much force and the lid flew off, showering the salt several feet behind me. "Crap," I muttered under my breath, realizing I must have hit someone with the salt.

I turned, apology on my lips, when I saw a beautiful young woman. She had just entered the pub, standing there wet and a bit bedraggled, but stunning, nonetheless. "My dear, I apologize. Please let me buy you a drink to make it up for you."

She brushed at the tiny granules of salt clinging to her curls and gave me a small smile. "It's okay, no need to do that. But maybe grab the lid from the salt shaker?" she said, pointing to the floor.

"Right. But, please, sit. I'll get some towels," I replied, pulling out the chair next to me and quickly brushing salt off the seat.

"How about I get the towels?" Stan said as he got to his feet. "Please, miss, have a seat."

The woman's unique, brandy-colored eyes shifted from Stan to me, and she nodded, "Okay, thanks. The weather is terrible out there," she said as she sat down while Stan headed to the bar.

"Yes, it is quite dreadful. May I explain what occurred here?" I said, chuckling. "When I inadvertently spilled salt on the table, my friend informed me I needed to throw some over my shoulder to dodge any bad luck." I gestured towards Stan, who was speaking with the bartender. "As bad luck would have it, the lid wasn't secure and...well, you know the rest." I shrugged my shoulders.

"I understand," she said, her voice tinged with amusement. "I'm London," she introduced herself.

My eyebrows went up in surprise. "You're having a go at me," I said with a chuckle.

She shook her head and laughed. "I swear. My name is London McCrae," she said.

"A Scottish last name with an English first name?" I teased, unable to resist a bit of playful banter.

"My father's from Scotland," she explained. "And I'm guessing you're from London, based on your reaction to my name," she said, smiling.

"That's right." I leaned back in my chair.

"Have you been in New York for long?" she asked, tucking a strand of wet hair behind her ear.

"Just arrived yesterday," I chuckled. "I seem to have brought the London rain with me."

She laughed, and before we could continue our conversation, Stan returned with towels. While London dried off, I signaled the waiter and ordered her a drink.

"I didn't catch your name," she said when the server left. "We were too busy talking about my strange name."

"Spencer York," I said, giving her a charming grin and leaning closer. "Nice to meet you, London."

"Likewise, Spencer," she smiled, her brandy-colored eyes sparkling.

"And I'm Stan Longley," Stan interjected, also leaning in closer and giving her a charming smile.

A strange sensation washed over me as I watched Stan flirt with London. "So, London," I said, steering the conversation back in my direction. "What brings you to this little pub tonight?"

"Just needed a break from the rain," she replied, taking a sip of her drink.

"Well, lucky for you, you found the entertainment of the evening," Stan said smoothly. "Don't you agree, Spencer?"

I gave him a playful glare. "Indeed. But I have a hunch that London will find British humor to be more to her taste, given her first name."

"Oh, I can handle both American and British humor," London said with a chuckle. "Alright. Enough about my name."

As Stan burst out laughing, I leaned in closer to London. "Certainly," I replied with a nod of my head. "I shall refrain from making any further jests about your name."

I could see the amusement in her eyes as she took a sip of her drink, and I knew I had caught her attention. I was determined to keep it that way.

Our conversation flowed as easily as the beer, and London's sparkling eyes and infectious laughter captivated me. She shared stories about her brother Carson and sister Maggie, both of whom lived in Manhattan.

"What a fascinating family you have, London," I said, intrigued. "You've got me curious. Any other hidden gems?"

"You ain't seen nothing yet," London said with a laugh, her eyes twinkling.

"I can't wait to uncover them all," I said, the words slipping out before I could stop myself. I glanced over at Stan, who was sitting there with a smirk on his face.

"I think it's time for me to hit the road," he said, pushing back from the table. "Miss McCrae, it was a pleasure. And

Spencer, I'll see you bright and early Monday. I'll bring the caffeine." He gave me a mischievous smile as he stood up and made his way out of the pub.

The atmosphere between London and me shifted as we were left alone, while the noise of the pub faded into the background. I became solely focused on her, unable to look away from her alluring gaze. The brief silence between us could have been awkward, but it was charged, like the impending arrival of a lightning storm, filling the air with electricity. I had the sudden urge to reach out and touch her hand to see if we'd actually spark.

"Well, this is quite a change from my usual Saturday nights," I said with a chuckle, trying to ease the suddenly charged energy.

"You mentioned you just arrived in the city," London said, her voice drawing my gaze back to her. "Are you here for business or pleasure?"

The way she said the word "pleasure" sent a rush of anticipation through me, and I couldn't help but let out a laugh. "I can assure you, it's all business, but I must admit, the pleasure of your company is a delightful bonus," I said, smiling at her.

"What kind of business, if you don't mind me asking?" she asked, leaning in a little closer.

"Not at all," I replied. "I'm a producer, and my friend Stan is interested in a little show I did back in England."

"That's fantastic," she said.

"It is," I said, smiling. "But I'm afraid I can't say much more about it yet. The details are still being worked out." I changed the subject. "What about you? Are you a native New Yorker?"

She shook her head. "West Coast. From San Ramon, California."

"So far from home. How did you and your siblings end up in New York?"

"I have many siblings scattered around," she answered with a grin. "But those in New York came for the same reason I did. Career opportunities." After a pause, she added, "I'm an actress."

"That makes sense," I said, trying to hide my curiosity. "You're all artists in your own right."

She smiled. "Not everyone would consider what Carson does to be art," she said, with a touch of sarcasm.

"Well, I'm not just anyone," I replied, leaning in closer.

Just then, her phone buzzed, disrupting our moment. "Sorry, I need to check this," she said, taking out her phone. After glancing at the message, she ignored it.

"Is everything alright?" I asked, hopeful that our evening wouldn't be cut short.

"Yes, just a friend checking in," she said, still smiling.

"Oh, I see," I said, not wanting to hold her back. "I didn't mean to keep you out so late. I'm sure you have a busy schedule."

"Not at all," she replied, her eyes shining. "I'm having a great time. How about you? Are you enjoying yourself?"

"Immensely," I said, feeling my pulse quicken. "I can't remember the last time I had such a delightful conversation with a beautiful woman."

"Flattery will get you everywhere," she said with a laugh.

"I hope it works its magic," I said, giving her a charming smile.

Her phone buzzed again. "Sorry," she said, glancing at it, this time typing a quick reply. "It's my friend Mercedes again. She's checking in to see how my date went." At the look of surprise on my face, she chuckled. "Earlier, I was on a blind date that didn't turn out so well. My date kept excusing himself to go to the restroom, and it was quite obvious he was indulging in something a bit more illicit than a quick wash-up."

London tapped her nose, and I got the hint. The bloke was snorting cocaine in the loo.

"So, I made my exit and ended up here."

"Blimey. Does your friend hate you?" I asked with a chuckle.

"At times, I do question it," London replied with a laugh. "In all seriousness, though, she just wants the best for me."

"She wants you to find love," I said.

London shook her head, her eyes sparkling. "She wants me to get laid," she said with a hint of sarcasm.

"I see," I said, raising my eyebrows in surprise. "And what about you? What do you want?"

London's gaze roamed over me, a look of appreciation on her face. "I'm thinking she might have had the right idea, just with the wrong guy."

As I heard London's words, my heart skipped a beat. "You're quite captivating, aren't you?" I said with a thrill of delight. "There's something about you that's entirely enchanting."

London raised an eyebrow. "Is that your way of saying you're interested?"

"I'm a man who knows what he wants," I replied with a charming grin. "And when I see something I want, I go after it."

She leaned in closer, her gaze fixed on mine. "And what is it you want, Spencer?"

"I want to know more about you, London," I said, my

voice low and husky. "I want to know your secrets, your desires, your passions."

I could see the wheels turning in her head. But then she let out a breathy laugh and said, "Well, I suppose we'll have to see where this goes, then, won't we?"

"How about we continue our evening at my hotel?" I suggested. "I've got a bottle of wine that the hotel gave me as some sort of welcome gift. It's probably terrible, but it's alcohol, so...," I said with a grin.

She hesitated for a moment, and I held my breath, wondering if I had overstepped my bounds. But then she smiled and nodded. "I'd like that. Let's go."

WE STUMBLED into my suite and threw off our coats, mouths together, hands tugging at clothes. She was surprisingly strong for such a tiny thing, and I chuckled as I heard buttons hitting the floor as they flew from my shirt. Her teeth sank into my bottom lip, possibly in retaliation for my laughter, but the jolt of pain and pleasure went straight through me, and I made a sound in the back of my throat.

I dug my fingers into her butt and lifted her. Her mouth didn't leave mine as she wrapped her legs around my waist. I could feel her heat through the thin fabric of our underwear, and my erection thickened. She ground against me as she leaned back, yanking her dress over her head and tossing it aside before bringing her lips back to mine. Her nipples were hard little bullet points as they rubbed against my chest and my mouth watered in anticipation.

She let out a startled yelp as I dropped her onto the bed, and I was momentarily distracted by how her breasts bounced. She was petite; her breasts a handful each, her waist narrow and limbs slender. The only thing hidden from me was the bit that her lace panties covered between her legs.

"You're gorgeous, you know that?" I said, barely recognizing my voice.

"Right back at you," she said. "And I wasn't expecting the tattoo."

I grinned. "Most people don't."

The intricate black pattern covered most of the left side of my torso, invisible even when I wore short sleeves, and I was careful to ensure no one in the press got even a whisper that I had ink. I doubted even my siblings or parents knew. Grandmother certainly didn't.

London's eyes took on a slightly glazed look, and I tapped her foot. "What's going on in that head of yours?"

"Mmm...I'd like to trace the entire thing with my tongue."

I let out a curse and crawled onto the bed, pausing only to retrieve a condom from the suitcase I hadn't yet unpacked. I tossed it next to London and leaned over her, taking her mouth again. My hands roamed over her bare skin, fingers teasing her nipples until she writhed underneath me.

I moved my lips from hers, kissing my way down her throat, flicking my tongue across her skin to taste her. Her fingers slid through my hair as I reached her breasts, fingernails digging into my scalp when I began to lick and suck my way across that soft flesh to the pale pink nubs of her nipples.

Taking one of those tight bits between my lips, I sucked on it, teasing with my teeth and tongue. London's moans filled my ears even as the scent and taste of her consumed my other senses. I slid my hand over her stomach and between her legs, fingers moving under black lace, and then a finger slipped between her folds, the slick, wet heat making me groan.

The moment my finger ghosted over her clit, she gasped, her back arching.

"So sensitive," I murmured against her breast. "Will you come for me before I get inside you?"

"Keep that up and probably." Her voice was breathless, which pleased me, but that she could still give a coherent answer told me she wasn't as far gone as I wanted her to be.

Not yet, anyway.

I rubbed her clit harder until I found exactly what she liked. Repeating the motions with my hand, I switched to her other nipple, worrying at it with my teeth until the sensitive flesh was swollen and she was panting. Tension radiated through her, and I could tell she was close to climax.

She cried out, an inarticulate sound of pure pleasure, and her entire body tensed. I pushed harder, wringing out another shout before I sat back and watched her ride her bliss, rolling onto her stomach and burying her face in a pillow. By the time her body stopped twitching, I was nude and had put on the condom.

She looked over her shoulder at me. "I feel like I should thank you for that."

Before I could figure out how to respond, she pushed herself up on her hands and knees, presenting me with a very nice ass and a pair of soaked knickers. The heat in her eyes said it all.

I moved behind her and hooked my fingers into the waistband, and lowered her knickers. I got a glimpse of flushed skin.

For a moment, it tempted me to lean down and lick her, but then she wiggled her ass at me, and I was lost.

Sliding inside her with one smooth thrust was like nothing I had ever felt before. Perfection. She was tight, but we fit together as if made for it. The way she caught her breath told me she felt it too, and it wasn't just physical. The weight of that realization only stayed on me for a moment before my body's more primal needs took precedence, and I started to move.

SEVEN
LONDON

THE MONDAY MORNING SUN BROUGHT A FEELING OF bliss. The memory of the incredibly intimate experience I had two nights before lingered, reminding me of my encounter with the charming Englishman. Though I knew we would never meet again, our night together had left a lasting impression. My frustration with my friend Mercedes for setting me up with the biggest jerk on earth was gone, as it ultimately led me to meeting Spencer.

I savored the beauty of the day as I strolled from the subway station to the theater for the open casting calls. Despite the chill, the sun had been shining brightly enough to melt away the remnants of the slushy snow from my journey out of Spencer's hotel the previous morning. The brightness of the day was almost overwhelming, making me regret not bringing sunglasses to protect my eyes. However, a sudden gust of wind reminded me that winter was still very much here.

The queue for the open casting calls was shorter than I expected, considering no appointments were necessary. I wasn't sure whether to interpret this as a positive or a negative sign, but I was determined to stick with it. Not because I direly needed a job for financial reasons, but I'd reached a point of frustration in my career that had me questioning my choice of profession. I needed to land a role, even a small one, in a small play.

An hour later, I faced a panel of four people introducing themselves. I recognized the casting director and the director's names, but I couldn't remember if I had auditioned for them before. The two producers were unfamiliar to me, but they seemed friendly enough.

However, none of them showed any reaction as I read the script they'd provided. Not even a twitch of an eyelid to show which way they were leaning.

After I delivered my last line, the silence in the room was deafening, and I wondered if I had blown my chance.

"Allow me to escort you out," said Russ Heyworth, the casting director, as he rose from his seat. "This way, please."

I trailed behind him, maintaining my professional demeanor with a broad smile that concealed any hint of frustration or disappointment. If I had a nickel for every time, some man told me to smile, I would've been twice as rich as I was.

"You did a great job back there," Russ said as we reached the door to the outside. "You've got some genuine talent."

"Thanks," I replied, but as I reached for the door handle, he angled his body, blocking the exit.

"You know, there's a special event happening tonight," he said, his tone making me feel a little uneasy. "I think you'd have a good time if you went."

I nodded, trying to keep my smile in place. It wasn't unusual for casting directors to want to get to know actors before casting them, but something in Russ's tone made me feel uncomfortable.

"I hate to break it to you, but it's unlikely that you'll be getting the role," he continued, his eyes roaming down my body. "However, there's a way to change that."

"And what's that?" I asked, trying to keep my tone neutral as I already knew where this was heading.

"Join me as my date to the event tonight and show me just how committed you are to your craft," he said with a suggestive smile.

I shook my head and stepped around him, making my way to the door. "I appreciate the offer, but I think I'll have to pass. Both the invitation and the advice."

He grabbed my arm. "You're making a big fucking mistake," he said, his breath foul. "Trust me, you'll regret it."

"Hardly," I replied, wrestling my arm free. "Touch me again, and I'll report you for inappropriate conduct," I said, rushing away.

Once I was clear of him, I took a deep breath of fresh air, relieved to be away from the situation. Unfortunately, this wasn't the first time someone had propositioned me in such a manner, suggesting that my career could reach new heights if I just gave in to their advances. Regrettably, I knew it wouldn't be the last time, either.

People like Russ sometimes made me hate the entertainment industry.

EIGHT
SPENCER

I<small>T WAS A CRISP AND BEAUTIFUL WINTER MORNING IN</small> New York City, the sun already peeking over the skyscrapers. As I stepped out of the lift at the hotel and into the lobby, a tune involuntarily escaped from my lips. My musical moment was interrupted by the amused smile of a fellow guest who had caught my impromptu performance. I offered a sheepish grin to her and adjusted my wool cap before making my way across the lobby to the car that had been sent for me.

Making small talk with the driver, my mind couldn't shake the thoughts of London McCrae. It kept replaying the memories of our passionate night together, the taste of her, and how she had cried out a sound of pure pleasure, a memory that sent signals straight to my lower regions.

As we neared my destination, I shifted in my seat and took a deep breath, trying to refocus on the task at hand. Stan and I had an appointment with the Vice President of Theatre Operations for the Shubert Organization to pitch my show.

It was crucial to secure the Shubert Theatre as the

venue, since it was the only Broadway theater with no shows running. I knew I had to bring my A-game for this.

I stepped out of the car, admiring the grandeur of the building before me. My determination to make this my stage was unwavering.

Before I could reach the door, it swung open, and out stepped Stan with two cups of coffee in hand. "Come on, Spencer," he said, gesturing for me to enter the building. "He is waiting for us."

I checked my watch and frowned slightly. Despite its expense, it must be running behind schedule. "Am I late?" I asked as I stepped inside.

"He's known to be early," Stan replied, handing me a steaming cup of coffee. I took a sip, only to burn my tongue on the scalding liquid.

Minutes later, Stan and I sat across from the Vice President of Theatre Operations. The formalities were swiftly dispensed with, and I was then asked to explain my show. This was a moment I always feared, as some concepts, no matter how ingenious, could sound ridiculous when spoken out loud.

"It's a mash-up, a modern-day retelling of 'A Connecticut Yankee in King Arthur's Court' and 'The Prince and the Pauper,'" I began, bracing myself for any potential skepticism. "I know you might wonder how a time-travel story will translate to the stage, but before you write it off, look at these numbers from last year's run on the West End." I handed him a folder filled with ticket sales and profit margins.

He studied the information, his expression unreadable. Then he set down the folder and looked up at me. "I'm intrigued. Tell me more," he said.

It was hard not to smile at this encouraging response.

"The story starts in the present day with a young woman named Canty," I said, eager to delve deeper into the details of my production.

"WE NEED TO CELEBRATE," Stan declared as we left the office.

"Indeed, we do," I agreed, my spirits lifted by the success of my pitch. The VP was so impressed that he brought in a few other executives for me to present my show to. By the end, they were already talking about contracts, casting, and crew. The cherry on top was that I would get the space I wanted: The Shubert Theatre.

"Where do you want to go to celebrate?" Stan asked. "A fancy restaurant?"

"I was thinking more of a pub," I responded impulsively. "Nothing beats a pint of ale and some fish and chips to celebrate a job well done, right?"

Stan gave me a playful grin. "You just want to see if the girl from the other night is there. I get it. My driver is outside. Let's have him take us there."

Not wanting to acknowledge Stan's accurate observation, I redirected the conversation to the show. "Can you get me a list of crew members you think would be the best fit? If the Shubert Organization wants to have our first open casting call on Thursday, we need to have our director and casting director booked by then at the least."

"I know a few directors who are between projects right now," Stan replied. "Some of them even have nearly full crews that they work with regularly. We might as well take advantage of that."

I agreed, and we continued our discussion as Stan's driver took us to the pub.

When we arrived, the familiar smell of chips and beer greeted us. It wasn't as busy as last time, with only a few patrons scattered around the tables, since it was still early for the lunch crowd. I searched the room for signs of London, but my heart sank as she was nowhere to be seen.

"You're not really hoping to find her here, are you?" Stan asked with a chuckle.

"Of course not. Why would she be hanging around a pub at this hour? That would make her a drunk... like us," I said with a grin.

Stan laughed and patted my shoulder. "Why don't you call her and invite her to celebrate with us?"

"I can't," I said, shaking my head. "I don't even have her number. She left my hotel room in the middle of the night without a word."

Whoops. I didn't mean to let that slip.

Stan looked at me in surprise. "You slept with her? You devil. I'm impressed," he said with a chuckle. "Don't worry. If it's meant to be, you'll find each other again."

I rolled my eyes and gave him a playful grin. "When did you become such a romantic, old friend?"

"I've always been a romantic," Stan replied with a chuckle. "Well then, since she's not here, let's just enjoy our pint and watch the soccer game," he said, gesturing to the match playing on the TV.

"Football," I corrected him with a grin. "It's football, not soccer. I am British after all."

"Ha! Touché, my friend," Stan replied with a playful smirk. "I stand corrected. Football it is." He raised his glass in a mock toast. "Here's to football and finding love, even if it's just for one night."

We ordered our lunch and settled in to watch the match, but my mind kept drifting back to London. As we chatted and enjoyed our meal, I couldn't shake the feeling of hope that she might walk in and our paths would cross once again. Although I knew deep down that it was unlikely, I still kept an eye on the door, just in case.

NINE

LONDON

THE FOUR OF US WERE ON OUR WAY TO THE SHUBERT Theatre after Rocio had shared the news of an open audition for a new show headed straight to Broadway. My friends were over the moon. However, I was less excited, still feeling the impact of my recent setbacks. And I knew that getting into this show would be a real challenge.

The concept was certainly intriguing, but I wasn't foolish enough to believe that I had anything more than a slim chance of getting the lead role. The understudy role, on the other hand, was a possibility. If only my luck would change and I could avoid creepy directors trying to get into my pants.

"There's the theater," Rocio gestured ahead. "Aw, damn. Look at that line."

Gin let out a low whistle, and Mercedes and I both expressed our frustration. With the wide range of roles they were casting for, I had expected a large turnout, but it was the second day of open auditions. We had all waited and come today, hoping that the turnout on the last day would be smaller.

We found the end of the line and huddled there, grateful that the building was blocking the wind as we waited. The people in front of us were already chatting, but I didn't get the impression that they knew each other. That wasn't uncommon. We were all competing for the same roles, and the difference was between those who were friendly with their competition and those who were not.

Three hours later, my name was finally called, and I stepped into the audition room, taking a deep breath. As I always did, I made eye contact with the person closest to the door and smiled at them. After that, as I walked to the center of the designated area, I let my gaze travel down the line of people. Then I saw a familiar face.

Spencer.

What the hell?

My mind went blank, my heart started racing, and I froze. I couldn't think, couldn't breathe, couldn't move. It felt like someone had pulled the ground out from under me, and I was falling into an endless pit.

What was going on? Why was he here? Was this just a twisted coincidence or had the immortal gods on Broadway decided to decapitate my career with one fatal blow?

"London McCrae?" Spencer said my name as if he hadn't been murmuring it in my ear just a week ago. His voice was emotionless, and it hit me like a slap in the face. "You may start whenever you're ready."

Ready? Oh, right. The audition.

I felt like I was moving in a daze. I took the audition sheet from the assistant and quickly skimmed it as I walked back to the marked spot on the floor. By the time I reached my mark, I realized I couldn't remember anything from what I'd just read.

I tried reading the sheet again, but my mind was too

clouded with confusion and fear. When I looked up, all eyes were on me, and I could sense their judgment and curiosity. I did not know what Spencer was doing because I couldn't bring myself to even glance in his direction.

I cleared my throat to start my audition, but my voice was barely above a murmur. After the first sentence, I knew I was in trouble. My mind was racing, my heart pounding, and I felt sweat forming on my forehead. I stumbled over my words, my voice quivering with emotion. I kept feeling Spencer's eyes on me, and couldn't shake the sense of being utterly exposed and vulnerable. My performance was truly a disaster.

As soon as the last word had left my lips, I practically fled from the room. I couldn't bear to face Spencer or the panel again. There was a sense of being in a trance as I stumbled out into the hallway, my mind and heart in turmoil. The sight of Spencer had completely thrown me off my game, leaving me feeling embarrassed and disappointed.

I knew deep down that I had lost any chance of getting the role. Spencer had been my downfall, and I was certain this was some cruel twist of fate, telling me it was time to find an alternative career path. I felt tears welling up in my eyes as I walked away, my career and my heart in ruins.

TEN

SPENCER

It surprised me to see London McCrae audition for my show, but I shouldn't have been. After all, she had mentioned being an actress, and we had one of the biggest turnouts Broadway had seen in quite a while for our casting call. The likelihood of her hearing about it, and me seeing her here, was higher than accidentally bumping into her at the pub where we first met.

But, even with that knowledge, the intense mix of emotions that hit me when she walked into the room still caught me off-guard. My heart raced, and my stomach flipped. I was in disbelief that she was here, right in front of me.

I gazed at her, noticing her disheveled hair and rosy cheeks. My mind immediately traveled back to memories of her soft skin and moans of pleasure, as if time had stood still and she was back in my hotel room.

However, the shock and confusion in her eyes made my heart sink. She was clearly taken aback, and I knew I was the reason. Although I had never expected to see her again, I felt terribly responsible for contributing to her distress.

"London McCrae?" I said her name, trying to keep my voice even. I wanted to give her a moment to compose herself.

As she spoke her lines, I saw the panic and fear in her eyes. Her words stumbled, and her voice wavered. My heart ached for her as I watched her try to save her audition, but it was a disaster, and then, as soon as she finished, she fled.

"That's too bad," Jerry Niyaz, the casting director, said from his seat next to me. "She was pretty to look at."

"She's the one!" I snapped and rose from my chair.

The director, Darrel Wyndham, gave me a skeptical look. "Are you joking?"

"My gut tells me she's it, and I'm going to get her back to try again."

I quickly left the room and entered the hallway, just as I saw London exiting the theater. "London, wait!" I called out, jogging to catch up to her.

She stopped, but didn't turn around. "I apologize if my being here caused you any problems," she said in a calm tone.

"I didn't tell them we know each other," I said as I reached her side. "And I'm sorry. I'm the one who caused you a problem."

She shook her head. "No need to worry about it. I should have been able to handle it better."

"Regardless, I'd like you to come back and give it another shot," I said, offering her a second chance.

She looked taken aback. "Really?"

"Yes, please return with me and audition again," I repeated. "If you don't feel comfortable or don't want to, I understand, and I won't pressure you."

"That's really kind of you," she said hesitantly, still wary of the situation.

"I just want to see everyone perform at their best so we can make the right casting decisions," I said, trying to reassure her with a warm smile. "We want the show to be a success."

"They don't know about our...." She gestured between us, referring to our past encounter.

"No, it's none of their business," I said, gesturing back the way we came. "Shall we?"

She nodded, and we made our way back to the audition room.

My colleagues were waiting, looking curious and amused.

"Miss McCrae," I said, returning to my seat, beaming. "We would like for you to give the audition another go. We didn't quite get a good understanding of your talent the first time around."

"Thank you," London responded, her eyes shining with determination. "I'm not sure what happened earlier."

She took a deep breath and began, "You can't reason with your heart, Lance. You should know this better than anyone by now..."

The difference between her first and second readings was stark. She was confident, and as she finished, I almost let out a small cheer. It filled me with pride and, I'll admit, the urge to sweep her up in my arms and plant a kiss on her cheek...and other places.

"Miss McCrae, that was fantastic," I said with a genuine smile.

"Thank you for giving me another shot," she replied, gratitude clear in her eyes.

"We'll be deciding soon," Jerry added.

I was eager to talk more about London with the group, but we still had other people to evaluate. I didn't want to draw more attention to London than I already had. Considering who was up next, I could be patient and wait a little longer. The Shubert Organization had requested that we consider Timothy Von Vierson as the male lead. Apparently, one of their executives was a big fan and thought Von Vierson would bring recognition to the cast.

After Timothy entered, he stepped forward to shake our hands before glancing at the male audition piece. Less than a minute into his audition, I could tell he was perfect for the role of Lance.

"That was fantastic, Timothy," Darrel said, clearly impressed.

I nodded in agreement, but kept my thoughts to myself. Instead, I said, "We'll have to schedule callbacks, especially to have a chemistry read with the female lead."

Timothy nodded. "Sure thing. My schedule is open all next week. Just let my agent know."

While nothing was set in stone, everyone realized Timothy was the one for the role of Lance.

"So, Jerry," I said, turning to my colleague after Timothy had left. "What do you think of him?"

"I like him," Jerry said, sporting a grin as he placed his pen on the table. "Check out my top picks," he said, gesturing to the paper in front of him.

My smile faded when I saw Jerry hadn't selected London McCrae as his top pick for the female lead. I raised an eyebrow and asked, "Why not London?"

"I'm still not sure why you had her read again, Spencer," Jerry said. "She's certainly talented, but she must have some emotional issues giving such a poor first audition. What if she freezes up like that in front of a full house?"

"Oh, I'm confident it was just a onetime thing," I

replied, trying to reassure him. "She probably just had a rough day. That's all."

"I like her," Darrel said. "It'll come down to how she reads against Timothy, but I agree with Spencer. She's my top pick."

Jerry and Darrel and I went through the rest of the audition lists, and though we had a few minor differences, we could come to a consensus.

We made a list of callbacks for the next week, and they looked excellent. I was happy about all the promising callbacks, but if I was being honest, I couldn't shake the excitement I felt for one specific reading. The thought of seeing London again was definitely intriguing.

I quickly reminded myself of the rule I had to never get involved with cast members in the shows I produced. London would be off-limits if she got the part.

I understood this potential obstacle, but dismissed it for now, knowing that I would have to face it if the time came.

ELEVEN
LONDON

I received the callback.

As I walked into the audition room, I steeled myself for the sight of Spencer at the table. He was there, his eyes on me as I entered. I also noticed another familiar face - Timothy Von Vierson, a well-known actor on the Broadway scene. Being slightly awestruck, I assumed they had cast him as Lance, and this callback was to assess our chemistry as the lead actors. If we didn't have that spark on stage, I wouldn't get the female lead role.

Timothy's good looks couldn't be denied. It was always a bonus when your leading man was easy on the eyes, and despite my nerves, I looked forward to performing with him.

"So good to see you again, Miss McCrae," Spencer said, his smile polite and professional, with a hint of passion in his gaze.

As I approached Timothy and introduced myself, I forced myself to focus on the task at hand.

"Hi, I'm London," I said with a warm smile.

"Timothy. It's great to meet you," he replied, his smile appearing forced, but he fixed his eyes on me, sizing me up.

I'd heard the rumors about Timothy's arrogance, that he was a diva. I wasn't sure if they were true, but I knew how to handle powerful personalities. Growing up around confident people had taught me how to hold my own and not be intimidated by their presence.

"Here's your copy of the audition piece." Jerry, the casting director, handed me the script, his face expressionless.

I thanked him and quickly scanned it before turning to Timothy. "Ready when you are."

He stood, and a change came over him. Gone was any arrogance that came with being a talented and attractive actor.

In its place was Lance, a completely different character.

I was impressed and followed suit, transforming into Canty. I glanced at the script a few times, as the words flowed naturally this time. My eyes met Timothy's and the energy between us was palpable as he leaned in for the kiss. His hands grasped my upper arms, and his mouth found mine. We held the embrace for a moment before stepping back and letting go of our characters.

I couldn't hold back a smile after our performance, but my excitement faded as I saw the expressions on the faces of the three men in front of me. Something in Spencer's expression made me uneasy. Jerry leaned back in his seat and commented, "I'm glad you didn't need to ask for a second chance this time." My smile faltered; that wasn't what had happened.

Spencer chimed in, "She didn't ask for a second chance. I offered her one because I believed she had more to offer. And it's clear that she did."

Jerry responded, "Maybe. Or maybe what Russ Heyworth said was true." My heart sank at the mention of the name.

"Who's Russ Heyworth?" Spencer asked.

"A fellow casting director," Jerry replied. "He told me an interesting story about Miss McCrae." He gave me a quick glance, but I couldn't read his expression.

"Miss McCrae auditioned for him a couple of weeks ago," Jerry continued. "According to Russ, she wasn't happy when she wasn't offered the part and proposed to sleep with him in exchange for the role. When he declined, she threatened to report him for inappropriate conduct."

I was shocked. "That's not what happened," I said, my voice shaking. "I would never offer something like that. He made inappropriate advances towards me. He even grabbed my arm when I refused."

"I believe her," Spencer said firmly. "Miss McCrae is a highly talented actress. Why would she need to proposition someone for a part?"

"Oh, come on, Spencer. You're telling me she didn't offer you anything for that second shot the other day?" Jerry asked with a smirk. "Afterwards, you were so insistent it had to be her."

"Because none of the others had Miss McCrae's potential," Spencer replied, his face set in determination. "Not that it matters. I don't need to explain myself to you, because you're no longer working on this project."

"I don't understand," Jerry said.

Spencer raised an eyebrow. "You're fired," he said succinctly.

"You can't fire–"

"I can," Spencer cut in. "I'm the sole producer and the fact that you just suggested that I took advantage of an actress, or even accused her of making an offer, is enough reason for me to fire your ass." He looked at me. "And just to be clear, I don't believe any of the nonsense that Russ Heyworth says."

"You're making a big mistake," Jerry warned as he stood up abruptly from his seat. "I'll make sure everyone knows how unprofessional you are. Good luck finding success on Broadway after that."

Darrel chuckled. "You're out of your freaking mind, Jerry. You don't have the influence to damage Spencer's reputation."

I looked at Spencer, curious, but he'd turned his attention back to the now-fuming Jerry.

"Do I need to call for security?" Spencer asked.

Jerry muttered some obscenities, gathered his things, and left the room.

Spencer turned his attention to me. "I'm sorry about what he said." His voice was full of genuine concern.

"Thank you," I replied, still a bit shaken from the entire ordeal.

Darrel, the director, spoke up. "That was a great audition, London. But we have other candidates to see, even without a casting director."

Spencer nodded in agreement. "Yes, but we'll be deciding soon. Thank you for your time today, Miss McCrae."

I understood the need for Spencer to keep our interaction professional, especially with the rumors about me that were now circulating in the theater community. I looked at Timothy and thanked him for his help with the scene. Despite my best efforts, I couldn't shake the uncertainty of what lay ahead. Spencer's reputation was on the line, and while he may have defended me, that didn't guarantee that he would take the risk of hiring me.

But I tried not to dwell on it. I was proud of standing up for myself and wouldn't regret turning down Russ's inappropriate proposal, even if it meant missing out on this opportunity.

AFTER A FITFUL NIGHT'S SLEEP, I was in the middle of making breakfast when the phone rang. I answered, "Hello?"

"London, it's Spencer York," his distinctive voice came through the line. "We've made our decision, and we want you to play Canty," he said.

"Really?" I couldn't contain my excitement.

"Yes, really. If you're still interested, of course," he added.

"Of course I am!" I exclaimed, doing a little dance in my bathrobe and slippers.

"Excellent! We'll have our first full-cast read-through next Tuesday at the Shubert Theatre," Spencer informed me.

"Perfect," I replied, still in disbelief at the good news.

"And just to be clear, the casting decision was based solely on your talent and fit for the role. Our personal relationship had no influence on the decision. Timothy, Darrel, and I all agreed that you were the best choice," Spencer added.

"I understand," I said, taking a moment to absorb the news that even Timothy believed I was the right candidate for the part.

"We'll see you next Tuesday, then. And London, congratulations on the role," Spencer said.

"Thank you, Spencer. I can't wait to start," I said before hanging up the phone, still in a state of elation. I felt like a kid on Christmas morning, eager to share the good news with my friends.

TWELVE

SPENCER

It was the Tuesday before Christmas, and the sky was an ominous shade of gray, signaling a potential snowstorm. I pulled my coat tighter around me and hailed a passing cab.

Settling into the back seat, I checked my phone for any messages. There was a text from my sister, Anne, asking about my arrival time at Heathrow. I sighed and turned off my phone. I had no plans to return to London for the holidays.

The cab made its way through the bustling streets of New York, and I felt a mixture of excitement and nervousness. Today was the first cast read-through of my play, and I had been eagerly anticipating this moment all week.

The biting winter air whipped past the windows as I reflected on my grandmother's attempts to set me up with wealthy aristocrats. It was always about maintaining the family's status in high society in England, but I refused to be a mere piece in her game. I had forged my path on the West End and was now making a name for myself on

Broadway. I wouldn't allow her to dictate my romantic life or my future.

But the real reason I didn't want to go back for Christmas was because of London McCrae. Ever since our encounter, I wasn't able to shake her from my thoughts. Now that she was the female lead, I knew I couldn't pursue a relationship with her because of my rule about not fraternizing with cast members. However, I still wanted to support her. It wasn't just because she was beautiful and I desired her, but because I truly believed she was a talented actress who deserved a shot on Broadway. At least, that's what I kept telling myself.

The cab pulled to the sidewalk, and as I stepped out onto the bustling streets of New York, I had to let out a chuckle. Me, Spencer York, the man who had once sworn off love and the societal expectations placed on me by my grandmother, now found himself captivated by the talents and charm of a stunning actress. It was quite an amusing turn of events.

Before entering the theater, I admired its beauty, feeling a buzz of excitement and energy in the air. I knew that this was where I wanted to spend my Christmas, surrounded by like-minded individuals who shared my passion for storytelling and theater.

With a whistle, I entered the lobby of the Shubert Theatre, my footsteps echoing off the marble floor. As I made my way up the steps, I heard someone call out my name.

"Spencer, my man!" Darrel greeted me, striding over with a hand extended for a shake.

"Darrel, good to see you," I replied, giving his hand a firm squeeze.

"How are you this morning?" he asked.

"Can't complain. Excited for the read-through?" I responded.

"Absolutely!" Darrel exclaimed. "Now that we're all set with casting without further incidents, thanks to your quick thinking of firing that Jerry guy. What a creep."

I chuckled. "Yeah, I couldn't tolerate his rude behavior."

"Definitely the right call," Darrel said, patting my back. "It was the only way to handle such a sticky situation."

"Thanks, Darrel," I said. "By the way, have you seen Stan around?"

Darrel shook his head. "Nah, I haven't seen him all week, but I'm sure he'll show up today."

Just as Darrel finished his sentence, Stan walked in, coffee in hand. "Morning, Spencer! I brought you a coffee, thought you might need it before the read-through," he said, handing me a coffee.

"Thanks, Stan, you're a lifesaver," I replied, taking a sip of the hot coffee, careful not to burn my tongue this time.

As we made our way up the stairs, Darrel and Stan discussed the plans for the day's read-through while I listened in. When we finally reached the top, I felt a rush of excitement in my chest. Today was a big day, not just because of the read-through, but also because I'd get to see London again.

"Alright, let's get started," Darrel said as he pushed open the double doors of the theater. The cast and crew were already there, setting up and chatting amongst themselves. I scanned the room, my gaze finally landing on London, seated in the front row, studying her lines. Our eyes met, and she gave me a small smile that made my heart skip a beat.

"Alright, everyone, take your seats," Darrel called out, breaking my thoughts. "We're starting now."

THE READ-THROUGH WAS GOING SMOOTHLY, and London's performance entranced me. Her eyes sparkled when she spoke her lines, and her voice carried with ease throughout the theater. I was becoming increasingly aware that I was in trouble. For years, talented and beautiful women had surrounded me, but I had always maintained a professional demeanor and keep my feelings separate from my work. But with London, things were different.

As Darrel called for lunch, a catered event in the lobby, I knew I had to speak with her. I was burning with curiosity to find out if she felt the same way I did or if our previous encounter had only been a one-night stand. The uncertainty was driving me crazy. As I spotted her in conversation with one of the other cast members, who I believed to be a friend of hers, I approached, but before I could reach her, Stan intercepted me.

"Spencer, listen up," Stan said, with a concerned look on his face. "I heard about the situation with Jerry, and I totally agree with your decision to fire him." He leaned in, lowering his voice. "But you've got to be careful with London. That guy wouldn't hesitate to go to the gossip press to get revenge for being fired. If they found out about your one-night stand, it could create a media frenzy that could harm the success of the show."

I knew Stan was right. Despite my attraction to London, I couldn't let it jeopardize her career or the success of the show.

"Of course, Stan," I replied with a sigh. "You're right. I need to stay professional with London and not let my personal feelings impede the show's success."

But even as I said the words, I couldn't take my eyes off of her as she laughed and chatted with the other cast members. The sight of Timothy flirting with her sent a pang of jealousy through me.

"Is everything alright, Spencer?" Stan asked, noticing my mood change.

"Yeah, just thinking," I replied, forcing a smile. "Maybe going back to England for Christmas wouldn't be such a bad idea after all."

"Well, if that's what you need, then do it," Stan encouraged, patting my back. "Just make sure you come back ready to give this show everything you've got."

I NODDED, knowing he was right. Some distance from London was exactly what I needed. But as I watched her walk away, my heart heavy with longing, I wondered if I would ever be able to truly let her go.

No matter what, I had to pull my shit together while I was in England and come back to New York with a clear head.

I could do that.

THIRTEEN
LONDON

The read-through the other day had gone really well, and today was our first real rehearsal on the stage. When I arrived at the theater with my friend Mercedes, it was with a mix of nerves and excitement. Mercedes had also landed a small part in the musical, but she was most excited about my lead role next to Timothy.

"Girl, you are in for a treat," Mercedes gushed as we walked into the theater to see a shirtless Timothy rehearsing a dance move on the stage. "Timothy is like a dream come true. He's got the looks, the talent, and the charm. I mean, have you seen those abs? And that voice, it's like liquid gold. And the way he moves on stage, it's like he's dancing just for you. I'm so envious! You're so lucky to be working with him," she said as we made our way to the backstage area.

"You make it sound like I'll be performing with Channing Tatum or Ryan Gosling," I said with a laugh, trying to downplay the hype surrounding Timothy. "Don't get me wrong, he's talented, but let's not put him on a pedestal just yet. I'm just grateful you're here, too."

"No way, even if I hadn't gotten a part, I wouldn't miss

this for anything!" Mercedes said, her eyes sparkling with excitement. "Can you believe we're both in a Broadway show together?"

I smiled, grateful for the support from my friends. They had always been there for me, even when I was just starting out in the industry.

"I'm just a little nervous," I admitted, biting my lip.

"Oh, stop it," Mercedes said, giving me a playful shove. "You've got this. Even if you mess up, who cares? It's just the first rehearsal. You'll be too busy stealing the show to worry about any mistakes."

I chuckled, feeling my nerves ease a little. "You're right. I'm just being paranoid."

"It's all part of the game," Mercedes said with a shrug. "But I know you'll do great."

Taking a deep breath, I squared my shoulders and said, "Okay, let's do this."

Mercedes grinned and gave me a quick hug. "Let's do it!"

As I stepped onto the stage, I noticed Spencer wasn't in his seat, and I felt a twinge of disappointment. However, I pushed it aside and focused on the task at hand, finding my spot next to Timothy.

"Places, everyone!" the director called out.

We ran through the scene, and once again Timothy impressed me. Despite the rumors I had heard about him being a prima donna, he was a dedicated performer and we worked well together to bring out the emotions of our characters in the singing. The choreography was challenging, but we moved in sync with the rhythm of the song, our bodies working together seamlessly.

When we reached the last notes of the duet and our

characters shared a kiss, I definitely felt a spark between us, and I could tell Timothy did too. However, I knew I couldn't act on it outside of the performance. The last thing I needed was more distractions that could affect my performance.

Darrel, our director, was ecstatic. "Wow, that was fantastic! The chemistry between you two is electric!" he exclaimed, before turning to Timothy to give him some direction.

With the final notes still ringing in my ears, I walked over to Stan, who was wearing a big smile on his face, and pulled him aside. "What happened to Spencer?" I asked. "Is everything okay?"

"Don't worry about Spencer," Stan reassured me. "He had to go back to England for Christmas to be with his family. But he'll be back after New Year's."

"Family?" I asked, surprised.

Of course, he has a family. He's probably married with kids.

"Yeah, his siblings, mother, and grandmother," Stan explained. "Apparently, his grandmother is causing him some stress. She summoned him home for the holidays." He gave me a knowing smile.

A sense of relief washed over me as I walked away from Stan. Spencer wasn't married, and he would return to New York soon.

The memories of our night together came back to me, but I quickly pushed them aside. Although it had been a thrilling experience, I realized in hindsight that it had also been a mistake. But how could I have known we would work together one day?

"What happened, happened," I told myself as I dismissed any more thoughts of my night with Spencer.

Now was the time to focus on the present and my performance in the show.

A few hours later, Mercedes sauntered over to me with a playful grin on her face. "Wow, London! That duet with Timothy was hot! Still denying his good looks and stage presence?" she said, teasing me.

It was impossible not to roll my eyes and laugh at her comment. "Mercedes, please. I'm a professional. I can separate my personal feelings from my work."

"Sure you can," she said with a smirk. "But I'm not blind. I saw the chemistry between you two. And let's be real, he is pretty easy on the eyes."

I laughed along with her, the relief and excitement of the successful rehearsal still coursing through my veins. "I'll admit, he's not half bad," I said with a smile. "But I'm done talking about Timothy. Let's focus on the show."

Mercedes grinned and nodded in agreement, "Of course, but let's not pretend like you didn't enjoy that duet just as much as I did."

She was right, of course. But I had the sense that with both Spencer and Timothy vying for my attention, the future was set for an intense and thrilling ride, both on and off the stage.

FOURTEEN
SPENCER

As a young boy, the sight of Christmas decorations in the city captivated me. The houses with the most impressive lights held a special appeal to me, and I often wondered why our own home didn't have similar decorations.

In a moment of youthful excitement, I suggested to my grandmother that we follow the trend and decorate our home as well. However, my suggestion was met with a stern lecture on how the Yorks were not common people, and therefore, should not engage in common practices such as decorating one's house.

However, these days, our home was beautifully decorated with all sorts of adornments. As I approached the front door, I admired the hard work put in by our staff. But despite their best efforts, something was missing - the decorations lacked warmth and charm.

Inside, the evergreen wreaths and boughs were artificial, and the pinecones and holly berries were equally fake. The cinnamon and pine scents that filled the house resulted from carefully placed essential oils, lacking the comfort of the real thing.

The Christmas tree was also an artificial creation, and while it looked realistic enough to fool the untrained eye, it was too perfect to be touched. Each ornament was flawless, and every placement was impeccable. Despite its beauty, the tree lacked the charm and warmth that one would expect from a real Christmas tree.

As I approached the front door, it opened before I could even reach it, and I stepped inside.

"Merry Christmas, Benedict," I greeted our butler politely, wiping my feet on the rug. The rain had left a mess outside, including on my shoes.

"Merry Christmas, Sir," Benedict replied, his formal greeting meant for all of tonight's guests. I knew that many of them would ignore him, but Benedict was always unfazed by it.

Benedict and his family had served the Yorks for generations, but I knew very little about him. I once tried to ask him about his family, but the look he gave me was so intimidating that I never dared to ask again. Even now, I still felt nervous around him.

I straightened my tuxedo jacket and headed for the sitting room where the rest of my family had assembled. I was the last to arrive, but I had still managed to beat the other guests, which would hopefully appease my grandmother. However, I knew she would inevitably find something to criticize, such as my hair being overdue for a cut.

"There you are," my grandmother greeted me as I entered the room, her tone stern. "I almost thought you missed your flight."

"Ah, but you know me, Grandmother," I replied with a

charming smile. "I couldn't miss the opportunity to bask in your delightful company for a whole evening."

She gave me a small, tight-lipped smile in response. "Do make sure you freshen up before the other guests arrive. I wouldn't want them to think we don't know how to groom ourselves."

I chuckled lightly. "I'll make sure to put in extra effort for your sake, dear Grandmother," I said, and turned my attention to my younger sister. "Gabriella, my dear sister, always looking lovely as ever. Though perhaps a quick touch-up before Grandmother catches sight of that stray lock?"

Gabriella shot me a glare, but I could see the hint of amusement in her eyes. "Thanks for the tip, dear brother. And don't worry, I'll keep my language ladylike for the evening." The sarcasm in her voice made me chuckle, but my amusement was short-lived as Grandmother's stern voice interrupted us.

"Gabriella, I expect you to conduct yourself with decorum this evening. We are not commoners to be throwing around coarse language."

"Of course, Grandmother," Gabriella replied, her tone respectful but with a hint of rebellion in her eyes.

As I made my way to freshen up, a sense of dismay creeped up on me. The evening promised to be filled with stilted conversation, forced smiles and thinly veiled criticisms. But I reminded myself, as always, that this was the life I was born into. And I was a York, after all. We knew how to put on a good show.

Upstairs, I found myself in my childhood room, and memories flooded my mind. The room was filled with my old belongings from my teens, from the worn books on the bookshelves to the posters on the walls. Now, my room seemed smaller than I remembered, but the cozy atmosphere brought back a sense of comfort. I recalled my grandmother back then. She seemed kinder, and our relationship wasn't as strained as it was now. I sighed and ran my hand over the spines of the many classic tales. While other kids had been playing football in the yards, I had escaped into grand stories of kingdoms, desires, and betrayals. Why couldn't we go back to those simpler times?

Ten minutes later, I was back downstairs and mingling with the guests as they arrived. Benedict made the usual formal announcements, and familiar faces and forced smiles filled the room.

However, I suspected Grandmother had added a few unexpected names to my parents' guest list. And I confirmed it when she introduced me to several adult daughters and their parents. One after another.

"Spencer, I would like you to meet Lorinda Grenville. Her family has just moved down from Newcastle." The young woman gave me a tentative smile that took her from plain to pretty in an instant, making me note her thick lashes and dark curls.

"Pleased to meet you, Lorinda," I said, taking her hand and giving it a polite kiss, as I'd been taught. Grandmother would approve, I thought. "How are you finding London?"

But as I asked the question, my mind immediately went to another London, and I didn't catch a single word Lorinda said in response. Fortunately, her parents called for her, and I could bid her farewell for the moment.

My relief was short-lived, however, as Grandmother appeared with another young woman in tow - a tall blonde with piercing eyes. Bloody hell.

"May I present my grandson, Spencer York," she said, before introducing me to the woman, Bethanie Neville.

"Happy Christmas," I said, brushing my lips across her knuckles in greeting. I wondered what London would make of the gesture - would it be charming or would it be met with rolled eyes?

"Your grandmother mentioned that you've only just arrived back in London after some time in America," Bethanie said, drawing me out of my thoughts.

"Yes, I was over there for business," I replied.

"Let's not have any of that," Grandmother said firmly. "No business discussion during the party."

"Understood, Grandmother," I replied, trying to appease her before she could decide whether to believe me. Just then, Benedict announced another family, and Grandmother excused herself. As was often the case at family gatherings, she seemed to take control of the party, despite my parents being the hosts.

I winced at the thought of what Grandmother would do if I ever were to get married. She had taken control of my sister Fleur's wedding, and I knew unless I chose a bride of higher status, she would treat my partner with the same disdain she showed my mother- and brother-in-law.

The thought of London facing off against my grandmother crossed my mind. Based on the strength I had seen in her, she might just be able to stand her ground.

"Well, if we're not allowed to discuss work, what shall we talk about?" Bethanie asked, a hint of playfulness in her tone. She leaned closer and lowered her voice. "To be honest, I already know about your work in theater. I'm more interested in getting to know the man behind the fame."

If I didn't know better, I would have thought that Bethanie was fed the line to flatter me. "May I ask you a question?" I said.

She looked surprised, but nodded. "What, exactly, did my grandmother tell you about me?" I asked.

Bethanie glanced over to where Grandmother was engaged in conversation with a viscount and viscountess. "Nothing directly," she said. "You know how these things go."

"I do," I agreed, my suspicions about her being fed information about me only growing stronger. Grandmother's attempts at matchmaking were common knowledge, but they were never openly discussed. Negotiations were hinted at, but never candidly addressed, as that would be considered uncouth.

"But, it's been implied that you will soon take your place in the family's affairs," Bethanie said, her tone coy. "And that you'll soon be looking for a proper wife."

I let out a sigh. This wasn't anything I hadn't already suspected, but that didn't make the prospect any more appealing to me.

"Are you're hoping to become that wife?" I asked, getting straight to the point.

"I can't say I wouldn't like the idea," she said with a suggestive look. "All the aspects of it."

Once upon a time, that might have set my pulse racing, but at the moment, I felt nothing.

"And I'm open to a bit of a trial run, if you're interested."

I gave her a polite smile. "I'm afraid I'm not, but thank you for the offer."

Her smile faltered. "I see. Now, if you'll excuse me, I know of some other gentleman who might be interested in a bit of holiday fun."

I nodded, silently wishing her the best of luck. I secretly

hoped she might cause a bit of a scandal, anything to take Grandmother's focus off of me.

As I heard my name being called, I put on my best "charming and debonair" smile. After all, as the heir to the York fortune, I knew my role to play at this party. I'd be expected to make small talk, charm the ladies, and be the life of the party. But it was tiring work with all the pretending. I mean, I'm only human, aren't I?

Just as I was pondering a quick escape to the bar, Grandmother appeared with yet another "suitable" young lady. I sighed inwardly but put on my charming smile, bracing myself for another round of tedious small talk.

I had a plan, though. I would go along with this charade for the next few days, but then I would make a hasty exit back to New York City earlier than planned. There was a certain woman there who had captured my attention, and I preferred spending my time with her over these stuffy socialites. I just hoped she felt the same.

FIFTEEN
LONDON

As the year came to a close, I was in awe of the transformations that had taken place in my life. The start of the year had presented its own set of challenges, but somehow things had fallen into place. My friend Gin had predicted it all along.

After our successful rehearsal, I spent a joyful Christmas in California with my family. There, I received some amazing news: my older brother Alec had finally proposed to his girlfriend, Lumen. We had started a friendly bet to guess when he would pop the question, and my brother Sean had won, gloating about it until Alec threatened to post some baby photos of him online.

But the excitement didn't stop there - my brother Brody announced that his wife Freedom was pregnant. We had a similar bet going on, which my brother Xander had won.

A few days after Christmas, I headed back to the city for more rehearsals. The only thing that kept everything from feeling perfect was Spencer's absence. I knew from Stan that he wouldn't be back until after the holidays. But I had been hoping that he'd return in time for New Year's Eve. Apparently not.

It surprised me how much I missed Spencer. Sure, he was incredibly attractive, with a charming smile and a talent for making me laugh like no one else. And I couldn't deny the amazing sex we'd had. But there was more to it than that. I missed his presence, the way he made me feel just by being near.

"Are you ready to party?!" Mercedes bounced into my apartment, her cleavage nearly spilling out of her dress - or was it a shirt?

"You're going to freeze your ass off," Rocio said. "Or maybe your boobs. It'll depend on whether you pull that thing up or down."

"We will not be outside for long," Mercedes said. "I'm springing for an Uber."

"Where are we going again?" I asked. "You just said to wear something nice."

"I said to wear something that'll get you laid," Mercedes said with a wink. "And it's still a surprise."

"As long as we're not going to Times Square again," Gin said with a groan. "I had to throw out my new dress shoes last year because I couldn't get the puke smell out."

I nodded, knowing the story all too well, but I was usually spending New Year's with my family in California, so I hadn't seen it happen firsthand.

"Nope." Mercedes threw her arms around us. "It's so much better than Times Square."

THE LINE TO get into The Velvet Rope, the exclusive and trendy Manhattan club, stretched around the block, as party-goers dressed in their finest attire eagerly awaited their turn to enter. Mercedes, who had somehow secured us a spot on the coveted guest list, led the way as we bypassed the long line and made our way straight to the bouncer.

After checking the guest list, he stepped aside and let us through the velvet rope and into the club's luxurious interior. The glittering chandeliers, plush furnishings, and state-of-the-art sound system were even more stunning than the exterior. We were finally here, ready to ring in the New Year with style at one of the city's hottest clubs.

As we made our way through the crowded dance floor, my heart raced and a grin spread across my face as I took in the sights and sounds of the bustling club. The throngs of people were a pulsating, vibrant sea, the music a driving, electrifying force that seemed to flow through every vein. The bass was a physical presence, a deep, relentless rhythm that shook the very foundations of the building. It was a seductive call that drew me in, making my body move to the beat. The lights were a dizzying display of colors, flashing and strobing in time with the music, casting a hypnotic spell over the crowd. The energy in the room was electric, a wild and frenetic energy that was both exhilarating and dangerous. I was completely caught up in it all, every sense alive with the excitement of the music, the crowd, and the moment. We laughed, talked, and let ourselves get lost in the rhythm as we danced together. Time flew by as we enjoyed the night until it was finally time to ring in the New Year in style.

As midnight approached, my friends drifted off, searching for someone to kiss and make the night even more memorable. I, however, had opted to move into the shadows, taking a break from the chaos.

Surrounded by couples eagerly awaiting the countdown to the new year, a twinge of unease came over me. I didn't want to have to explain why I would not grab just anyone for a New Year's kiss.

Because I simply couldn't.

My mind was a jumbled mess every time I tried to make sense of my feelings for Spencer. Despite being drawn to him, I knew nothing could happen between us. It would not only be unprofessional, but could also ruin the show, leading to headlines like "Broadway show caught up in a sex scandal! Producer seduces the lead actor!"

Tim, my co-star in the musical and the object of many women's affections, had been flirting with me since rehearsals started. While dating between the leads in a romantic musical could add to the show's realism, Tim was just as off-limits as Spencer. Besides, I suspected that his flirting was more about creating stage chemistry rather than a genuine interest in me.

So, I decided to spend the last moments of the old year alone, sipping my drink and pondering the past and future. I realized that, while I couldn't have the man I desired, I was content with my choice. I was elated about the role I had landed and eager for the opportunities that the new year would bring.

Lost in thought, a familiar voice interrupted me.

"I was terribly worried you had gone."

My heart skipped a beat. At first, I thought it was my imagination playing tricks on me, but then he stepped into view and my gaze met his.

Spencer.

The sight of him took my breath away, and I couldn't help but gawk. Standing in front of me, he was even more handsome than I remembered, with his dark hair falling in a wave across his forehead and his eyes sparkling with a touch of mischievousness.

I regained my composure and felt a familiar flutter in my stomach. "How did you end up here?" I asked Spencer as he approached me with a warm smile. "I thought you were still in England."

"I was," Spencer answered, his voice filled with amusement. "But I decided to come back early. And I'm glad Mercedes posted a picture of you all on Instagram and tagged your location, or I might have had to spend all night searching from club to club to find you." He chuckled, his charming smile making my heart skip a beat.

The DJ's voice cut through the music, "All right folks, we've got thirty seconds until midnight, so find the person you want to kiss and get ready to count down from ten."

Spencer's smile wavered slightly as he said, "Seems like I made it just in time. Unless you have other plans?"

I couldn't resist him any longer, and I shook my head, trying to clear my thoughts. As I stepped forward, our eyes locked. I saw the desire in his gaze, a reflection of my own intense feelings, and I closed the gap between us, my body drawn to him like a magnet.

My hands trembled as I placed them on Spencer's chest, feeling the contours of his muscles through his shirt. I could sense his heart pounding just as fast as mine. The warmth of his skin seeped into mine, making my senses come alive.

Electricity pulsed between us as I gazed into his eyes, and I saw he felt it too. He inched closer, his breath hot on my face, and I felt the tension inside me rising, my body yearning for his touch. There was no going back now.

He met my lips on the count of two, unable to wait those last seconds. The kiss was firm yet gentle, his tongue lightly grazing the seam of my lips, teasing with the promise of more, hinting at the intimacy to come. I was enwrapped in the moment, my mind consumed by the way he was kissing me.

When we parted, I was barely aware of the cheers and excitement surrounding us. But then he leaned in again, and I thought he was going to repeat the kiss. Instead, he whispered into my ear.

"This takes me back to our night together. I haven't been able to get you out of my mind."

I struggled to catch my breath, my heart racing as I told him I felt the same way.

"Why don't we go outside and take in the New Year's Eve festivities?" he suggested, his eyes alight with excitement as he offered me his arm. A smile spread across my face at the prospect, and as I took his hand, I felt weightless with happiness.

We walked out of the club and the noise and heat from the place immediately dissipated, replaced by the cool night air and the sounds of the city coming to life. Spencer confidently led the way through the bustling crowds, his arm wrapped around me.

"Ah, my dear, what a night this is turning out to be," Spencer said, a smile lighting up his face. "The crowds are thick, but don't worry, I'll expertly navigate us through."

I laughed, feeling at ease with him. "You seem quite the expert, Spencer. I've never seen this many people in Times Square," I said as we made our way through the throngs of people. "This is my first time being here on New Year's Eve."

"Well, then I'm glad I'm here to show it to you," he replied, as he took my hand and pulled me close to him.

His embrace warmed me as the sound of horns and cheers filled the air, the bright lights of Times Square illuminating us.

It wasn't just Spencer's warm body that caught my attention, but also the way he looked at me, with a sparkle in his eyes and a smile on his face, like he was seeing me for the first time.

"I couldn't stop thinking about you the whole time I was in England," Spencer whispered. "I had to come back and see you."

"I'm glad you did," I replied, as we locked lips amidst the chaos of the New Year's Eve celebrations. His soft, warm lips moved against mine in perfect harmony, making me shiver.

When we broke apart, Spencer gazed into my eyes with a look of pure longing. "I know this may not be the simplest situation, but my feelings for you are irrefutable," he said in a hushed voice. "I want to spend this night with you and bask in the warmth of our connection. Will you come with me to my hotel?"

I stood before him, my heart pounding in my chest. Spencer's eyes were locked onto mine, his gaze intense and filled with a longing that matched my own. I wanted to respond to him, to give in to the desires that had been building inside of me, but I hesitated. The musical was my top priority, and I couldn't risk it all for just another one-night stand.

"What's wrong?" Spencer asked, his voice a low rumble that sent shivers down my spine.

I shook my head, struggling to find the words. "I just can't, Spencer. The show has to come first."

He stepped closer, his hand reaching out to tuck a strand of hair behind my ear. "I understand that, London, but I can't ignore the way I feel about you. The chemistry between us is undeniable."

I closed my eyes, feeling torn. Part of me wanted to throw caution to the wind and give in to the passion that was crackling between us, but the rational part of me feared the consequences.

Spencer must have sensed my inner turmoil, because he leaned in, his lips brushing against my ear. "I promise you, London, I won't let anything get in the way of the show. I just want to bask in this moment with you."

I couldn't resist his words any longer. With a soft sigh, I gave in and pressed my lips to his. The kiss was electric, a perfect storm of desire and need. I wrapped my arms around his neck, pulling him closer as I lost myself in the moment.

"I've been waiting for this for so long," Spencer whispered as we broke apart, his breath hot against my cheek.

I smiled, feeling a thrill of excitement as I realized I had, too. "Me too," I replied, and as he took my hand, I knew I was ready to take a chance on something truly magnificent.

As we walked hand in hand, the rest of the world became a blur. The sounds and lights faded into the background as I focused on the feeling of Spencer's fingers entwined with mine. My heart was pounding and my palms were sweating with the anticipation of what was to come.

We finally arrived at his hotel and as we stepped into the elevator, he pulled me close. He caressed my cheek as he leaned in and whispered, "This elevator is moving too slow. I don't know how much longer I can wait."

He pressed his lips to mine.

As the elevator doors opened, we stepped out, hand in

hand, and made our way to the Pulitzer Suite. The world faded as we focused on each other, our hearts racing with anticipation.

Once inside, Spencer tenderly cupped my face in his hands, his soft lips barely brushing mine in a teasing touch that sent shivers down my spine. I couldn't help but pull him closer, my arms wrapping tightly around his waist as we got lost in each other.

"More, please," I murmured, slipping my hands under the back of his shirt. I could feel the heat of his skin under my palms, the muscles tensing at my touch.

"As you wish," he whispered, leaning in for another kiss.

His mouth moved against mine, his tongue seeking entrance. I parted my lips, making a contented sound. As his hands stroked along my spine, I deepened the kiss, exploring his mouth and running my own hands up and down his back. Between us, his cock pressed against my stomach, growing hard and thick.

I wanted him in my mouth.

I tugged on his shirt. "Need you naked."

He chuckled, that deep, masculine sound that men sometimes made when they knew a woman desired them. "Thrilled to oblige."

I took a step back and enjoyed watching his clothes come off, running my eyes over every gorgeous inch of his body, from those long, muscular legs to the narrow waist and broad chest with the dark curls. My gaze followed the trail of hair down to a thick cock, straining up toward his flat stomach.

"I believe it's your turn," he said.

I shook my head and put my hand on his chest, giving him a little push backward. "Not yet."

He raised an eyebrow but took the hint, moving back

onto the bed until he was stretched out. I wasn't ready to get naked yet, but I wanted to move more easily, so I reached behind me to unzip my dress, welcoming the weight of Spencer's gaze on me. He muttered a low curse, making me thankful I'd taken my friends' advice and worn my sexiest lace and silk lingerie tonight.

I climbed onto the bed slowly, letting him look his fill as I moved to straddle his thighs. Smiling down at him, I reached up to release my hair from the clips that'd held it in place all night. With the curls cascading down my shoulders, I leaned over, not to take him in my mouth yet, but to let my hair trail across his skin. He sucked in a breath, his hips jerking when the strands brushed his cock.

Pleased with the reaction, I blew gently on his skin and earned a growl. This was the most responsive I'd ever had a man be to my touch. And I hadn't even really touched him yet.

I ran my fingers up and down his length once, then twice, before tracing the same path with my tongue. He cursed, and I could feel the muscles in his thighs tensing beneath me. Wrapping one hand around the thick base, I took the tip of his cock between my lips, barely resisting the urge to smile when he let out an inarticulate yell.

He was too large for me to fit all of him in my mouth, but I lowered the circle of my lips over him as far as I could, letting the weight of him slide over my tongue until my jaw couldn't open any wider. I held him there for a few seconds before raising my head and repeating the entire thing quickly. With my hand working the part of him I couldn't suck on, I used my tongue along with suction to send him hurtling toward the edge.

"Stop." His hand came down on my head, fingers tangling in my curls. "Stop, or I'll come in your mouth."

I looked up, at last, finding the blue of his irises reduced to only the thinnest circle around pupils blown wide with desire. The near-wild expression on his face made things low inside me clench. I let his cock slip from between my lips.

"I wouldn't mind," I said.

"I would." He sat up, catching my chin in his hand. His thumb brushed across my swollen bottom lip. "As much as I love what you're doing, I want to be inside you when we come."

"Condom?"

Less than a minute later, I was above him. The damp fabric of my panties simply moved aside to give him the room I needed to lower myself onto him. We both groaned at the tight fit. My hands went to his stomach for balance, and as I had to work to take the last couple of inches, my nails dug into the firm muscles. His hands moved up and down my thighs, fingers flexing as if he wanted to bury them in my flesh the same way my nails were embedding in him, but he held back.

I wanted to see him lose that control. I didn't want the contained, professional man in the suits who gave everyone the same polished smile. I wanted the man who'd gotten that tattoo. The one who came looking for me tonight, even though he knew it was a bad idea.

With his eyes on me, I rocked back and forth, letting my body adjust to the fullness of having something that large inside me. I took my hands from him and moved them up my body until I cupped my breasts. When I was certain I had his full attention where I wanted it, I unhooked the front clasp and let my bra drop away.

"Oh, London." He reached for me, his touch a bit too gentle, too controlled. "You're so fuckin' gorgeous."

While his fingers teased my nipples, I began to ride him, finding a rhythm that would keep us both right on the edge. Pleasure rippled out along my nerves, but never enough to release the pressure building inside me. I stopped when I felt his hips push up to meet me and his hands were squeezing my breasts.

He groaned, his head falling back. "You're going to be the death of me, London."

"Look at me," I said, and waited until his eyes opened and found mine. "I want you to fuck me."

He looked confused, so I leaned down and lightly bit one flat nipple. He hissed.

"Get on top of me and fuck me hard." I tightened around him and that was all it took for that restraint to snap.

He surged up, one arm going around my waist as his mouth slammed into mine. He turned us but didn't put me beneath him like I'd thought he would. Instead, I found myself with my back against the headboard, my legs automatically going around his waist. Without taking his lips from mine, he drove into me, short, hard thrusts that drove the air from my lungs. What little air I'd been able to get, anyway. The angle had the right pressure and friction on my clit so that, suddenly, nothing was building slowly. Pleasure so intense it was almost painful ripped and clawed its way through me until I was whimpering, my body literally shaking with need.

He finally took his mouth from mine and I gasped in air, but every sound that escaped was more a cry than an exhalation. Then his teeth found my neck, and I came with a scream. He drove into me two more times, each one deeper than the last, and then called out my name. His entire body shuddered with the force of his climax, and we collapsed together in a tangle of limbs.

I heard a soft chuckle and then "Happy New Year" before my exhausted body and mind demanded I rest.

SIXTEEN

SPENCER

I GROANED AS I ROLLED OVER; THE ACHE JOLTING ME awake. My mind raced for a moment as I tried to recall what had happened, and then I felt bare skin against mine as a body shifted next to me. Soft strawberry blonde curls tickled my cheek as she snuggled closer, resting her head on my chest.

Right.

I'd slept with London McCrae again.

And this time, I deliberately sought her out, despite knowing better.

I closed my eyes and mentally cursed myself. Not that I wasn't a good person with no real vices and a few solid rules I never broke.

But sleeping with the actresses who worked for me? Twice? I knew I shouldn't have had her in my bed, but I couldn't help myself. She drew me in.

I sighed and ran my hand through my hair, trying to clear my mind. I was the producer of the play, and she was the lead actress. This was not a good situation. I was the one who made the rules about fraternizing with the cast, and now I was breaking them.

I had to find a way to make this work, to keep the production from falling apart and to not let my feelings for her interfere with my job.

"I can hear you thinking." London's sleep-thick voice sounded amused.

I opened my eyes and found those brandy-colored eyes dancing with humor, and I couldn't help but smile back. Maybe having a good shagging wasn't brilliant, but how could I regret it?

"I'll be back in a minute," she said right before rolling off the bed.

I watched as she moved because no straight man in his right mind would reject the opportunity to gaze at a lovely woman like that walking around naked. She was so small, more than a foot shorter than I was, and slim.

"You bit me in a fairly visible place," she said as she returned from the loo. "I'm going to have to wear high necks or scarves for the next few days."

"My sincere apologies." My grin probably gave away the fact that I wasn't sorry, but she didn't seem like it genuinely bothered her.

She climbed onto the bed, but then glanced at my back and frowned. "Oh no."

"Oh yes, I think you left your own mark at the end," I said with a chuckle.

"Shit. I'm sorry." The bed dipped, and a moment later, I felt the ghost of a touch on my back.

"No worries. I don't mind it." I rolled over, not bothering to hide how her touch affected my body. "Actually, I rather enjoyed it."

"Really? You did?" She blushed and then whisked her fingertips over the bruise-like mark on her neck. "Me too."

I reached up and touched it. "You like how it...felt, or you like wearing my mark?"

"Both."

My cock hardened more, but I ignored it. "I feel the same."

After a moment of silence, she spoke. "All right, I'll ask it. What does this mean? Or does it mean anything?"

I decided. "I'd like it to mean something."

I pushed myself into a sitting position, and she sat next to me, pulling the sheet to cover herself, though I didn't know if it was discomfort at being naked or the chill in the air. Either way, it was probably a good idea. Easier to talk if I wasn't distracted by her breasts.

"I don't usually sleep with women who work on my show," I said. "For obvious reasons."

"Yeah." She looked sheepish. "I don't make a habit of sleeping with producers or anyone involved in shows I'm in."

"It does...complicate things," I said. "But it didn't play any role in you getting cast, and it won't get you preferential treatment."

"And I wouldn't expect it," she said.

"We both know other people might not see it that way," I said. "But I can't say that I care."

She smiled. "Me either."

"I'd like to see where this goes," I continued.

"Like out in public?" she asked.

"I think we should keep things low-key," I admitted. "No displays of affection at work, that sort of thing."

She studied me for a minute and then smiled. "I think

I'd like that." Then, without another word, she bounced up off the bed. "I'm hungry. We should order breakfast."

As I studied her walk over to the desk to pick up the phone, her confident stride sending her hips swaying, I felt a sense of excitement and calm wash over me at the same time. Something about being in her presence made all of my anxieties fade away. Perhaps I could even allow myself to consider the possibility of a relationship. One that could bring true happiness.

But as I thought of my grandmother and her expectations for me to continue climbing the social ladder, I realized I needed to be upfront with London about my family's wealth and status. I knew she deserved to know what she was getting into, but as she stood before me, her nipples tight and her body inviting, I couldn't bring myself to mention it. I told myself that if things between us only led to a few more dates, it would be silly to bring my family's baggage into it. When the time was right, I would let her know.

"Hey London," I said, reaching for her hand. "I have dinner plans with Stan tonight, but I'd love to spend tomorrow and Sunday with you if that's okay."

"That sounds great," she replied, a smile spreading across her face. "I'm meeting my brother and sister today, so those days work for me."

I grinned in response. "Perfect."

"Now," she purred, her sultry gaze locked onto mine. "Breakfast will be here in about forty minutes. And I wonder, what do you propose we do with all that time?"

I let out a low growl as I reached for her, pulling her close to me. The heat radiating from her body was palpable, and I couldn't wait to feel her soft curves pressed against mine. "I have a few ideas," I murmured, my lips trailing down her neck. The way she let out a soft sigh in response sent a jolt of desire through my body, fueling my hunger for her even more.

AS I ENTERED the restaurant for my appointment with Stan, I felt a small twinge of discomfort when my shirt brushed against the nail marks from last night's fiery encounter. I quickly dismissed the feeling, knowing that the passionate night and morning with London was well worth it.

"You seem in good spirits," Stan commented as I took my seat across from him. "I know you were dreading going back to England, but it looks like something, or someone, put a pep in your step."

"I was dreading it," I admitted. "So much so that I returned to New York early."

Stan's grin widened. "And I have a feeling I know what, or rather who, was behind that change of heart," he said in a knowing tone. "Don't tell me it's London?"

I gave a nonchalant shrug, trying to play it cool. "Oh, come on, Stan. Don't be ridiculous," I said with a chuckle. "But enough about me. Let's talk about the rehearsals. How are they shaping up? I'm all ears."

"The rehearsals are going great," Stan said. "Timothy and London have amazing chemistry. It's almost as if they're not acting." He shot me a searching look and continued, "It's impressive to watch." As he spoke, I felt a pang of jealousy. I knew their chemistry was just part of the job, but the image of London enjoying Timothy's kisses wouldn't leave my mind. Just as I was struggling to shake it off, a boisterous man plopped down in the seat behind me, his loud laughter drowning out Stan's words. I turned around, giving the man a pointed look, trying to convey that his behavior was disruptive, but he and his companion seemed entirely unaware.

"It's the best gig," the man boasted. "I mean, I can offer them what no other man can, and they're so grateful. They all end up in bed with me."

"All of them?" The other man's doubt was obvious in his tone.

"Well, if they're uncooperative, I make sure everyone knows it," the man said with a laugh. "Like at the start of December, there was this one bitch."

At the disrespectful term, Stan and I both stiffened.

"She was auditioning for a role and I told her she needed to show her commitment," he boasted. "But she refused. Dumb move on her part. Now, I'll make sure the only job she can get is as a subpar fluffer in porn. I've already alerted all the casting directors I know about how she tried to falsely accuse me and warned them to steer clear of her."

I looked at Stan and saw my shock mirrored in his expression.

The other guy spoke. "Thanks for the heads up. I'll keep my distance. What's her name again?"

"Boston? Paris? Some fucking city," the first man replied carelessly. "London? That's it. Her name was Lon–"

Unable to contain my disgust any longer, I jumped out of my seat and loomed over the man, my voice firm and accusatory. "You must be Russ Heyworth?"

The man frowned at me, with no fear or intimidation in his eyes. "I am, and who the fuck are you?"

My hands balled into fists, but I suppressed the urge to strike Russ. "Listen closely," I said, my voice low and dangerous. "If I hear one more lie from you about London McCrae, there will be consequences. And I guarantee you won't like them."

Russ let out a boisterous laugh, his double chin jiggling. "What, are you her uncle or something?"

"I'm Spencer York," I replied, my voice firm. "The same Spencer York who fired your friend Jerry Niyaz from my show just last week."

"The producer?" Russ's lunch companion looked increasingly uneasy.

"That's right," said Stan, standing behind me. "And I'm Stan Longley."

Russ's face turned an unsightly shade of gray, and he appeared to struggle for breath. "I see," he muttered. "My apologies. I had no intention of causing any trouble."

Russ started to rise from his seat, but I stepped forward, towering over him. "Mr. Heyworth," I warned, my voice still low and menacing. "I won't hesitate to destroy your career if you persist in your vendetta against London or anyone else associated with my show."

His lunch companion, looking increasingly uncomfortable, grabbed his arm and pulled him away, mumbling something about needing to leave. Russ shot me a final, resentful look before allowing himself to be dragged away.

"Well, that was intense," Stan said, breaking the silence.

I let out a deep sigh and sat back down in my seat. "I won't tolerate anyone trying to ruin our show," I said. "London is a talented actress, and she doesn't deserve to have her reputation tarnished by people like that."

"I completely understand," Stan said. "And I'm glad you stuck up for her."

As I sat there in the café, nursing my coffee, I felt a sense of satisfaction after putting that guy in his place. Not that I would ever tell her, but I knew it would please London that I had defended her reputation and set the record straight with that jerk.

SEVENTEEN
LONDON

A MIXTURE OF EXCITEMENT AND NERVES FILLED ME AS I led Spencer through the bustling city streets, pointing out all the famous landmarks and tourist attractions along the way. We strolled through Central Park, took a ferry ride to the Statue of Liberty, and even stopped for a bite to eat at a charming little sidewalk café.

But despite all the amazing sights we saw, my mind was focused solely on our next stop: my brother Carson's apartment. I was eager to introduce Spencer to a small part of my family, but I was worried about how he would react to him. Would he like him? Would he think he was good enough for me? These thoughts swirled in my head, causing my nerves to get the better of me. But as I looked over at Spencer, his hand clasped in mine, I knew I had nothing to fear. Together, we could conquer anything.

Today was my brother's thirty-first birthday, and I wanted to give him a present. It wasn't anything big because none of us siblings did major gifts, but I liked to find little things that showed I was thinking of them.

"Are you certain he won't mind you bringing me along?" Spencer asked. "I don't want to intrude."

"He won't mind." I smiled and tugged on his hand. "Besides, I want to show you off." He laughed as I pulled him out towards my brother's building.

A few minutes later, Carson opened the door with a warm smile. He hugged me, but his demeanor changed slightly when he saw Spencer. I pulled back and introduced them.

"Carson, this is my friend Spencer York. Spencer, this is my brother, Carson McCrae."

They shook hands and Carson welcomed us into his apartment.

"London tells me you're a designer," Spencer said in his charming English accent.

"And you're English," Carson replied, raising an eyebrow. "Oh, Dad's going to love that," he added with a twinkle in his eye.

"Don't be stupid, Carson," I interjected. "Da's never cared about that kind of thing."

"Your father is the founder of MIRI, correct?" Spencer continued, unfazed. "I've heard wonderful things about it."

"How did you know that?" my brother asked, intrigued.

Spencer flushed ever so slightly. "Well, I may have done a bit of research on the flight over here."

"So you know the family's worth a pretty penny," Carson said, his tone slightly guarded.

"Carson," I warned. "Don't be rude."

But before I could say more, Spencer spoke up. "I can assure you, I'm not after your sister's wealth. I have more than enough of my own," he said with a charmingly roguish grin.

Carson regarded him with a narrow gaze. "I'll be checking into you, you know."

Spencer simply chuckled. "I would expect nothing less. I have sisters too, after all."

"In that case, you won't mind if I ask if you have a criminal record," Carson challenged.

"Carson!" I smacked my brother's arm. "Honestly!"

But Spencer remained undaunted. "I could simply lie, of course," he said with a wry smile.

"And I could have a private investigator look into you," Carson retorted.

Spencer held up his hands in mock surrender. "I've got nothing to hide."

"Is that so?" Carson said skeptically.

"All right," I stepped in. "That's enough macho posturing for today." I pointed at Carson. "You're lucky it's your birthday, or I'd kick your ass."

Carson laughed and raised his hands. "Okay, you win. I'll be on my best behavior."

"I mean it, Carson. Be nice," I warned. "I apologize for that. I should've expected he'd be protective of me."

"It's all right," Spencer said with a smile. "Like I said, I understand the guarding nature of siblings."

Carson offered his hand again. "No hard feelings then?"

"Not at all," Spencer replied, shaking Carson's hand with a chuckle.

While the two of them struck up a casual conversation, I shook my head and muttered, "Men are idiots."

Less than ten minutes later, we were all in the living room, basked in the warm atmosphere of laughter and easy conversation. I watched with a smile as Carson and Spencer hit it off, their effortless banter and shared interests bringing them closer together. My heart swelled with hope, as I dared to imagine a future where Spencer would be accepted by the rest of my family, just as he was by Carson.

I heard footsteps and, based on the way my brother's face lit up, I knew who was coming. Vixen Teal, my brother's muse and partner in life.

"Perfect timing," he said as he rose to his feet. "We were just talking about how it's the beautiful people in my life who make my designs so appealing."

"Well, don't let him fool you," I teased. "He was actually just practicing his compliments for you, Vix."

"Ha ha, hilarious," Carson shot back with a grin. "Vix, this is Spencer York. Spencer, meet Vix Teal."

I watched as Spencer took in Vix's stunning appearance, her long, white-blonde hair and light violet eyes contrasting against her porcelain skin. The dress she wore was one of Carson's designs, fitted to her curves with the precision only custom-made clothes could provide.

Spencer turned to Vix with a charming smile. "Vix, I have to ask, do you act? I love your look and I think you'd be perfect for the production."

Vix raised an eyebrow, her lips curling into a small smile. "I've always dreamed of acting. But why, may I ask, are you so interested?"

"I just got a call from my director this morning," Spencer explained. "One of our ensemble actors had to drop out unexpectedly, and I think you could fit the part."

Carson's jaw tensed, and he crossed his arms over his chest. "Vix has a successful career as a model. Why change it?" he asked, a hint of possessiveness in his voice.

"Carson, I can make my own decisions," Vix said, her tone firm but still friendly. "I appreciate the offer, Spencer. What would I have to do to audition?"

As Spencer shared with Vix everything auditioning

would entail, Carson's expression softened. Afterwards, he looked at Vix. "I just don't want you to take on too much and spread yourself thin," he said, his voice low and sincere.

Vix walked over to Carson and wrapped her arms around him. "I know, but I need to make my own choices," she said, kissing his cheek.

Carson hugged her back and turned his attention to me.

"So, you're sure this guy's all right?" my brother asked, with a hint of concern in his eyes.

"Positive. He's a good man," I replied, trying to ease his worries.

When Carson looked like he was about to argue further, I handed him his birthday gift, hoping to change the subject. "Happy birthday."

He opened the gift and looked at me, puzzled. "Thank you? It's a lovely tape measure."

I rolled my eyes. "It's not just any tape measure, Carson. That's the tape measure Irene Sharaff used when she designed Anna Leonowens' 'Shall We Dance' dress for The King and I in 1951."

Carson's jaw dropped, and I couldn't help but laugh at his reaction.

"How did you... I mean... wow, London," he said, giving me a hug. "Thank you."

"Talk about setting the bar high," Vix teased as she sat next to Carson.

"Where did you find that?" Spencer asked, looking intrigued.

"I know someone who collects and sells Broadway memorabilia, and when she found it, she called me."

The look on Carson's face was worth the trip to New Jersey to pick it up.

"I just had a brilliant idea," Spencer said excitedly. "Have you ever considered delving into costume design?"

Carson appeared surprised. "Costumes? I've always thought of that as more of a Halloween thing, you know? Not something to take seriously."

"Well, that's where you're mistaken," Spencer said with a smile. "I've heard from London that your dress designs are stunning. And I need some special dresses designed for the play. I want something that truly embodies London's essence and sets her apart on stage."

Carson's eyes lit up at the prospect. "I've designed clothing for London before," he said, glancing at me.

"Would you be interested in giving it a go? I can provide some concepts and notes, and you can see if you can bring the character to life through her costumes."

When they both looked at me for my input, I felt my heart swell with pride at my brother's talent and I nodded encouragingly. "I think he'd be perfect for the job," I said.

Carson smiled. "I love challenges. I'll do my best."

As the two men delved into the details of stage costumes, Vix and I discussed acting. Before we knew it, the conversation had turned into a dinner invitation, and I watched Spencer, considering the possibilities of a future between us. I felt a spark of something deep and intense, a connection that I couldn't ignore. Could this be the start of something real and long-lasting? There was a part of me that wanted to hope.

EIGHTEEN
SPENCER

It had been two whirlwind weeks since London and I took the plunge and decided to explore a potential relationship. Despite some fun, casual dates, I was determined to take her somewhere truly unforgettable. So, I turned to my trusty business partner, Stan, for his expert recommendation on the best dining spot in the city.

To my delight, not only did he provide the name of a highly acclaimed restaurant, but he also went above and beyond to secure us coveted reservations. This was the type of place that was renowned for its extensive waitlist and typically required months of planning to secure a table. I couldn't wait to sweep London off her feet and make this an evening she'd never forget.

Excited for a night to remember, I eagerly approached London's apartment. As I rang the doorbell, I grew nervous with anticipation. The moment she stepped out, my nerves melted away. She was a vision in a deep blue dress; the fabric hugging her curves in all the right places.

I suspected her talented brother was behind the creation of this masterpiece. The plunging neckline hinted at the possibility of her going braless, sending my imagination into overdrive with inappropriate thoughts.

Arm in arm, we stepped into the luxurious car service and were whisked away to the highly anticipated restaurant. I felt every eye upon us as we entered the establishment, but I was certain that most of the attention was directed towards the stunning woman by my side.

"The name on your reservation?" the hostess asked with a bland expression on her face.

"Spencer York," I replied with a charming smile.

She took her time searching for our reservation, but before I could become too impatient, she spoke again, "Here you are. If you'll follow me."

At first, I thought we would be seated at a private table at the back of the restaurant. However, to my surprise, the hostess led us to a tiny table right beside the kitchen. I was about to request a better table and offer a substantial tip, but the hostess walked away without even giving me a second look.

I took a deep breath, determined not to let this spoil our evening. With a charming grin, I pulled out a chair for London and sat across from her, quickly moving my seat just in time to avoid a near miss with the swinging kitchen door. "This is...cozy," I said with a chuckle, trying to make light of the situation.

London laughed. "Someone has to sit here, right?" she said with a smile, making me grateful for her easy-going nature.

I reached across the table and took her hand. "You're quite the woman, you know that?"

"I do, but it never hurts to hear it," she teased.

A waiter appeared with two glasses of water and took our drink orders.

"Perhaps this will mean we'll get our orders faster," I said as the waiter walked away.

"Maybe," she agreed.

A burst of noise accompanied the doors opening behind me, and I suppressed my annoyance as we paused our conversation until it was quiet again.

"So, how did you and Stan meet?" London asked. "I don't think you ever told me."

"It's quite a story," I said with a grin. "Stan came to the UK to check out the West End a few years ago, and I, being the charming devil I am, swept him off his feet."

London giggled. "That sounds like the start of a beautiful love affair."

"Hardly," I chuckled, and continued with a grin. "He had just purchased an off-Broadway theater and came to London to steal all my secrets." I paused as the kitchen doors swung open again, slamming into the back of my chair. I turned around, expecting an apology, but the server continued without even acknowledging us.

I sighed and took a sip of my drink. "After he left, we stayed in touch," I said.

"So, you called him when you decided to bring your show to the US?" London asked.

"No, actually," I replied with a chuckle. "It was Stan who rang me up and suggested that my show could be a tremendous success on the bright lights of Broadway."

We paused again as our server came out of the kitchen and I expected our drinks being delivered. However, he passed us with a tray of food, which left me slightly disappointed.

"How's your brother doing with the costumes?" I asked. "Didn't you see him yesterday?"

"I did," London replied with a twinkle in her eye. "At

the last fitting, he told me I could pick up the dresses tomorrow before our big rehearsal."

"Fantastic," I said, already having seen the preliminary designs and loving them. "They will be a hit on stage."

Just then, the kitchen door swung open, banging into the back of my chair and jolting me forward. I barely pushed back when our waiter set down our drinks on the table.

"I'll be back in a moment to take your orders," he said before hurrying off.

I raised an eyebrow and turned to London. "I apologize for this poor experience. Stan highly recommended this restaurant, and it has received glowing reviews. Perhaps they're just having an off night."

"Or maybe it's one of those over-hyped things," London added, "like caviar."

"Caviar?" I asked, intrigued.

"Yes, you know, the wealthy people love to have it on hand, but in reality, it's just fish eggs and can be quite disappointing," she said with a delicate frown.

"I couldn't agree more," I chuckled. "I've never been a fan myself."

Just then, two more waiters rushed in and out of the kitchen, and our server still hadn't returned. I let out a sigh and said, "Perhaps it would be better if we moved on to another establishment. What do you think?"

"Certainly," London said, grabbing her purse. "How about that charming pub where we first met?"

I smiled. Every time I thought she couldn't be more perfect, she surprised me with something like this. She took pleasure in just being in each other's company and not seeking anything more.

As we left the restaurant, I left enough money to cover

the drinks we never got to enjoy. The hostess looked at us with confusion as we passed her by, but I simply smiled and said, "Thanks for the entertainment. It's been quite a show!"

London giggled beside me as we walked away, leaving the hostess standing there in disbelief. What a breath of fresh air she was, making this evening just as memorable as our first date at the pub.

As we walked away from the restaurant, London looked up at me with a playful glint in her eye. "You know, Spencer," she said, "I think this is just the beginning of our own little Monty Python adventure." And with a laugh, she took my hand, and we headed off to the pub.

We hailed a cab and as the vehicle started moving, I couldn't resist the temptation to lean in and kiss London. Her lips were soft and warm, and the aroma of her perfume filled my nostrils. I wrapped my arm around her waist and pulled her close, deepening the kiss. London responded eagerly, her fingers entangled in my hair.

The cab driver's clearing of his throat brought us back to reality. I reluctantly ended the kiss, but kept my arm around London as we laughed and regained our composure. The rest of the ride was a blur of whispered words and stolen kisses. By the time we arrived at the pub, I was completely enamored with this incredible woman at my side.

As we settled into a cozy booth in the corner, London leaned back and took a deep breath, her contented smile spreading across her face. After placing our orders with a much more amiable server, we enjoyed an uninterrupted conversation.

"You mentioned that your father's from Scotland. Have you ever been there yourself?" I asked.

"I've been there enough to feel comfortable," she replied. "All of my siblings on my dad's side were born in Scotland, and he wanted us to keep that part of our heritage. Plus, he wanted my older siblings to feel close to their mom."

"Is Carson one of them?"

London nodded. "I only have two full biological brothers, Sean and Xander. They're twins and older than me. The three of us were born in California."

"Have you ever been to any other part of the UK, like London?" I asked with a chuckle, considering her name.

She laughed and shook her head. "No, I haven't had the chance to venture outside of Scotland. I've been all over Edinburgh and Glasgow, but never beyond."

"An idea just hit me," I said. "With the start of the preview phase of the show next week, this weekend is our last chance to travel for a while. I was thinking of going back home to London for a few days. Would you like to join me? You could see some of the city and, if you're comfortable, meet my parents."

London's eyes widened. "Your parents?"

"Yes, my parents," I replied with a grin. "I can't very well go to London and not see my mum. Although, I'll admit it might be soon for the whole 'meet the parents' talk. But I'd love for my mum to meet you."

I brought our hands to my lips and gently kissed her knuckles. "So, what do you say? Are you up for a trip to England this weekend?"

NINETEEN
LONDON

When Spencer invited me to join him on a trip to London, the thought of meeting his parents made my nerves kick in. I couldn't believe he was already thinking about introducing me to the most important people in his life. On the one hand, I felt flattered and liked he was taking our relationship seriously, but I was scared. What if they didn't like me? What if I said something awkward or embarrassing? And meeting the parents was a big step, which made me question if I was ready for it so soon.

However, I understood Spencer's reasoning for wanting to see his parents while he was in London. It would be a waste for him to travel all that way and not visit with them.

Despite my apprehension, the idea of exploring a new city with Spencer was too tempting to resist. Deep down, I also wanted to meet the people who had helped shape him into the person he was today. So, I told Spencer that I would accompany him to London.

Now, as we traveled to the airport, I sat in the town car, feeling a mix of excitement and nerves. My jaw dropped as

I realized we would fly on Spencer's private jet. Technically, it belonged to his family, but it was my first time experiencing this level of luxury.

As I looked out the window, I was struck by how much my life had changed since I met Spencer. He was unlike any other person I had dated before, and the thought both scared and exhilarated me.

"Nervous?" Spencer asked, covering my hand with his.

I turned to him and smiled. "A little. I've never been on a private jet before."

"Don't worry," he said, his tone reassuring. "You'll love it. It's much more comfortable than flying commercially."

"I'm sure it is," I replied, still feeling a little overwhelmed.

When we pulled up to the private terminal, I couldn't help but gawk at the sleek white plane waiting for us. A uniformed attendant greeted us and showed us to our seats.

The interior of the plane was even more luxurious than I could have imagined, with plush leather seats, a fully stocked bar, and even a bedroom. I felt like I was in a movie.

"This is amazing," I said, unable to hide my amazement.

Spencer grinned at me. "I'm glad you like it."

As the plane took off and I leaned back in my seat, the flight attendant approached us with a tray of champagne flutes. Spencer raised his glass, a mischievous glint in his eye. "To new adventures," he said, clinking his glass against mine.

I took a sip of the bubbles, feeling their effervescence tickle my nose, and gazed at Spencer, who was watching me with a look of pure adoration. It was hard not to feel grateful for this moment; for this man by my side.

As the flight continued, a delicious meal was served,

and I savored every bite. The conversation flowed easily, making me laugh more than I had in a long time.

After we finished our meal, Spencer suggested we take a little "nap" in the plane's bedroom. I raised an eyebrow, wondering if this was going to be our mile-high club moment. But Spencer simply took my hand and led me to the back of the plane, where the cozy bedroom awaited.

I lay down on the bed, feeling the softness of the sheets and the gentle rocking of the plane as it flew through the evening. Spencer lay down beside me, and as I drifted off to sleep, it was impossible not to think how lucky I was to be here.

WHEN WE TOUCHED down in London early on a Saturday morning, a sleek car awaited us at the private terminal at Heathrow. The driver was on hand to whisk us away to Spencer's luxurious apartment in the heart of the city.

As the driver navigated the bustling streets of London, the vibrant sights and sounds of the city captivated me. I was in awe of the historic buildings, busy street markets, and the hustle and bustle of everyday life. And, all the while, Spencer was by my side, pointing out all the sights and sharing stories about his life in the city.

When we arrived at Spencer's apartment, its elegance and sophistication struck me. The spacious living room was filled with natural light and furnished with plush sofas and modern art. The open kitchen was a chef's dream, with gleaming countertops and state-of-the-art appliances.

As we settled in, Spencer showed me around the apartment, pointing out all of his favorite features. He even took me up to the rooftop terrace, where we enjoyed a stunning view of the city.

"This is incredible," I said, taking in the view. "I feel like I'm on top of the world."

Spencer smiled and wrapped his arm around me. "I've arranged for lunch to be delivered from the hotel next door," he informed me. "It should arrive shortly. After we've eaten, I have a meeting with the theater owners to go over the renovation progress. It won't take long, but I had the maid make the bedroom ready for you if you'd like to take a nap? We have a long evening with my parents ahead of us tonight."

I nodded, feeling a bit overwhelmed by the excitement and anticipation of the day. After a satisfying lunch, Spencer bid me farewell, and I retreated to the main bedroom, relishing the tranquil and serene surroundings. I was eager to embrace the peace and make the most of this idyllic space.

———

"HEY THERE, SLEEPYHEAD," Spencer grinned as he walked into the bedroom, waking me from my nap.

"Oh, hi," I rubbed my eyes, feeling a bit disoriented.

"I've got something for you," he said, handing me a small, elegant box. "I know we haven't been together long, but when I saw this, I thought of you."

I opened the box to reveal a delicate gold bracelet with an infinity symbol, similar to the one on my necklace. It even had a diamond in the center.

"It's beautiful," I said, admiring the delicate gem. "It goes perfectly with my necklace. I'm speechless."

Spencer beamed with pride. "Excellent, because I wanted to take your breath away," Spencer chuckled in his signature charming manner, and kissed me before he fastened the bracelet around my wrist, his fingers manipulating the clasp with surprising dexterity.

"So, how did the meeting about the theater renovation go?" I asked, tearing my gaze away from the beautiful bracelet to admire Spencer.

"It was good," Spencer replied, his eyes shining with excitement. "The owners are determined to spare no expense to make the theater truly magnificent. I'm eager to see the finished product and relaunch the production." He leaned in and gave me a kiss before helping me out of bed. "But let's not talk about work now. We have a big night ahead of us with my parents. Let's get ready."

As I stood in front of the bathroom mirror, I couldn't help but feel a twinge of sadness. Despite all our hard work and dedication, I knew that our Broadway production would never hold the same place in Spencer's heart as his first West End show. But I pushed the thought aside, determined to enjoy this special evening for what it was. I had planned my outfit carefully, choosing a sleek black dress from Carson's collection that accentuated my curves and complemented my braided updo. A pair of understated heels and a new bracelet completed the look, and I felt confident and elegant as I stepped out of the bathroom to join Spencer.

He was waiting for me by the door, his eyes lighting up as he took in my appearance. "You look absolutely stunning," he said, running his hand up my arm and sending a thrill through my body. "Shall we go?"

I nodded, my heart racing with anticipation. Tonight was more than just dinner - it was a chance for me to meet

Spencer's parents and learn more about the man I was falling for from a different perspective. I had heard so little about them from Spencer, but I was eager to put faces to the names and see how they had influenced the person he had become.

"I'm as ready as I'll ever be," I replied, sensing some tension in the corners of Spencer's eyes. It seemed like he was more nervous about this dinner with his parents than I was. I took his hand, hoping to ease some of his anxiety.

"Shall we?" I asked, a hint of excitement in my voice.

"Our car's waiting," Spencer replied, a smile playing on his lips.

"A car? I expected a royal carriage," I teased, trying to lighten the mood.

"I'm so sorry to disappoint," he chuckled. "But I'll do my best to make it up to you."

I grinned back at him, feeling a sense of comfort in his presence. "I have no doubt about that. I already have a few ideas about how you can do that," I said with a mischievous twinkle in my eye. "Just you wait."

"Bloody hell, London," Spencer said, his tone equal parts amusement and exasperation. "You never cease to surprise me. Now I'm going to be wondering what inventive, filthy things you have planned for later. Not exactly ideal when we're having dinner with my parents."

I grinned mischievously. "Then I probably shouldn't tell you what I'm not wearing," I teased, winking at him. "But maybe I should. It's your call."

Spencer let out a deep, guttural sound that was part growl, part laughter. "You're trouble," he said, shaking his head. "Pure trouble."

I laughed along with him, feeling a sense of warmth and

connection between us. Despite the nervousness that still lingered in the back of my mind, I couldn't help but feel excited about the night ahead. This was another adventure in our relationship, and I was ready to face it with Spencer by my side. Whatever challenges or surprises lay in store, we would tackle them together. It was going to be a night to remember. In a good way, I hoped.

I STARED AT THE HOUSE, feeling a mix of nerves and awe as I waited for Spencer to come around and open my door. The front entrance was grand, with double doors made of polished mahogany that looked like they belonged in a palace. The windows were large and adorned with intricate scrollwork, allowing the soft glow of interior lighting to spill out onto the street. This was a house that commanded attention and spoke to the wealth and prestige of its owners.

Spencer had spent the drive here filling me in on the various forms of proper etiquette his family would expect, from letting him open the door and pull out my chair to the way to greet his parents. It felt like playing a role, and I couldn't help but feel a sense of nervousness as I mentally rehearsed the steps in my head. But I tried to remind myself that he wasn't asking me to be someone else. He just wanted me to be myself, but with a few extra touches of elegance and poise.

With that firmly in mind, I walked up to the door, my arm linked with Spencer's. As we approached, the sheer size of the place blew me away. This wasn't just a house, it was a mansion. I wondered what it would be like to grow up in such opulence, with every comfort and privilege at your fingertips. But as we walked to the front doors, I felt my nerves fray once again. The stakes were high, and I couldn't afford to mess this up. I took a deep breath and reminded myself to stay calm and focused.

The man who answered the door was an honest-to-goodness butler, complete with a black suit, white tie, and everything. His name tag read "Benedict."

"Good evening, Benedict," Spencer said politely.

"Sir." Benedict's eyes flicked to me. "Miss."

"Good evening," I said with a smile, but Benedict didn't even blink in response. Based on what Spencer had told me, that was normal.

As the butler closed the door behind us, I found myself face-to-face with Spencer's parents. The resemblance between father and son was striking, from the clear blue eyes to the sandy brown hair, now silver-streaked with age. The man was tall and heavyset, with broad shoulders that gave him a commanding presence. Next to him stood a slender woman with blue-black hair and dimples that looked all too familiar. It was clear that Spencer got his good looks from both sides of the family.

"London, may I present my parents, Raynard and Eloise York. Dad, Mum, this is London McCrae," Spencer introduced me with a polite bow of his own.

"Pleased to make your acquaintance," I said with a smile and a nod, not offering a handshake since I knew it was not the proper greeting for this situation.

"If you'll join us in the drawing room while we wait for dinner to be announced," Eloise said with a polite smile directed at both of us.

Spencer and I followed his parents into an elaborately decorated room, where two more adults and three children sat quietly on a couch. The opulent decor was impressive, but even more remarkable was the sight of the children, who sat with their hands folded neatly in their laps, as if they were afraid to move on the expensive piece of furniture.

The children's faces lit up as they saw Spencer, and the boys looked over at a woman with dark brown hair and blue eyes, silently asking for permission to approach. The youngest child, a girl who couldn't have been more than three years old, didn't hesitate and ran straight towards Spencer.

"Uncle Spencer!" She leaped into his waiting arms and hugged him tightly around the neck.

"Have you been behaving yourself, Jane?" Spencer asked with a smile.

She nodded enthusiastically before leaning close to him and whispering at a typical little kid whispering volume, "I try, but it's really hard."

"I know," Spencer whispered back. "I try too."

Damn, if that wasn't the cutest thing I'd ever seen.

"Aren't you going to introduce us to your friend?" The dark-haired woman's bitter tone chilled me to the bone, her back stiff in a chair that was probably older than my entire apartment building.

"Fleur, this is London McCrae," Spencer introduced me, his arm sliding around my waist. "London, my sister Fleur and her husband Parker Linden. The boys are Harrison and Matthew." Spencer kissed Jane's cheek and set her down.

"Pleased to meet you," I said warmly, trying to break the ice. Spencer had warned me that his oldest sister would be harder to win over than his mother, and the way Fleur looked at me made me think Spencer might have down-played it.

"How did the Blackwell Charity Auction go?" Spencer asked Fleur, trying to shift the focus.

"Grandmother was pleased," Fleur said smugly. "Quite a bit more than she was with you after our Christmas party."

Spencer's expression tightened, and I saw color tinging his cheeks. "I conducted myself appropriately."

"Are you certain she thought so?" Fleur asked, her eyes challenging him. "Or were you in such a hurry to return to New York that you didn't speak with her after that night?"

"Fleur, this isn't the time for this discussion," Raynard interrupted, trying to diffuse the tension in the room. He didn't look in my direction, but Fleur's eyes were still fixed on me.

After a moment of awkward silence, Eloise spoke up. "London, my dear, may I ask about your name? I find it quite intriguing."

"My mother has a fondness for city names and chose them for all her children," I replied. "Austin, Rome, Paris, Aspen, and me."

"Ah, I see," Eloise nodded, her eyes brightening with interest. "You have four siblings?"

"More, actually. I come from a large blended family," I said with a smile.

Before I could say more, Benedict entered the drawing room to announce that dinner was served. As we made our way to the dining room, Spencer leaned in and whispered, "Are you okay?"

"I'm fine," I replied, giving him a reassuring smile. "What about you?"

He chuckled. "Oh, this is just another typical dinner

with my family," he said, his tone a mix of amusement and resignation.

I nodded, understanding Spencer. Family dynamics could be complex and difficult for outsiders to navigate.

My jaw dropped when I entered the dining room in Spencer's family home in York. Instead of the functional dining room I was used to in my parents' house in San Ramon, or the similar one in the family's house in Scotland, I found myself in a room that seemed straight out of a Regency romance novel. The giant table had to be antique, and there were paintings on the walls that my sister Aspen would have gone crazy over.

"Are you familiar with art?" Fleur asked as if she already knew the answer and it wasn't flattering to me.

"A little," I said honestly. "My older sister, Aspen, owns an art restoration company based out of San Ramon. She'd love these." I gestured to the artwork.

"San Ramon?" Eloise asked.

"Yes, it's a city in California." I sat in the chair Spencer had pulled out for me and hoped the movement didn't look as awkward as it felt. "Her business is called Carideo Restorations."

"Why Carideo?" Raynard asked. "Isn't that Italian?"

"Yes, Aspen's father was Marcus Carideo, and I think he was of Italian and Spanish heritage. I'm not positive, though."

"And you?" Fleur asked. "What are you?"

"Fleur." Spencer's voice was sharp.

His sister rolled her eyes. "I apologize. That wasn't politically correct of me. What I meant to ask is where your family comes from. McCrae is Scottish, but you sound American."

"I am." I could feel the tension radiating off Spencer,

and reached over to put my hand on his knee. "My father's from Scotland and moved to the US after he met my mom. I was born in California."

"So, what is it you do for a living?" Eloise's smile made me think maybe she wasn't simply trying to find something else to pick at.

"I'm an actress," I said, trying to keep my tone light and pleasant.

Eloise's smile tightened. "Is that how you and my son met? Did you audition for his show?" she asked, her eyes boring into me.

Spencer spoke up quickly. "No, actually. We met at a pub on my second day in America," he said, his voice firm.

But Fleur wasn't convinced. "But she is in your show, right?" she sneered, her lips twisting into an unattractive scowl.

Spencer's jaw tightened, but he kept his composure. "Yes, she is. But it's not because we're dating. London more than earned it. Something you'd all be able to experience if you come to New York to see the show."

Fleur made it clear that she had no intention of doing so, but Eloise intervened with a stern look. Raynard then picked up the questioning, asking about my parents' occupation.

I replied with a polite smile. "My father created the McCrae International Research Institute, but he's retired now and my older brother Alec has taken over."

"McCrae International Research Institute? That's MIRI, right? Based in Scotland?" Parker's eyes lit up with curiosity.

"Yes, that's the one," I replied, glad somebody recognized the name.

"I've always wondered what–"

But before Parker could finish his sentence, Fleur cut in, interrupting as if it was a regular occurrence.

"Mum, I've been meaning to talk to you about our annual donation to the British Museum. The curator would like to come on Monday to review our collection," she said, her tone firm and commanding.

I looked around the dining room, feeling more and more out of place. It was obvious that Spencer's family was wealthy and cultured, and I couldn't shake the feeling that I didn't belong there with my American accent and background in acting. I tried to put on a brave face and be polite, hoping to make a good impression. Spencer's hand found mine under the table, and I squeezed it in gratitude for his comforting touch. I could tell that he was also feeling the pressure of his family's scrutiny, but he handled it with grace and dignity, which only made me admire him more.

As dinner ended, I was relieved that the conversation hadn't turned into a full-blown interrogation. But by the time we said our goodbyes, I had to force a smile on my face. I felt like a little girl who didn't fit in with the other kids at school. The Yorks were like a clique of the most exclusive social circle, and I knew I was the outsider who would never belong.

Spencer had been so confident and determined about our relationship, but now I wondered if we had a future together. His family's expectations were clear - they wanted someone from their social circle to be by his side. The thought of Spencer only being with me to defy his family was painful.

A little voice in my head whispered that this would not work, that I should leave before it shattered my heart into a million pieces. Despite hoping that we were building something real, tonight's dinner with his family crushed that hope. Their rejection of me was palpable, and I couldn't bear the thought of forcing Spencer to choose between them and me. Our relationship felt like nothing more than an illusion, and I didn't know how to move forward from here.

TWENTY

SPENCER

As I sat on the flight back to New York with London, something felt off. She had barely spoken, and when she did, her responses were short and to the point. I assumed she was just exhausted from the trip, as she had slept for most of the flight.

However, the next morning, I sent her a couple of texts but received no response. I could tell she had read them, but there was still no reply. With rehearsals starting the following day, I had no chance to see her in person. I knew I had to reach out to her, so I called her.

For a moment, I thought she wouldn't answer. But then, I heard her voice on the other end of the line, "Hi."

"Hey, I just wanted to make sure everything was okay since I didn't hear from you," I said, trying to keep my tone light.

"I'm fine, just busy," she replied, her voice sounding distant.

I was taken aback by her response. "Well, I have you on the phone, so would you like to have dinner with me tonight?"

After a long pause, she declined. "No, thank you. I need to focus on the previews and make sure I'm prepared."

I was disappointed, but I didn't let her rejection discourage me. "Okay, what if I bring dinner to you and help you run lines?"

"Um, I don't think that's a good idea. You'd just distract me," she said curtly.

I didn't know how to react to her words. It didn't sound like a compliment, and I felt uneasy.

"Spencer, I've got to go. I'll see you at previews tomorrow," she cut off the call, without waiting for my response.

I sat in silence for a moment, staring at my phone. What had just happened? I couldn't understand it. I had felt her distancing from me, but I never expected her to go from meeting my parents to completely blowing me off.

Frustrated, I headed to the minibar to find a stronger drink than beer. I needed to take the edge off and clear my head. The situation was confusing, and I couldn't wrap my head around it. She had talked about wanting to meet my parents, and now, suddenly, she seemed to pull away.

Damn.

Maybe I had been moving too fast? Perhaps my invitation to England was a significant step in our relationship, rather than just me wanting to spend some time with her and show off my home.

The more I thought about it, the more I realized what a fool I'd been. I should have clarified what I was asking and set the proper expectations. She and I had agreed on quiet and casual. I should have let her know my invite changed nothing.

There was only one way to fix this. I had to apologize for the misunderstanding and talk to her. Clearly, she didn't want to talk to me over the phone, so I'd catch her tomorrow at previews, explain everything, and then things would return to the way they were.

———

"LONDON, MY DEAR," I said, sounding like a perfect gentleman. "I want to apologize for any confusion I may have caused. I understand we agreed on taking things slow, and I should have made sure we were on the same page before extending the invitation to England. Can we find a way to move forward at a pace that is comfortable for both of us?"

I sighed, feeling ridiculous for talking to myself, rehearsing this conversation out loud. But I knew I had to make things right with her, and I didn't want to mess up my words.

Leaving my quiet hotel suite, I made my way to the theater for the first night of previews. I had decided it would be best to give her space before the show, and approach her after. We both needed to focus on the performance, as previews were crucial for fine-tuning the production before opening night. While this was a reproduction of my West End show, we still needed to be attentive to the audience's reactions and make any necessary adjustments.

As I went about my day, I attempted to keep my distance from London. I had to focus on my responsibilities at the theater, which included meetings with donors and investors. Having grown up in the family business, I knew how to put on a charming facade and pretend to enjoy these meetings, even when I wasn't feeling it.

But as the lights went down for the first night of previews, I was relieved to finally find my seat in the box. It was a prime location to observe the entire audience and take in the full stage.

As the music started and the curtain rose, I felt myself being drawn into the world of the musical. It was as if the outside world faded away, and all that mattered was what was happening on the stage. And then London stepped out, and her performance completely captivated me. Her presence was commanding, her voice divine, and she brought a depth to her character that I had not expected.

The first act came to a close with a sense of satisfaction and pride. The hard work we had put into the show had paid off, and I was confident that it would succeed on Broadway.

During intermission, I chatted with some investors and donors, all of whom were thrilled with what they had seen so far. Despite that, I kept thinking about London, how I would confront her after the show, give her my apology for everything that happened back home and try to figure out what's bothering her.

As the lights dimmed and the second act began, I settled back into my seat, and once again, London's performance left me breathless. Every moment on stage was captivating, and I knew that she was destined for greatness. But it wasn't just London. Every member brought a unique energy to the stage that lifted the show into something truly phenomenal. While we might need to make a few minor tweaks in the coming weeks, I was confident that this show was going to be a hit.

After the final curtain call, I sat still for a moment, taking in the audience's energy and noting who left in a hurry versus who lingered. Once I was ready, I hurried to the stage, using a secret passage to avoid the throngs of admirers that had gathered.

My only focus was finding London. I had to catch her before she slipped away again.

As I made my way through the backstage area, Tomma Ackman, an ensemble member and also London's understudy, stopped me. "Mr. York, what did you think?" she asked with a smile.

"Everyone was brilliant," I replied politely. "Excuse me, I need to find someone."

I didn't wait for her to answer, though I spared a thought to hope I wasn't being terribly rude. Instead, I hurried on, my mind racing with what I would say when I finally found London.

I walked through the throng of performers and crew, avoiding eye contact but acknowledging their hard work with a small smile. My gaze darted around the room, searching for the one person who mattered most to me. And there she was, standing next to Timothy. The man I had always suspected had feelings for her.

My pace quickened as I made my way over to them, hoping for a moment alone with London. But before I could reach her, Timothy's arm snaked around her waist, pulling her in close. My heart sank as I watched her smile up at him, seemingly oblivious to my presence.

I stood there, frozen in place, unable to look away as Timothy's hand moved up her back. My mind raced with questions and doubts, wondering what had happened to the connection London and I had shared. Had I been imagining things, or was this the end of our relationship? My thoughts were a jumbled mess as I tried to process what I was seeing, unsure of what to do next.

Fuck.

My jaw clenched, and I struggled to keep my emotions

in check. Was this really happening? Had I misjudged everything so badly?

As Timothy leaned in to whisper something in her ear, I saw London's eyes flicker in my direction, and my heart lurched, hoping she would see me and come over. But she was acting as if I wasn't even there.

With a deep breath, I turned and made my way out of the theater. I needed space to clear my head and figure out what I was going to do next.

TWENTY-ONE
LONDON

W‍HEN M‍ERCEDES AND I HAD ARRIVED AT THE S‍HUBERT Theatre for the preview of the show, I hadn't fully considered the consequences of avoiding Spencer. Ignoring texts and phone calls was one thing, but avoiding him at work would prove more challenging. With his hands-on approach to production, I knew it was only a matter of time before I would have to face him.

All day, I was able to push thoughts of Spencer and his perfect family to the back of my mind and focus on the performance. However, as the final bow was taken, my first thought was what Spencer thought of my performance.

As I walked off the stage, my immediate attention was drawn to the fact that Timothy was still holding my hand. I didn't want to jerk it away and risk someone thinking there was bad blood between us. While critics didn't come to previews, the media could still quickly get wind of any hint of scandal. Sure, bad press could bring more attention, but I didn't think that was the way Spencer wanted the word to get out about the show.

"Great work!" Darrel came up to Timothy and me, his expression the happiest I'd seen. "You were magnificent!"

"Thanks." I used the opportunity to take my hand from Timothy's, and then I shook our director's hand.

"Yeah, thank you," Timothy chimed in, a wide grin spreading across his face. "But I couldn't have done it without London here."

Inwardly, I smirked at Timothy's confidence. Even though Darrel was addressing both of us, Timothy assumed the compliment was solely for him. Although I'd come to appreciate him over the weeks, his ego was still larger than anyone I had ever met.

Darrel's eyes sparkled with amusement, as if he was having the same thoughts.

Timothy placed his arm around my waist and pulled me close. "With this much chemistry, it's impossible not to create magic."

I resisted the urge to roll my eyes. This was just Timothy's personality. I doubted he even realized how he came off.

"You two look great together," Darrel said. "The press is going to love you guys."

I tensed as Timothy's hand slid up my back, the proprietary touch pushing the boundaries of appropriate behavior. In character, it may have been acceptable on stage, but now it was overstepping. I wanted to give myself space and reinforce my boundaries, but confronting Timothy in public wasn't the smartest approach. He was simply making an assumption, not actively pressuring me. I could handle this privately, without jeopardizing the success of our performance or my working relationship with my co-star.

I awkwardly patted Darrel on the shoulder and offered a

polite, "You did a great job tonight too," as I made my excuses to leave. But before I could turn around, Timothy held me tighter and whispered something into my ear. Not hearing much of what he said, I noticed Spencer watching us.

His expression tightened, and a flash of jealousy crossed his face. Our eyes met, and we locked gazes for a moment before he turned and walked away.

Damnit.

I was the one who put the brakes on our relationship with Spencer, but I never intended for it to come to a full stop. I just needed time to catch my breath and determine what I truly wanted.

I realized maybe that had been a mistake. It would have been smarter to act like an adult and communicate with him.

It was time to make things right before I lost my courage or talked myself out of it.

"I'm sorry, Tim. I didn't hear what you said, but if you'll excuse--"

"I said, how about I buy you a nightcap, and we can chat about tonight's success?" Timothy interrupted me before I could finish.

"What?" I looked at him, confused.

"A nightcap," he repeated, flashing a charming smile. "A drink. Maybe back at my place?"

I understood that his offer to help me relax likely had more to do with intimacy than with the alcohol, but that didn't make me any more likely to accept. Hooking up with a co-star could only lead to trouble, especially if things didn't go well. At best, it would be awkward. At worst, it could damage my performance and reputation.

As much as I appreciated Timothy's attention, he just

didn't tempt me. Despite him standing right in front of me, all I could think about was finding Spencer.

"No, thank you," I said, forcing a smile to soften the rejection. "If you'll excuse me, I need to speak with someone."

I left before Timothy or Darrel could ask questions. Making my way to where I'd last seen Spencer, a quick look around told me he'd left. I doubted he'd left the building, though. Not considering how important tonight was.

I spotted Stan and approached him, hoping he might have a clue about where Spencer went.

Stan was deep in conversation with a beautiful brunette, dressed in a form-fitting red dress that accentuated her curves, and she had a sparkling smile that lit up her face.

As I caught up to them, the woman looked up and smiled at me. "There she is! The star of the show!" Her eyes sparkled with excitement.

"London, what a performance. Congratulations," Stan said, with a big smile on his face as he gave me a hug. "Have you met Alice?" he continued. "She's a dear friend of mine and one of our biggest sponsors."

"It's nice to meet you, Alice," I replied, extending a hand.

Alice took my hand and squeezed it, still beaming with excitement. "I just wanted to say your performance was amazing! You were absolutely breathtaking."

"Oh, thank you," I said, feeling a warm flush of pride.

"So, I need some insight," Alice said, pulling me out of Stan's hearing range. "There's this gentleman here tonight I have had my eye on for a while, and I was hoping you might have some advice on how to get his attention."

I raised an eyebrow in surprise. "Really? Who is he?"

"I really shouldn't say out loud here, but he's so hand-some," Alice said, her cheeks flushing pink as she glanced toward Stan. "I was hoping you might have some tips on how to persuade someone who works with theater, and has little time for anything else?"

I smiled, realizing she must be talking about Stan. "Well, sometimes a little flattery can go a long way. And if all else fails, just be yourself. People can sense when someone is genuine and sincere."

"Thank you, London," Alice said, her eyes shining with gratitude. "I really appreciate your advice. And once again, congratulations on the show."

"Thank you, so nice to meet you," I said, glancing around the room. I still needed to find Spencer. "Good luck with your gentleman. I hope everything goes well."

Avoiding the cast and crew who wanted to congratulate me on a job well done, I slipped along the edges of the crowd to make my way to the dressing rooms. If Spencer wanted to greet everyone, that would be a good place to be.

Ten minutes later, after searching everywhere back-stage, I'd almost given up, thinking he must have left, and then suddenly, I spotted him.

Butterflies fluttered in my stomach as I walked toward him. I needed to apologize first, and tell him I should have talked to him instead of pushing him away. Then I had to let him know that what she saw with Timothy and me–

All thoughts flew out of my head as the same tall, slen-der, beautiful brunette from before kissed Spencer on the cheek.

Alice. What the...

I blinked and froze in my tracks as I watched. That could have been simply a friendly greeting.

Except she put her hand on his arm and laughed. There

was no mistaking the flirtation in that sound or the way she tossed her hair. Stan wasn't the man she had been after. It was Spencer.

I suddenly felt the grime of caked-on theater make-up on my face, the way my costume clung to me, fabric damp with sweat. Alice looked cool and fresh, not a hair out of place. She probably smelled a lot better than I did, too.

She laughed again and leaned into Spencer enough to press her breasts against his arm. I waited for him to tell her he was seeing someone, or at least offer a polite smile and step back. Instead, he just stood and smiled. And it was a nice one with warmth to it.

Then he took her hand in his.

"There you are!" Timothy's voice boomed behind me.

Color flooded my face as Spencer and Alice turned in my direction. I didn't look to see if he was still holding her hand. I didn't want to know, and I definitely didn't want to hear anything he had to say.

I spun on my heel and stalked toward Timothy. Grabbing his arm, I said, "Let's go."

If Spencer wanted to spend time with another woman, well, I had another man who wanted to be with me.

TWENTY-TWO

SPENCER

ALICE SARGENT WAS AN ATTRACTIVE, WELL-DRESSED woman with deep pockets and an affinity for the theater. Stan had introduced me to her shortly after we'd secured the backing of the Shubert Foundation, and she'd since become one of our top sponsors.

It was clear, however, that she was interested in more than just my show. She had not been bold enough to make her intentions clear while I was with Stan, but I was unsure how long her discretion would last. To maintain professionalism, I had limited our interactions to emails through my business account.

But now, as I stood waiting for the cast to return to the dressing rooms, Alice approached me.

"You look so hot tonight," she said as she leaned in to kiss my cheek. "Although I bet you look great every night."

"Thank you," I replied, offering a polite smile. "You look lovely as well."

Alice laughed, placing her hand on my arm. "Things always sound better with a British accent, don't you agree?"

I chuckled. "I suppose that depends on the region of England."

She laughed again and leaned closer, her breasts pressing against my arm. "Aren't you just precious?"

I chuckled. I'd been called a lot of things, but I didn't think a woman had ever called me precious.

"Things went so well tonight," she continued. "We should celebrate together."

Her fingers tightened on my arm, and I shifted, taking her hand between mine and holding it to keep her from wandering. "Ah, but I'm afraid I'm on a tight schedule tonight. A producer's work is never done, you know."

"There you are!" I heard Timothy's voice, and I breathed a sigh of relief. If he was looking for me, it gave me the perfect excuse to extricate myself from this situation.

But as I turned, I saw Timothy wasn't talking to me. London was just a few yards away, her face a delicate flush and her lips pressed together in a firm line. By the time I realized she had seen Alice flirting with me, London and Timothy had left—together.

Bollocks.

"So, what do you say?" Alice purred, pressing closer to me. "Shall we celebrate the successful preview with a bottle of the finest champagne money can buy?"

I raised an eyebrow, trying to keep my tone light. "I'm afraid I have to decline. Duty calls, you see."

"Oh, come on," Alice pressed, pouting slightly. "Surely you can spare a little time for some... celebration?"

"I'm sorry, but I have to go. My lead cast is waiting for me." I said firmly, extricating myself from her grasp.

"Well, a rain check then." Alice said, giving me a sly smile. "I'll hold you to it."

I didn't give her a response. My mind was already on

London, who I had spotted leaving with Timothy. I quickly made my way out of the theater, my heart racing as I tried to come up with a way to stop her and make her stay. But by the time I stepped out into the crisp winter night, they were nowhere to be found.

Bloody hell.

I stepped back inside but didn't return to the chaos and noise backstage. Instead, I ducked into an alcove where I knew I'd have some privacy, and I took out my mobile and rang her. Straight to voicemail. I didn't leave a message. This wasn't the sort of thing to be discussed over the phone.

I tried not to be too discouraged as I emerged from my hiding place and headed back the way I'd come. Cast and crew turned their phones—or at least their ringers—off during performances. I doubted London had even looked at her mobile yet, let alone turned it back on. I'd wait a bit and ring her again.

I only made it halfway down the corridor before I tried again. As before, the call went straight to voicemail.

Fuck.

I FINALLY MADE my way back to my hotel room after what felt like an eternity. The entire night, people wouldn't stop congratulating me for producing a marvelous show. Every time I thought I had a chance to slip away, someone else would grab my arm, telling me how amazing the performance was.

By the time I made it to my room, I was ready for a stiff drink. On my way back, I'd picked up a bottle of whiskey from the liquor store, and I didn't waste any time pouring myself a glass. I was halfway through it when my phone rang. I didn't even bother to look at the caller ID. I just answered.

"Hello?" I slurred into the phone.

"Is that how a York answers the telephone?" My grandmother's sharp voice was like ice water or coffee when it came to sober a person. "Grandmother?"

"Do you always answer the phone sounding like a drunken person?"

"What time is it?" I squinted at my watch.

"Seven-thirty. A perfectly reasonable time for the day to begin."

I closed my eyes and decided not to remind her it wasn't seven-thirty in the morning here.

"Is something wrong, Grandmother?"

"Why would something be wrong? Can't a grandmother call her grandson?"

"At seven-thirty in the morning?" I couldn't keep the skepticism from my voice.

"I like to get unpleasant tasks out of the way first thing."

"Thanks, Grandmother," I muttered.

"What did you say?"

"Nothing." I paused. "What is it you wanted to talk to me about?"

"It's time for you to return home and select an appropriate bride."

At least she got straight to the point.

"I'll be back after things get started here," I said. "Just like I told you before."

"And when, exactly, will that be?"

"A few more weeks. I don't know exactly. It all depends on how previews go. I'll be home before spring for certain."

"After hearing about your most recent trip home, I've decided that simply won't do. You're to return at once, leaving that woman behind for good. You will work alongside your father to prepare for your future, and you will choose a suitable partner from a group of women I have selected."

I was not up to having this conversation. Not because I could barely think straight, but because I was losing the filter that usually kept me from saying what I truly thought to my grandmother.

"Do you understand me?"

I sighed. "Yes, Grandmother, I understand you."

"Good. Then you'll be home by the end of the week."

"No." I shook my head, even though she couldn't see me. "No, I won't. I'll be home when I'm ready. And I'll continue living my life the way I want. You need to stop interfering."

And then I ended the call without giving her the chance to answer.

I'd either done the bravest or the most foolish thing ever. Only time would tell which it was.

TWENTY-THREE

LONDON

"MY PLACE IS THAT WAY," I SAID AND POINTED BEHIND me as I settled into the passenger seat of Timothy's car. I'd been a bit surprised he had a car since most New Yorkers didn't, but that it was a Lamborghini made complete sense.

"Do you have a roommate?" he asked as he turned in the direction I'd pointed. "I noticed you come in a lot with a redhead. Mercedes, right?"

"We're friends, but we don't live together," I said, half answering his question.

"So you're the queen of your own castle, huh?" Timothy chuckled, his eyes sparkling as he sped up. "I hear your brother designed your costumes. I like them. Talent runs in the family, it seems." He flashed me a winning smile.

"Thanks. I'll pass that along."

I didn't feel like making small talk, but I didn't want to be rude either, so I followed Timothy's lead and answered his questions about my brother and then about what other family members lived in the city.

As we approached my building, I said, "You can just drop me off here."

Timothy seemed surprised by my words, but he covered it with a charming smile. "Aren't you going to invite me up for a drink?"

Shit.

"I'm sorry. I didn't mean to make you think...." I shook my head. "I meant what I said about not having a late night before a show."

The confusion in his eyes was brief. "Are you seeing someone?"

"No." The denial slipped out before I could decide what I wanted to say. Then again, considering how things were between Spencer and me, I honestly didn't know what that answer would've been.

"So, you're into women?"

It was all I could do not to roll my eyes. Of course, he'd think that the only reason I turned him down was that I was dating someone or gay. "It's late, Timothy, and I'm tired."

"Of course, I should have realized. This is your first time as a lead in a big show. You're not used to this."

Timothy's words dripped with condescension, but I let it go. I wanted to take a shower and go to bed. Alone.

"I'll see you tomorrow." I reached for the door handle.

"Just something to think about," he said. "The press always loves it when a pretend love story turns into a real one. It could be good for the show if the two of us spent some time together. Even a casual thing would be good publicity."

I smiled but didn't answer as I got out of the car. As if my life wasn't complicated enough at the moment.

THROUGHOUT THE REST of the week, no one noticed the strain between Spencer and me, but it was a constant reminder of why I should never have gotten involved with a coworker. By Saturday, I was almost hoping he would return to England soon.

When Darrel called the cast together for our last preview of the week, I was more than ready to have some time off. I loved the show but needed time away, even if only for a day.

Lost in my thoughts, I didn't realize we had a visitor backstage until I heard a flirty laugh. When I glanced over, I saw Alice hanging all over Spencer again. I turned away, hoping he hadn't seen me looking. The last thing I wanted was for him to know it bothered me to see him with someone else.

Hell, I didn't even want to acknowledge to myself how much it hurt.

I had to stay focused and make it through the night. With the successful previews, we might open on Broadway as soon as next week, and I didn't want to be the reason for any delay.

"Alright, everyone," Darrel gathered us. "Our producer wants to address us."

I clenched my jaw and fixed my gaze on a spot above Spencer's shoulder as he approached us. The brunette lingered behind him, but I didn't dare make eye contact with her either, unsure if I could completely conceal my feelings towards her.

"We've had a fantastic week," Spencer started. "I've heard people saying that our previews are the best New York has seen since a certain hit musical about one of America's Founding Fathers."

A buzz of excitement filled the group.

"In fact," Spencer continued, "they're so good that, provided tonight goes just as smoothly, we'll be officially opening at the Shubert Theatre this coming Friday."

The cheers were almost deafening as Mercedes hugged me tightly. She whispered in my ear, "This is all because of you. No one else could have made this happen."

Though I wasn't entirely convinced, I held her tighter in gratitude.

"You've all done an exceptional job." Spencer raised his voice over the cheers. "And to show my appreciation and to let you all relax before the work starts again on Tuesday to prepare for opening night, I'm inviting all cast and crew to King's Ransom after tonight's performance. There'll be dancing and an open bar."

"Is he serious?" Mercedes asked. "An open bar at King's Ransom?"

"Okay, people, I need you to focus again," Darrel shouted. After everyone quieted down, he continued, "we still have a performance to put on, and I don't want anyone slacking off now that we've had good news. Let's finish as strong as we started and not make Mr. York regret his generosity."

As Spencer and Alice left, I turned my attention back to the task at hand, preparing for the night's work.

I WAS STILL RIDING HIGH on my performance rush when Mercedes and I walked into King's Ransom. It's hard to believe, but tonight's performance was our best yet, and I could feel that we were still right at the edge of everything we could accomplish. If we polished a bit more this week, we could have the most incredible opening night ever.

As for tonight, I planned to have a good time.

Mercedes and I made our way to the bar and placed our orders. Once we had our drinks—a strawberry-lemonade vodka for me and a French 75 for Mercedes—we checked out the dance floor where some others were already dancing. The music was at just the right volume where a person could get lost in it, but conversations were still possible.

I scanned the crowd absently, not looking for anyone in particular, and that was when I saw him.

Spencer.

I had figured he would be here and show off his new whatever-she-was. I automatically looked around him, expecting to see Alice at his side.

Except she wasn't.

"What are you looking so serious about?" Mercedes asked. "This is supposed to be a party."

I couldn't do this. I couldn't stand here and be excited about what was coming while things were still unsettled with Spencer. I needed to talk to him, and this seemed as good a time as any.

"I'll be back." I set down my now-empty glass. "Go have some fun."

"Don't do anything I wouldn't do," Mercedes called after me.

"That's a very short list of restrictions," I muttered as I left her and walked over to where Spencer stood next to Darrel. The director raised an eyebrow in question while Spencer pretended to ignore me.

I knew he was pretending because I could sense the tension in every line of his body, and I knew I was the reason for it.

"Hi, Darrel." I nodded at him and then walked around

to stand directly in Spencer's line of sight. "Spencer, can we talk? Maybe somewhere quieter?"

He frowned, but nodded. I motioned for him to follow me and the two of us walked around the edge of the club until we were in the short corridor where the bathrooms were located.

"We can't keep doing this," I said. "There's at least a few more weeks before you return to England, right? We need to be fully focused, and I don't know about you, but I can't do that unless we clear the air."

"I agree," he said tightly.

"You've clarified that you want to pursue 'other interests', so why don't we just keep it simple."

"Other interests?" Spencer's eyes flashed, surprising me with his anger. "I'm not the one who went home with a co-star."

My jaw dropped, and I stared at him. I would've asked if he was serious, but it was clear from his expression he was.

"I didn't *go home* with anyone. Timothy took me back to my place." I didn't hide my anger. Finally, letting it out felt good.

"Yes, that's much better." Spencer crossed his arms. "The two of you went back to your apartment."

I mimicked his pose. "I'm surprised you even noticed. You seemed pretty *busy* yourself. In fact, you've been *busy* a lot lately with your pretty little brunette."

"My what?"

The shock on his face threw me enough to shake my certainty about his relationship with the mysterious woman.

"Your girlfriend, Alice, who's been hanging all over you every night," I said.

"Alice isn't my girlfriend." Spencer took a step toward

me. "Not that it's any of your business, considering you haven't talked to me since we got back from England."

"I came to talk to you, but you were already talking with someone else," I shot back, taking a step toward him.

"And you couldn't have waited instead of making assumptions?"

"You're one to talk," I snapped. "You assumed I slept with Timothy because you saw us leave together."

"What was I supposed to think? You ignored me and have been spending so much time with *him*." Spencer was so close to me now, I could smell that spicy, masculine scent that was him. "And every time I had to watch you kiss him on that bloody stage, it drove me mad. All I wanted to do–"

"What did you want to do?" I demanded. "What, Spencer? What the hell did you–"

His mouth slammed down on mine, cutting off the rest of what I intended to say. Hands found my waist, pulled me tight against his body, and I leaned into him. My fingers curled into his shirt as my tongue danced with his. Desire burned through me, a fire so fierce I didn't know if I'd survive. Only when my lungs burned, too, did I pull back. Spencer's eyes were wide, his breathing as harsh as mine.

"I didn't sleep with Timothy," I said, my voice breathless. "I didn't even want to. I had him take me home because it pissed me off that you seemed to move on to someone else."

"Alice Sargent is one of our financial backers," he said. "She's been flirting with me, and I've had to be polite when turning her down. There's nothing between her and me."

Relief rushed through me. "I'm sorry I ignored your texts and calls. I was overwhelmed in England and should have talked to you about it."

That wasn't the whole truth, but this didn't feel like the right time or place to discuss my feelings about his family.

"I should have realized it was too soon to have you meet my family." He caught my hand and kissed my knuckles. "I'm sorry too."

"Are we okay?" I thought we were, but I needed to ask to be sure. Assumptions had given us both problems recently.

"We are." He put his hands on either side of my face, his fingers brushing my hairline. "I've missed you."

"I've missed you too," I admitted.

He rested his forehead against mine for a moment before speaking again. "I don't know about you, but I think I'd prefer somewhere a little less crowded."

I smiled. "I'd like that. Let's go to my hotel."

"No. Tonight, I'm taking you to my place."

TWENTY-FOUR

SPENCER

London surprised me when she said she wanted us to go to her apartment.

We slipped out without anyone noticing and quickly found a taxi. After giving the driver her address, London pulled out her phone.

"I'm just letting Mercedes know I left," she explained. "Don't want her to worry."

Realizing that I should probably have let Darrel know I was leaving, I busied myself on my phone until London finished.

As the taxi moved, London put away her phone and looked over at me. I could tell she was nervous by the way she was twisting her hands in her lap, and I wondered if this was a good idea after all.

"Is everything okay?" I asked, trying to break the silence.

London gave me a small smile and nodded. "Yeah, I just want you to know that I don't do this very often."

"Do what?"

"Invite a guy to my place."

I could feel my heart beating a little faster. This was a big step, and it honored me that she trusted me enough to do this. After everything.

"I understand," I said, giving her hand a gentle squeeze.

London's smile grew a little wider, and she leaned into me, resting her head on my shoulder, and let out a soft sigh. "I trust you," she said, and I felt a warmth spread through me.

Before I knew it, the taxi was pulling up to a nice apartment building on the Upper West Side. As we got out, London took my hand, and I couldn't help but smile. It felt like something special.

As we walked inside her apartment, I noticed everything here reflected London's personality.

"Want to see the bedroom?" London grinned at me. "It's nicer than all this. Definitely more comfortable."

I chuckled and followed her down a short hall and into a pale yellow bedroom dominated by a queen-sized bed with a floral bedspread. I was in awe as I looked around London's room. The walls were covered in all things Broadway, with posters, tickets, and programs ranging from "Waitress" to "Wicked." I saw autographs from Caroline Bowman, Adam Pascal, and a handful of other theater greats.

"Wow, you sure are a big fan of Broadway, huh?" I commented out loud, admiring the collection.

"That stuff would distract only a true theater nerd from *this*."

I turned toward her voice, and when I saw her stretched out on her bed, completely in the nude, my mind went blank.

"And that's the expression I was hoping to see." She

smiled at me, tracing a finger between her breasts, then around the small mounds, and up to one pale nipple. My eyes followed the path she made, lust hitting me like a punch in the gut.

Damn, she was beautiful.

"You're overdressed," she said.

I tossed my jacket and tie onto the chair in the corner and then got to work on my shirt. A burst of pride filled me at the hunger in London's eyes as she watched me unbutton my shirt. When I stripped off my trousers and pants, she made a soft sound that brought a smile to my face.

I was half-hard as I crawled onto the bed and pushed her legs apart. Prettily pink and nearly bare, her pussy made my mouth water. It'd been too long since I'd tasted her. I stretched out between her legs, curling my fingers over her thighs as I buried my face in her cunt and licked her from core to clit.

"Fuck!" Her back arched, and she came up off the mattress.

I chuckled and held her tighter, forcing her body back down onto the bed. I ran my tongue over and around that bundle of nerves, gauging her responses to the different levels of pressure, the different kinds of friction. As she grew wetter, I slipped a finger inside her, eliciting curses intermingled with her moans. My cock throbbed, pressing against the bedspread as blood rushed south. Working a second finger into her, I twisted the digits with each thrust and steadily pushed her toward climax until she finally came with a scream that made me wonder just how thin her walls were.

I moved over her, covering her mouth with mine. She kissed me eagerly, her hands gripping my shoulders even as she hooked one leg over my hip. The tip of my cock brushed against her, nudged between her folds, and I groaned.

"Inside me." She nipped at my bottom lip. "I want you inside me."

She raised the lower half of her body, and the head of my cock slipped inside her entrance. I cursed, my hips jerking involuntarily and pushing me deeper. I cursed, squeezing my eyes closed as I fought for control. She felt too good. Slick and hot, skin against skin–

Shite.

My eyes flew open. "Condom."

I started to pull back, but London tightened her hold on me, wrapping both legs around my waist and digging her nails into my shoulders.

"I'm on the pill," she said. "Please."

How could I argue when we fit together so perfectly? When it felt right to drive deep into her and make her mine?

I took her mouth again, my tongue thrusting between her lips. Long, slow strokes sent ripples of pleasure over and through me, building the pressure in me even as I stoked the fire in her.

My hand found her breast, her nipple a hard point against my palm. Rolling the sensitive skin between my finger and thumb, I tugged on her nipple until she cried out, then bent my head to take her into my mouth. I sucked on the tight flesh, scraping my teeth over it as she writhed beneath me. Then, between one heartbeat and the next, the muscles in her body tensed, and her pussy clamped down on me. I bit her nipple, and she keened, completely coming apart.

The gasp of my name pushed me over the edge, and I

came with a groan, pressing my face against the side of her neck as I emptied myself inside her.

We clung to each other, shuddering through the aftereffects of orgasms so intense we nearly passed out. I knew my feelings for her were strong, but it wasn't until this moment that I realized how badly I was lost.

TWENTY-FIVE

SPENCER

Opening night on the West End had been nerve-wracking because it was my first big production. Tonight's opening night was nerve-wracking for being my first Broadway production, but also for a different reason. It was London's first lead role on the biggest stage, and I wanted everything to go well for her sake and my own.

I had a completely different reason to be nervous, too. London's parents were here, and she wanted me to meet them after the show.

In England, I would've known what to expect, having been born into the aristocracy. Here, I was a theater producer, and I had no idea what her family would think of that.

Then the music began, the curtain went up, and all my anxious thoughts disappeared. I let myself get caught up in the magic London made with a story I'd seen hundreds of times before.

She was perfection, embodying the role in a way that I hadn't even seen Anjelika do. And London made Timothy better. The man was a brilliant actor in his own right, but seeing the two of them together...I felt like I was watching something special.

So special that I pushed aside even the first hint of jealousy that reared its head when they kissed, and people cheered.

Their chemistry was only for the stage. I was the one meeting London's family tonight. And even if Timothy was introduced, it'd be as her co-star, not her boyfriend.

After the curtain call, I met her backstage, hating that I was empty-handed. While we weren't exactly hiding our relationship, it wasn't wise to reveal anything to the cast on opening night. So, I had to be content with sending flowers to her apartment earlier today rather than giving them to her after the show.

Her face practically glowed as she came over to where I stood, and I could see the restraint it took for her not to reach for me.

"Did it look as good as it felt?" she asked. "Because it felt amazing."

"I haven't seen it done any better," I said honestly. "Not here, and not on the West End, either."

She beamed even more. "Really?"

I nodded. I wanted so badly to lift her up and steal her away to somewhere private.

"C'mon, Let's find my parents. I want to hear what my family thinks." She started to reach out her hand, then dropped it, her smile dimming. "Sorry."

I shook my head as I followed her. Pitching my voice low, I said, "I'm practically dying to kiss you right now, and if I thought I could without revealing our secret to the cast members and crew, I'd do it."

The pleased expression on her face told me I'd said the right thing. It was the truth, too.

Then I spotted Carson and saw Vix with him, her arms full of flowers. Next to them was a slender blonde woman who shared enough features with London for me to know that was her sister, Maggie, the violinist. I assumed the tall, auburn-haired man beside her was her husband, Drake Mac Gilleain.

Then we were standing in front of a man and woman who could only be Patrick and Theresa McCrae.

Patrick, at least double my age, was in great shape. Theresa was slender, and I could see London got her beauty from her mum. London's features, however, were just Patrick's features feminized.

"Mom, Da." London hugged them both. "What did you think?"

"You were brilliant, lass." Patrick's accent was still fairly thick, even though he'd been in the US many years.

"Aye," Drake spoke up from his place next to Maggie. "I've never seen better."

"Good work," Carson said, holding out his hand.

It took me a moment to realize that he was speaking to me. "Thank you." I shook his hand.

"Mom, Da, this is Spencer York." London put her hand on my arm, the touch brief but reassuring. "He's the show's producer...and my boyfriend."

"Is that so?" Theresa's eyes narrowed. "Boyfriend *and* producer."

"When did this happen?" Maggie asked, eyes wide with surprise.

"It's a fairly recent development," London said.

"Nice to meet you." Drake held out a hand. His tone was polite enough, but the pressure he put on my hand as we shook left little doubt that he was taking my measure. "I'm Drake."

"London has told me a lot about you," I said. "About all of you."

"You're English." Patrick's words were mild.

"I am." I smiled. "Londoner, ironically enough."

"And you met my daughter when she auditioned for your show," Patrick continued. "A show in which she just so happened to get the lead."

"I assure you, Mr. McCrae, that London earned her role through pure talent." I gave her a soft look. "She's a wonderful actress."

"She is," Maggie agreed. "I'm glad you saw that."

"I've heard you're quite the musician," I said to Maggie. "Perhaps one day I can persuade you to share your talents in a new way."

"You seem to have something for everyone in London's life," Theresa said. "I noticed her friend Mercedes also had a role in tonight's show."

"Mercedes earned her role as well," I said.

"Convenient." Theresa's smile was tight.

"Mom," London said, mortification in her voice. "If you must know, Gin and Rocio auditioned, too, and didn't get parts. Besides, Spencer would never give someone a job to impress me."

"And from what I know of your daughter, that sort of thing wouldn't ingratiate me to her at all," I pointed out.

"But she is technically your employee, is she not?" Patrick asked.

"Spencer and I met before I auditioned for him," London said. "We had no idea we'd see each other again."

"The choice wasn't mine alone, either," I added. "The director and the lead male both wanted London for the part, too."

"And is she an investor in your show as well?" Patrick asked.

"Da!" London's face was bright red.

"You can't be too careful," Theresa said.

"Mom, Da, I've checked him out," Carson cut in before London had to respond.

"You did what?" London turned on her brother.

"I checked him out," Carson repeated. "He gave me permission."

Everyone looked at me, and I shrugged. "I have nothing to hide."

That wasn't entirely true, considering I hadn't yet told London about my family's insistence that I marry a particular type of woman, but her family wasn't worried about that. They wanted to ensure I didn't have a wife, or I was after London's money.

"No skeletons in the closet," Carson said. "He's a good guy."

Patrick gave me a searching look. "I'll trust my boy, but if you hurt my daughter, I guarantee you they'll never find your body."

"Da!"

"Understood," I said.

As Patrick and Theresa turned their attention to their daughter's performance, I went to Carson.

"Thank you."

"I meant what I said." He shrugged. "You're a good guy."

I was grateful for Carson's support. Now, I only hoped I could be the man he and London believed me to be.

When I spotted Stan entering the room, I took London to the side. "I'll see you in a bit, darling," I said, giving her a mischievous smile. "I've got to have a quick word with Stan."

With a hint of excitement in her voice, she whispered back, "Don't be too long. I've got something special planned for us later."

I nodded eagerly, feeling the anticipation building within me. I excused myself from London's family and made my way over to Stan, who was deep in conversation with a beautiful couple.

"Ah, Stan, what have you got there?" I said, trying to play it cool.

"Spencer, may I introduce Gavin and Carrie Manning, the owners of the most exclusive nightclubs in town," Stan said, turning to me.

My curiosity was piqued. "That's quite an accomplishment in one of the biggest entertainment capitals in the world. Do tell, what's the secret to your success?"

Gavin chuckled, handing me a sleek black card with golden lettering. "We simply provide a safe place for people to enjoy the best of what life has to offer with no judgment. Please join us next week for the private opening of our latest club, Show and Tell."

I couldn't resist a smile as I took the invitation. "Show and Tell, what a clever name."

We continued chatting with Gavin and Carrie for a couple more minutes, and after they walked away, Stan, always the cryptic one, warned me about their clubs. They were not the typical nightclubs.

I leaned in closer. "What do you mean, Stan? Are they dangerous or something?" I asked, my tone curious but also skeptical. "They are not being run by mobs, are they?"

Stan let out a laugh. "No, Spencer. They are not part of the mob," Stan replied, a mysterious glint in his eye. "Let's just say, these clubs cater to a very specific type of clientele, people who like to indulge in their desires and darkest fantasies with others who share similar interests."

I felt a rush of excitement, mixed with a hint of uncertainty. "What kind of fantasies?" I pressed.

Stan let out a deep, hearty laugh. "My dear boy, that's half the fun, discovering what goes on behind those doors," he said, tapping the invitation in my hand. "All I can say is, be prepared for the unexpected. And keep it on the low. Like I said, this is not your typical night club."

I nodded, taking in Stan's words, but my excitement was uncontainable. I was ready for an adventure, to push the boundaries and live a little. With a grin on my face, I made my way back to London.

Despite Stan's warnings, I intended to bring her to the event. It had been too long since we last let loose, and I was tired of playing it safe and following everyone else's rules, starting with my demanding grandmother.

I gazed once more at the invitation, which stated I could bring a plus-one, and my pulse raced with the idea of a night of pure joy, sprinkled with a hint of danger.

"Why do you look so excited?" London asked with a playful smile, her eyes sparkling with curiosity.

"It's just a surprise I have in mind for us," I replied, slipping the invitation into my pocket. "Where are your family members?"

"They had to leave. My parents are flying back to California in the morning." She sighed, but I caught a hint of relief in her voice. "Now, spill the details about this surprise that you've got up your sleeve," she said, her eyes twinkling with anticipation.

"We've been invited to the grand opening of a new club next week," I revealed. "I just met its owners, someone Stan knows. But enough about that, I want to know your surprise." I took a step closer, eager to hear what she had in mind.

"Oh, it's a good one," she said, a mischievous grin spreading across her face. "It involves The Plaza and the jacuzzi bath in your hotel suite. I believe there's room for two."

"Oh, I see," I said, my heart pounding with anticipation. "So, what are we waiting for?" And with that, I swept her off her feet and whisked her away to my hotel suite, eager to make the most of this unforgettable evening.

TWENTY-SIX
LONDON

I was sitting in a noisy café when I told my friend Mercedes about going to a new club called Show and Tell. Her shock was palpable, but not because Spencer and I were going out, because I hadn't told her who my date was. No, it was the specific club that caught her attention.

"I don't think you understand what kind of club this is," she said, giving me a stern look.

"It's just a private nightclub for the rich and famous. What's the big deal?" I replied, taking a sip of my coffee.

"Hold on, let me clarify for you," Mercedes said, scooting closer. "Show and Tell is Gavin Manning's latest venture. He's the mastermind behind Club Prive, one of the city's most prestigious and infamous private nightclubs. Are you aware of the reputation that comes with it, girl?"

Her words gave me pause. What reputation?

"Come on. How bad can it be? There'll be hundreds of people around me. I'll be fine," I said, trying to sound calm.

"I know you will, darling," she replied, her voice gentler. "Just be cautious, okay? Don't let anyone pressure you into doing something you're not comfortable with."

I nodded, taking a sip of my coffee, shaking off the unease that had settled in my chest. But the more she told me about the club, the more excited I became about exploring it with Spencer.

I PICKED out my outfit with great care, wanting the evening to be perfect. Considering what Mercedes had told me about the club, I'd decided to be bold and wear something *not* made for me by Carson; a daring emerald green mini dress with a halter lace-up back and diamond cut out just below my breasts. The glittering material made my legs appear longer and revealed a lot of skin. Ever since I bought the dress, I'd been waiting for the right occasion to wear it.

Upon Spencer's arrival, I knew I'd picked the right dress. "Bloody hell, London," he growled in a low voice as he saw me, revealing his amorous and possessive nature. I twirled slowly, allowing him to see the full length of my bare back and confirm that I was not wearing a bra. He caught my arm before I completed my rotation, stepping close enough that I could feel the heat from his body.

"You're testing my self-control," he said. "I don't know whether I want to take you against the wall right here or forbid you from going out in that dress so no one else can see you in it." His words sent a shiver down my spine.

"Well, the club is called Show & Tell," I replied.

He growled low in his throat and tightened his grip on my arm, making my heart race. "At least make sure you're wearing something to keep you warm," he said, releasing me and stepping back. I held up my long dress coat, showing him it would reach my knees.

"Good," he said, assisting me into my coat. "Let's keep the focus on that coat until we reach the club."

As we entered Show and Tell, it didn't surprise me to see how busy it was for a Sunday night. It was a private opening, after all. Spencer placed his hand possessively on the small of my back, sending shivers down my spine with his warm touch.

The interior decor was a perfect representation of the club's name, "Show & Tell." With the use of lighting and shadows, partially concealed alcoves, screens, and curtains, it offered a tantalizing glimpse into the activities taking place.

One wall was a dance floor, the other a bar, and in the center of the spacious room was a circular stage where two muscular men, dressed only in tight jeans, were setting up a performance. Knowing very little about this place or Club Privé, I was eager to grab a drink and find a seat to watch what was about to happen on stage.

Based on the very few hints Mercedes had given me, I knew the entertainment would be...*entertaining*.

"Do you want a drink?" Spencer leaned closer than necessary, and I couldn't help but smile at the little show of possession.

"Something fruity," I said. "I'll grab us a seat with a good view."

He gave me a puzzled look, and I gestured to the stage. His eyebrows went up as if he hadn't realized there was a show. As I made my way to a semi-private chaise large enough for two, I could feel him watching me. I enjoyed that.

I'd been stretched out on the chaise lounge for a few minutes when the curtain to my right moved. I opened my mouth to tell Spencer he was fast, but another man stood there. Insanely tall and muscular, he had a ruggedly handsome face and was wearing tight leather pants. In the dim lighting, I couldn't make out much else about him.

"Are you looking for some companionship tonight?"

That his eyes didn't stray from my face gave him serious points, but I had no hesitation when I shook my head.

"She already has a companion." Spencer's voice came from behind the mountain of a man. "And not just for tonight."

The man stepped to the side and raised his hands, a smile flashing dimples as he spoke. "No harm meant. I saw a beautiful woman sitting alone and thought I would ask. Have a great night."

Spencer watched as the other man walked away, a scowl etched onto his face. The expression was unusual for him. When the curtain fell back into place, Spencer turned to me and offered a glass of pinkish liquid.

"You made a new acquaintance," he said, a smile curling his lips.

I grinned. "I didn't even catch his name."

Spencer sat down next to me, draping his arm over my shoulder. "Do you want it?"

I leaned into him, feeling safe and protected.

"Not even a little." I chuckled.

As the music volume dropped, a tall, handsome man with dark hair climbed onto the stage. Spencer told me it was Gavin Manning, the owner of the club.

"Good evening, ladies and gentlemen. Welcome to the opening of Show & Tell. Please familiarize yourself with the rules in our private rooms, and ensure you seek verbal consent before participating in any activities. And now, let's welcome our first performance of the night, featuring Craig, Lacey, and Philip."

Applause erupted as the performers took the stage. Spencer turned to me with a look of surprise on his face. Mercedes had told me about these exhibitions, but I hadn't fully believed her until now.

Lacey, with her dark curls pulled back into a sleek ponytail, flaunted her hourglass figure in a glittering gold wrap dress. Her curves were accentuated as she confidently strode onto the stage and presented a pair of handcuffs with a mischievous glint in her eye. Standing next to her was a clean-shaven man with a muscular build, accentuated by the bold barbed wire tattoo circling his biceps. On the other hand, the shaggy-haired Philip, with his neatly trimmed beard and mustache, cut a tall and lanky silhouette in his well-tailored clothes.

Craig undressed, revealing an average body but a very above-average cock. He was huge.

"Bloody hell," Spencer said. "I never thought I'd feel inadequate in that area."

I laughed and put my hand on his thigh. "Frankly, I'd be a little scared of what that man's wielding."

Spencer's arm tightened around me, and he pulled me half onto his lap. Pressing his mouth against my ear, he said, "I'm terribly sorry for bringing you here. I had no idea it would be like this. Stan is such an ass for not mentioning it."

I turned and looked at him, and I could practically feel the heat of his gaze on me. "I love it, though." My hand slipped under his shirt, and I fingered the hard bulge of his pectoral muscle. "It kinda turns me on."

He kissed my jaw and moved one of his hands to cup my breast, his fingers brushing against uncovered skin. Flickers of heat followed his touch.

On the stage, Lacey had removed her dress and was bent over in front of Philip, her hands on his knees. Her face was inches from his, too far for them to kiss without her moving, but I figured that was the point.

Craig was on his knees behind Lacey, his face buried between her legs. From where we were sitting, we could see his tongue as it worked over smooth pink skin.

Spencer's fingers plucked at my nipple, every pinch and tug sending a jolt of pleasure straight through me. And the thick bulge beneath my ass was an indication that he was enjoying it.

My stomach twisted with excitement.

Craig was on his feet now, shoving two fingers in and out of Lacey while his other hand stroked that enormous cock. As Craig added two more fingers, Spencer's hand slid up my leg and under the hem of my dress, fingers dancing along the inside of my thigh. My breathing quickened, and I swallowed hard, my mind racing. I'd always enjoyed being in the spotlight, but I'd never thought about people watching me this way.

"I think I'll just start with one," Spencer whispered in my ear. "Four might be a stretch."

I laughed at his joke, but the sound turned into a moan as the tip of his finger slipped underneath the lace of my panties.

In front of us, the show continued with Craig now slamming that enormous cock into Lacey hard enough to make her squeal; the sound carrying even over the music.

"Could I get you to make a sound like that, I wonder?" Spencer kissed the spot under my ear, his tongue darting out to taste my skin even as his finger ghosted over my clit. "I know I can when we're in private, but would you be that loud here?"

I shifted, stretching my arms up behind me to touch

him. His soft hair. The rougher scruff on his cheeks. The warm skin of his neck.

On the stage, Lacey unzipped Philip's pants and reached inside, her hand moving in an unmistakable way even though his cock had yet to make an appearance. Even from where I was sitting, I could tell he was pulling against his restraints, desperate to touch her.

Spencer's fingers made circles over my clit, even as his teeth scraped and nipped at the side of my throat. The other hand still played with my breast, adding to the myriad sensations racing across every nerve. The hand in my panties dropped low enough for him to slide a single finger inside me.

I gasped, my eyes closing, and I pressed down on his erection.

"Not nearly loud enough."

A second finger joined the first, and I cried out, unable to hold in the sound. I had a flash of embarrassment mixed with my arousal, but it vanished beneath a new surge of pleasure.

"That's better." He pushed his fingers deeper, rubbing the heel of his hand on my clit with every stroke. "Come for me, London. I want to feel that hot pussy of yours squeeze my fingers."

Something else was happening on the stage, but I couldn't process it. I was barely aware of people around us, but all I could think about was what Spencer was doing to my body and how good it felt.

"Say my name." He pinched my nipple, drawing another noise from me I couldn't stifle. "Come and say my name so that everyone here knows that I'm the one bringing you that pleasure."

A twist of his fingers made me whimper. "Spencer."

"Almost," he coaxed. "Louder than that."

"So close."

"I know." His thumb stroked my clit. "Now, scream my name."

He bit the place where my shoulder met my neck, and I tipped over the edge. I might not have screamed, but I was loud enough to draw the attention of at least some people around us.

I couldn't find it in me to care. It added a little extra thrill that I hadn't expected.

Spencer drew his hand out from under my dress, and on the stage, Lacey climbed onto Philip's lap.

"I know the show hasn't reached its...*climax*, but what do you say we continue this back at my hotel room?"

TWENTY-SEVEN

SPENCER

London cries as I bring her to orgasm in the club.

I'm so fucking hard it hurts.

The jarring ringing of my mobile yanked me unceremoniously from an extremely pleasant dream about the night before at the club. I fumbled blindly for my phone, just wanting the noise to stop.

"Hello?"

"Spencer, thank heavens you answered."

The near-panic in Stan's voice chased away any sleepiness that lingered. "What's wrong?"

"I thought I told you to keep it on the low?!"

I closed my eyes and breathed a sigh of relief. "That's why you woke me this early?"

"This isn't funny, Spencer." Stan's disapproval dripped from every word. "What happened at Show & Tell last night?"

I couldn't resist tormenting him as I tried to ease away from London. "Indulging in some sexual fantasies, what else?"

"That's not funny, Spencer."

"It is a little funny," I said.

London spoke up from next to me. "Is everything all right?"

"Let me guess," Stan said, "that would be London McCrae in your bed."

"Shite," I muttered.

London's eyes flew open. "Who is it?"

"It's Stan," I said to her, before turning my attention back to the man on the phone. "How did you know I was with London?"

London's eyes went wide. "Shit."

"Because the same paparazzi who saw you going into Show & Tell also saw who you were with."

"Oh, bloody fuck."

London grabbed my arm, the sheets slipping from her breasts. Under other circumstances, I would've been distracted.

"What?" she asked.

"Reporters saw the two of us going into Show & Tell last night," I told her.

"Oh."

"How bad is it?" I asked Stan, rubbing my forehead.

"The pictures are online, and the press is having a field day with the type of club it is," he said. "Both of your names are out there, too. It was just rotten luck that someone who normally covers the theater was doing a story about Gavin Manning's new club."

"I thought you said Manning's clubs were the most exclusive private clubs in town," I said.

"They are," Stan agreed. "But they're still sex clubs."

I tried another angle of protest. "They're perfectly legal clubs, and we're consenting adults."

"But they're still sex clubs," he repeated. "Our views on sex here in the US are still quite puritanical compared to Europe."

"Fuck." I reached over to turn on the lamp. I won't be getting any more sleep this morning.

"Right now, it seems only the tabloids are running with it, but if it's a slow news day, it could hit major outlets before lunch," Stan continued. "That's why I called. You can still get ahead of it, give the press something else to talk about."

"How do you think the Foundation will respond?" As much as I didn't want a scandal dogging London and me, my primary concern was for my show and the people working on it. "There's no morality clause in our contract, but I'm sure they have skilled lawyers. How much ground do we have to stand on if they try to drop us?"

"To be honest, I think they'll have more of a problem with the fact that you took the lead in their show to a sex club than with what goes on at Show & Tell."

"I bloody botched this." We should have been more careful, being in disguise, going in and out, but it was too late to change anything now.

"Look Spencer, I don't know what's going on with you and London, but if you don't give the press something, they're going to make up shit and considering where you two were last night, I don't think you want that."

"You're right," I said. "But that's not a decision I can make on my own."

"Good answer." He paused, then continued, "Make sure you don't fuck up her career with this."

I didn't need the warning, but I appreciated he cared about what happened to London. "I won't."

We ended the call, and I took a deep breath before

turning to face London. She'd been sitting next to me, listening to my half of the conversation, and now I filled her in on what she hadn't been able to hear. Her cheeks flushed red, then paled as she realized how much damage this story could do if we didn't take action.

"We can tell them I'm the one who got the invitation to the club opening," she said once I'd finished the explanation. "That I invited you."

I shook my head. "I think that'll just make things worse for you."

"But that's better than them making it seem like you're corrupting me," she countered. "Because let's get real. That's exactly the spin the paparazzi are going to take. They'll point out that you're the producer of the show that I got the lead in, and you used that power to your advantage."

"But that's not what happened. They can write what they want. They do anyway. I am done caring about what other people think. I could not be bothered with my reputation anymore."

"You should," she said. "You have an entire cast and crew relying on you for income. If the show closes, many people will be out of work."

I shook my head and reached over to cup my cheek. "It shouldn't surprise me you're putting everyone else's well-being above your own."

"It's the smart thing to do." She smiled and put her hand over mine. "You know it is."

"The smart thing would've been for me to stay as far away from you as possible." I leaned forward and brushed my lips across hers. "But I didn't, and I don't regret my decision for a second."

She put her hand on my chest, and I watched her pupils

dilate for a moment before she gave me a gentle push. "I will not let you distract me with sex."

"You're right." I sat back. "We need to take this seriously and figure out what to do."

"I don't think anything short of a bigger story is going to get the spotlight off us," she said.

"What if we could tone down the sensationalism?" I suggested. "A producer and the lead in his show spotted at a sex club is a scandal. A producer who's dating an actress who is in his show isn't completely non-news, but it would change how people would view last night. We were a couple exploring things together, not two people sneaking around."

London frowned. "It still won't look good for either of us. It could hurt the show."

"It could," I agreed.

"Let's not make a rash decision," she said. "We agreed to keep things quiet for a reason, and I need to think about what changing that would mean for me."

"You're right," I agreed.

London climbed out of bed. "I'm going to tell my friends either way. Even if the story doesn't make headlines, they'll hear about it, and I want it to come from me. Especially Mercedes."

I reached across the bed and grabbed her hand. "It's going to be okay, London. We'll figure it out."

She nodded, but didn't look at me. I didn't blame her. Though it was unfair, the woman usually bore the brunt of these things. I'd be written off as another horny man getting his rocks off. She'd be labeled a slut and a deviant, especially if people thought we'd gone there as a one-off and not because we were a couple.

"If we're lucky," she added, "it won't be an issue because someone more important than us will do something notable, and we'll be worried about nothing."

Somehow, I didn't think it'd be that simple, but I didn't say it. I'd let her have hope as long as possible.

TWENTY-EIGHT
LONDON

I'D ALREADY CHECKED THE WORD ONLINE, AND IT wasn't good, but I didn't think my friends had seen it yet. At least, when we met at our usual diner for brunch, nobody mentioned anything, and that would have been the first thing out of their mouths.

Halfway through our meal, after my friends had filled me in on the latest news in their lives, I cleared my throat to get their attention. "There's something I need to tell you guys before you hear it from someone else." I looked at each of them, stopping at Mercedes, since what I had to say would affect her the most. "I'm dating Spencer York."

Three sets of eyes stared at me in stunned silence for a minute before Mercedes spoke. "Well, now things make more sense."

"What makes more sense?" Gin asked. "Because London dating the producer of her show makes no sense at all."

The shock in my friend's voice didn't surprise me. I would be shocked by my behavior too.

"I kept telling myself I was just imagining things,"

Mercedes said. "He looks at you differently than the other actresses, and you do the same when you look at him."

Rocio's eyes narrowed. "Yeah, you've been acting like you're getting laid lately."

I sighed. "Really, Rocio? That's your response?"

He shrugged. "I say more power to you."

"Can I ask a question?" Mercedes reached for her drink. "It might upset you."

I had a feeling I knew what was coming. "Go ahead. I won't get mad."

"Did you know him before we went to the audition?"

"Remember that terrible date you sent me on with the cokehead?"

"Yeah." Mercedes looked puzzled.

"Do you remember telling you about how I ducked into a pub when it started raining, and I met this handsome English guy who I slept with?" I used my straw to play with the ice in my glass.

"You're fuckin' with us," Mercedes said, frowning. "That was Spencer?"

"Yes," I nodded. The audition was the first time I learned he was producing the show.

"That also explains why you introduced him to your family on opening night," Mercedes said.

"We're not exactly trying to hide, but we're keeping things low-key," I explained. "Or, at least, we were."

"So...what happened?" Gin asked, her curiosity piqued. "You said you wanted to tell us before we heard it from somewhere else."

"Spencer and I went to a club opening last night, and the paparazzi spotted us," I replied.

Gin raised an eyebrow. "I love you, London, but you're not exactly a big enough name for that to make headlines."

"You and Spencer went to Show & Tell?" Mercedes asked, her eyes growing wide.

"What's Show & Tell?" Gin asked, unfamiliar with the name.

"It's a new private club where the daring and adventurous go to have some fun," Mercedes explained, a mischievous grin spreading across her face.

Rocio let out a low whistle. "Well, fuck. Rich British producer takes the young lead of his new show to a sex club. The headline writes itself."

Gin pulled out her phone. "I haven't heard anything about it. Are you sure it's going to be an issue?...Oh."

I sighed. "It's gaining more attention, isn't it?"

"I wouldn't say it's gained traction, but what's being said isn't good," Gin reported, her expression serious.

I reached for my phone, but then stopped and shook my head. "I don't want to know."

"You can't ignore it forever, though," Mercedes warned. "Even if it doesn't make the major news cycles, it'll get around."

"I know," I said, feeling a sense of dread wash over me. "We're trying to figure out the best way to handle the situation."

"How can you handle something like this?" Gin asked, her tone concerned.

"Spencer wants us to go public," I revealed.

Mercedes let out a low whistle. "That's a serious step to take."

I was so glad that my friends understood.

If Spencer hadn't been producing the show, I was in—I wouldn't have cared about people knowing we were dating. Getting involved with someone who was, in some ways, my boss, meant things were different.

"I don't even know if it'd make a difference," I said. "I mean, we still work together, and we were still at a sex club together. Would it be less scandalous if we were in a relationship?"

Mercedes shrugged. "Who knows? But I don't think it'd hurt. You'd be able to talk to reporters honestly without worrying about whether you accidentally revealed something. And it'll show you have nothing to hide."

She had a good point.

The problem was, as supportive as all three of my friends sounded, they weren't quite able to hide the wariness in their eyes. I didn't blame them. After all, I'd been one of the biggest opponents of relationships in the workplace, particularly between actors and the people in charge. And I still believed all the reasons why those relationships weren't wise.

"Whatever you decide to do, you know we've got your back, right?" Rocio put his hand over mine. "Just like you've always had ours.""Thanks," I smiled at him, then turned to my friends. "Now, I want to hear more about this walk-on role you got on a Dick Wolf show. That's big news."

Rocio blushed and tried to downplay it, but we managed to get him talking. "It's just a small part," he said modestly.

For a while, I forgot about my problems as we chatted. But the moment we stepped out of the diner, everything came rushing back.

"London! London!" someone shouted my name, and I turned toward the voice. A bright flash went off in front of me, and I squinted, trying to see who was talking.

"London, are you and Spencer York seeing each other?" another voice asked, accompanied by another flash.

I put up a hand, trying to shield my eyes. "Who's the

guy you're with right now? Are you cheating on Spencer with him?" a third voice called out.

I looked over at Rocio, who was staring at me with wide eyes. "Did Spencer force you to go to a sex club with him?" yet another voice asked.

My vision was still impaired by the flashes, and I couldn't see who was doing the talking. "Was your attendance at Show & Tell part of a bargain to get the lead in York's show?" another voice asked.

I glared in the direction of that voice. Multiple flashes kept my vision from returning to normal, but I could tell that at least half a dozen paparazzi were swarming around my friends and me. "Did you sleep your way to a leading role?" one of them asked rudely.

"That's enough!" Rocio stepped in front of me, shielding me from the paparazzi. "London has no comment on these absurd accusations. Please, back off." He took my hand and led us towards the curb where a cab was waiting.

The paparazzi continued to shout questions as Rocio opened the passenger door. "Get in the cab!" he shouted, gesturing for us to hurry. We scrambled into the cab, and I heard one reporter shout, "Is this your new boyfriend, London? What's his name?" Rocio slid into the cab beside me, slamming the door shut.

"Let's go!" he yelled to the driver, who nodded and sped away from the paparazzi.

I breathed a sigh of relief as the sounds of the paparazzi faded into the distance. I leaned back against the seat and closed my eyes, trying to calm my racing heart. "Are you okay?" Rocio asked, turning to face me.

"Yeah, I'm okay. Just a little shaken," I replied with a deep sigh.

Once I was alone in my apartment, I called Spencer. "I

just got mobbed by some reporters outside a diner," I said. "Be careful if you go out."

"I was worried about that," Spencer replied with a sigh. "I think, without any answers, they'll keep coming...and they'll make up whatever we don't tell them."

"Maybe what we need to do is go public in a big way," he suggested. "Find a place where a lot of reporters will show and answer a few questions. The truth isn't nearly as scandalous as what they think is happening."

"Will you go out with me tonight?" Spencer asked.

I paused for a moment, considering his proposal. Going public could solve our problem, but it was a big step. I took a deep breath and replied, "Yes. Let's go public."

TWENTY-NINE
SPENCER

Looking for the perfect restaurant for a high-profile dinner date was proving to be a challenge. Most celebrities preferred to dine in private, away from the prying eyes of the media, while some craved the attention. And while I understood the appeal of pandering to the press for exposure, I didn't want to be seen at a hotspot known for attracting celebrities. The delicate balance between subtlety and visibility, combined with a desire for good food, had consumed my entire afternoon.

Seeing London in her sleek black dress when I arrived at her apartment made everything worth it.

"You look breathtaking," I said, giving her a gentle kiss on the cheek to avoid smudging up her lipstick.

"So do you," she replied with a smile.

We made our way down to the lobby, nervous that reporters might wait outside. However, despite the growing media frenzy surrounding us, no one seemed to have uncovered London's address.

As we made our way to the restaurant, the tension

between us was palpable, but I didn't want the reason for our outing to cast a shadow over our evening. So, I took London's hand and said, "Let's not let the outside world interfere. I want to enjoy a romantic dinner with my girl-friend. Everything else can wait."

Her smile beamed. "I couldn't agree more."

The mood between us lightened as we were seated at our table, glasses of rich red wine in hand, and our meals on their way.

While we waited for our food, we continued our conversation, delving into lighter topics and letting go of the tension that had previously hung between us.

"I thought Da was going to kill the twins," London said with a laugh. "Or at the very least, ground them until they were thirty."

"What did he end up doing?" I asked, intrigued by her family dynamics.

"For the next week and a half, from sunrise to sunset, the twins had to muck out stalls at a local stable." She chuckled as she took a sip of her wine.

It surprised me how different her family was from my own. I could only imagine how my grandmother would react in a similar situation.

The server arrived with our dinners, interrupting my thoughts and pulling me back to the present. Things were going well and the last thing I needed to be thinking about was my family.

"Can I get you anything else?" the server asked.

"Not at the moment," I said after a glance at London.

As we started our meals, the only sounds were the clinks of our silverware against our plates and our quiet moans of delight at the delicious flavors of our risotto. If not for the need to be seen in public, we might have never discovered this little gem of a restaurant.

London broke the silence, a thoughtful look on her face. "I didn't see any reporters out there when we came in. I'm having a good time, don't get me wrong, but we picked this restaurant for a reason, right?"

I took a sip of my wine and nodded. "Stan's taking care of that. His publicist is currently alerting a few reporters of our dining experience here. They'll be eagerly awaiting our departure outside."

She raised an eyebrow. "Do you think this will really work?"

"To be honest, I'm not sure," I admitted, setting down my glass. "But I think it's the best option we have, besides lying about us being together or being at the club."

As we finished our meal and the waiter brought us the check, I felt a knot of nervousness form in my stomach. This was it. This was the moment that could either make or break our carefully crafted image.

London and I gathered our things and made our way out the door, taking deep breaths as we prepared to face the waiting crowd of reporters.

"Mr. York, are you and Miss McCrae dating?" one reporter asked, snapping a picture.

"Well, I must say, I never thought I'd be caught in the crosshairs of the paparazzi," I quipped. "But yes, we are dating. And before you ask, yes, we were at a club last night."

"Did you know it was a sex club?" a reporter asked.

"A sex club? Goodness me, I wasn't even aware you chaps had such clubs in America," I replied with a raised eyebrow, as if scandalized.

As we made our way to the waiting car, a photographer

shouted, "Mr. York, did you cast London in your show because she promised to sleep with you?"

I stopped and let out a deep, exaggerated sigh. "Oh dear, it's always the same old accusations, isn't it? No, I didn't cast London because she promised to sleep with me. London and I were already friends before the casting." I added with a wink, "And as you might have heard, she's a talented actress. If you've seen the show, you know she's absolutely brilliant in the role."

Before anyone could ask another question, London climbed into the car, and I followed, giving the reporters a wave and a charming smile.

"That was a close one, wasn't it?" London asked, her eyes shining with amusement.

"It was," I agreed, settling into the comfortable leather seat. "But with a little charm and wit, I think we can handle anything the reporters throw our way."

After dropping off London, I was halfway to my hotel when my phone rang. Considering the time difference, it surprised me to see my father's name on the screen.

"Father? Is everything okay?"

"It's time for you to come home."

For a moment, I was speechless. I really hadn't expected that.

He continued, "You've had your fun, and it's out there, splashed across the internet for everyone to see."

Bollocks.

I hadn't considered a minor story had traveled across the ocean.

"I've tolerated a lot from your little hobby, but this is too far," my father went on. "It's time to stop all of that nonsense and come home, take your place with the family."

I didn't even have to think about it. "No. Sorry, father, I'm staying as I planned."

He sighed. "I thought you might say that."

"And yet you still called," I said.

"I still called," he agreed. "Because I had to tell you that you'll be cut off if you refuse. Disinherited and cut off completely."

THIRTY
LONDON

THIS WAS IT. THE MOMENT I HAD BEEN WAITING FOR.

As I approached the theater, the excitement I felt was almost palpable. The Broadway marquee, with my name up in lights, was an indescribable feeling. I had worked so hard to get here, and to be the lead in a Broadway show was a dream come true.

And, of course, there was Spencer. Just the thought of seeing him again made my heart race.

But as I began my pre-show routine, I pushed thoughts of Spencer aside. Being in a relationship with the producer wouldn't be an excuse for me to slack off. I needed to be at my absolute best and show everyone that I deserved to be here.

I made my way to the backstage area where the cast gathered before each performance. As I took my spot next to Timothy, I noticed that my understudy, Tomma, was also there, looking as unapproachable as ever.

Tomma and I had competed for the same parts in the past, and she had always viewed me as competition, not just professionally but personally as well. I tried to maintain a cordial relationship with everyone, but she made it difficult.

"She's as unpleasant as ever," Mercedes muttered, shooting a glare in Tomma's direction. "Think your new boyfriend can do something about that?"

I elbowed her gently. "Shh, don't even joke about that. I wouldn't use a relationship for something like that."

"I know you wouldn't," Mercedes replied with a sigh. "It was just a wishful thought."

Darrel's assistant called for everyone's attention, and Darrel took the lead, reminding us of the great opening weekend and encouraging us to exceed the audience's expectations. As we joined hands, I felt a strange awkwardness from Timothy. Normally, he would hold my hand tightly during this pre-show ritual, but today his hand was limp.

I was so preoccupied with Timothy's strange behavior that I barely paid attention to the affirmations we all made. And as we finished, Timothy practically yanked his hand away from mine. Something was definitely wrong.

"Hey." I reached out to him, but he stepped back. "What's going on?"

"I need to be in the zone, and your presence is throwing me off." Timothy looked down at me with a cold and unfamiliar gaze, the disgust clear in his eyes. It was a far cry from the flirtatious and sexual looks he'd given me in the past.

"I'm sorry," I said, my voice quivering as I tried to sound apologetic. "Can we go over our scene together?"

"I need an actor who is fully invested and focused on the performance," he replied, turning his attention away from me and towards Tomma. "Tomma, you're ready, aren't you?"

She smiled seductively, tossing her hazelnut-colored

hair as she fluttered her lashes at him. "Of course, always ready for you, Timmy."

My heart sank as I watched the exchange. I knew dating Spencer, the producer, would cause some whispers, but I never expected it to affect my relationship with Timothy.

Mercedes, sensing my distress, came to my side. "Do you need help with your mic?" she asked softly.

"Yes, please," I said, gratefully accepting her offer. I took a deep breath, trying to push aside my worries and focus on the performance. If I didn't bring my A-game tonight, all my hard work would be for nothing.

IT COULD HAVE BEEN A DISASTER, but thankfully it wasn't. The audience seemed oblivious to any issues, judging by the enthusiastic applause. I wasn't sure if anyone in the cast had noticed, but I wasn't about to bring it to their attention.

After a quick change in the dressing room, I emerged to find that the backstage crowd had thinned. Spencer was waiting for me, as promised, but he looked just as preoccupied as he had all night.

"Thanks for sticking around," I said, kissing his cheek. "I'm more than ready to head home."

"Our car is waiting," he replied.

As we made our way towards the exit, I couldn't help asking, "Was it that terrible?"

"What are you referring to?" he asked.

"The performance between Timothy and me. It felt stilted and awkward."

Spencer frowned and gazed down at me. "Really?"

"You can't tell me you didn't notice," I said. "It's been bothering you all night."

"From where I was sitting, everything looked fine," he said, sounding genuinely surprised.

His sincere tone made it difficult for me to doubt him. If he had noticed nothing amiss, then something else must have been weighing on his mind.

"So, what's been bothering you?" I asked, taking his hand. I tried to keep my voice light, but I must have conveyed some concern because he forced a smile when he looked at me.

"I spoke with my father last night," he admitted. "He was making demands, but it's nothing for you to worry about."

I could tell he didn't want me to ask for details, which made me want to ask even more, but I didn't. Despite Spencer's reassurances, I couldn't shake the feeling that something was off. He was hiding something, and it was worrying me. I didn't want anything to be troubling him, especially not something as serious as his father making demands. I took his hand and looked up at him, my concern for him clear in my eyes. I didn't want to push him, but I couldn't ignore my instincts. I squeezed his hand, silently letting him know I was there for him, no matter what.

THIRTY-ONE
SPENCER

This was certainly turning out to be a week full of surprises. A text message from my twin, Anne, jolted me awake this morning. She and Gabriella would land at JFK and I should come to the airport to pick them up. This was more of a shock than anything else. Although my sisters had been to see my show on the West End, I had never expected any member of my family to visit the States to see the performance.

So, I summoned the car service I'd been using since I arrived in New York and made my way to JFK. As I waited for their private plane to touch down, I quickly tapped out a message to London.

"Two of my sisters have decided to pay me a visit. Would you be interested in meeting us for lunch? I'm sure Anne and Gabriella would love to meet you," I wrote.

London was quick to respond. "That sounds good. Want me to make a reservation?"

I sent her a quick message, thanking her and asking for the restaurant's name and when we should meet. Just as I finished my response, my sisters emerged from the plane, both looking far too fresh and radiant for having spent almost ten hours on a plane.

"Surprise!" Anne exclaimed as she hugged me tightly.

"It certainly is," I replied, hugging Gabriella next. "Not that I'm not thrilled to see both of you, but what brought on this sudden visit?"

"I told you he'd be suspicious," Gabriella said with a chuckle, turning to Anne. "We wanted to see your show... and maybe meet your leading lady."

"I figured as much, especially since both of you were unavailable when I took London home," I added with a smile. "That's why I asked London to make our lunch reservations. Do you have any other luggage?"

"Just what we have here," Anne replied, showing the suitcases she was pulling behind her. "We'll be flying back on Sunday afternoon."

"Alright, then let's go. I offered for you both to stay in the spare room in my suite, but I see you've already booked a suite of your own at the same hotel."

"Having it available on short notice sealed the deal for Gabriella and me. It was like fate," Anne said with a smile.

"If we believed in fate," Gabriella added drily.

As we made our way to the hotel, I pointed out the various landmarks of the city and shared personal stories about each place. I was pleased to be showing my sisters around, but I couldn't ignore the anxiousness that was building within me. The upcoming meeting with London was weighing heavily on my mind, and I didn't want my nerves to show.

Once we arrived at the hotel, I escorted my sisters to their luxurious suite on the floor below mine. "We have a couple of hours before meeting London," I said. "Maybe you two would like to rest a little before?"

"I'd love to see the city you've talked so much about," Gabriella replied. "If you don't mind?"

"Of course not," I replied with a warm smile. "Just give me fifteen minutes to make a few calls, and then we can go explore together."

I made the calls, and by the time we headed back down to the car, I had arranged for my sisters to join me in my private box for the performance tonight. In the meantime, I had planned a tour of some of the most beautiful and iconic locations in Manhattan.

By the time we arrived at the Royal 35 Steakhouse, my sisters were enamored by the city and the excitement of being in New York. I was as ready as I could be for them to meet London.

She was waiting for us inside, and I noticed a flicker of panic in her eyes before she quickly composed herself.

"You look stunning," I complimented her as I kissed her cheek. I then turned to my sisters and introduced them. "London, I'd like you to meet Anne and Gabriella. Ladies, this is London McCrae."

"It's a pleasure to meet you," Anne greeted London with a polite smile.

"It's great to meet you too," Gabriella echoed.

"The pleasure is mine," London replied, shooting me a quick glance.

"Your table is ready," the hostess informed us.

"Perfect timing," I said with a grin.

Our table was much grander than the one London and I had shared on our first date, and I was relieved that the atmosphere was more sophisticated. My sisters didn't have London's relaxed and easy-going nature, and here, in this setting, they would be comfortable.

We talked and ordered and talked some more, with

Anne taking the lead and directing the conversation by asking too many questions, all of them directed at London. I was worried for a bit that the third degree would freak London out, but she handled each question gracefully, even sending a few back to my sisters, who were less forthcoming. Overall, I thought things were going well.

"If you'll excuse me," London said, pushing back from the table. "I'll be back in a minute."

As she left, I turned my attention to my sisters, who were now watching me with careful expressions.

"She's brilliant, isn't she?" I asked with a smile. But my smile faded as I noticed my sisters exchanging glances. "What?"

"She's lovely," Anne said. "And I like her."

"I like her too," Gabriella said.

"Then what's with the look?" I asked, motioning between them.

"You know our parents won't let this get serious," Anne said frankly.

"They won't approve of anyone our grandmother doesn't set me up with," I pointed out. "And they know I will not marry someone random she picks for me."

"Maybe not," Gabriella said, "but that doesn't mean they'll accept an American actress."

"And it's not as if you're planning to stay here," Anne added softly. "How can you have a serious relationship with someone across an ocean?"

London came back before I could respond, but I had no answer for my sisters' observations. I already knew all of this, but I had been trying not to think about it too much. My sisters' words were echoing in my head as we headed to the theater, and I realized that no matter how much they liked London, my family would never approve.

As my sisters left us backstage shortly before the show was about to begin, I could tell that London had noticed their reluctance.

"I like them," she said. "But they seemed hesitant around me."

I pondered, but then decided to lie.

"That's just how upper-class Brits are," I said, forcing a smile. "Remember, the rest of my family was the same way."

"I think these sisters were nicer than the one in England," London said, giving me a mischievous grin.

I chuckled, but then made a decision, partly to distract her and partly because I realized what I truly wanted.

"I'm going to get an apartment in the city," I said.

Her eyes widened. "Seriously?"

"Seriously," I said, kissing her forehead. "Now, go break a leg."

As she walked away, I knew I needed to figure out if I was going to tell my sisters before they left for home or wait until I had a few thousand miles between us. Either way, they were going to be upset.

THIRTY-TWO
LONDON

SPENDING TIME WITH SPENCER'S SISTERS WAS A NERVE-wracking experience, but mostly because I wanted them to like me. The thoughts occupied my mind, but that changed when I went to the dressing room after Spencer left me backstage.

I could hear the whispers and murmurings all around me, my name and Spencer's name being mentioned. I could feel the gaze of the others on me, but whenever I looked at them, no one would meet my eyes. This only confirmed what I had been hearing.

"You should hurry and get ready," Tomma said as I walked past her and Timothy. "You don't want Darrel to think you're unprepared and replace you with someone else."

"At least then we'd know we have a professional on stage," Timothy added, his voice low but still loud enough for me to hear.

Tomma made sure everyone could hear her next remark, "Yeah, someone who's earned their role the right way."

I stopped and turned as Mercedes stepped forward and confronted Tomma.

"Watch yourself, Ackman," Mercedes warned. "You're not as untouchable as you think."

"What? Is London going to run to her boyfriend and get me fired?" Tomma retorted, seemingly unperturbed.

I placed a hand on Mercedes' arm. "It's okay."

"No, it's not okay," Mercedes replied, not taking her eyes off Tomma. "You work so hard and are ten times the actress this bitch is."

"What did you just call me?" Tomma stepped forward from Timothy.

"Mercedes," I said her name firmly. "Come help me get ready."

My tone got through to her this time, and she looked at me. I raised my eyebrows and gave her a pointed look over her shoulder. She turned to see some members of the cast watching us.

"Right," she stepped back. "This is not the right time or place."

Once we were in the dressing room, I said, "I appreciate you sticking up for me, but I don't want you to get into trouble because of it."

"Fine," she sighed. "At least Spencer will believe you when you tell him what she said."

"I will not tell him anything," I stated firmly. "It will only make everything she's saying look true and make the situation worse."

"So, you're just going to do nothing?" she asked.

I shook my head. "No, I'm going to do the only thing I can do."

"What's that?"

I replied determinedly, "Work my hardest and make it impossible for anyone to say that I don't deserve this role."

AFTER YET ANOTHER flawless performance on Saturday night, I was confident that my plan was working. No one who had seen the first week of shows could deny my talent and the reasons they had given me the lead.

However, that thought was soon dispelled when I turned to Timothy backstage and complimented his performance. "Great job tonight," I said.

The look Timothy gave me was filled with disgust and scorn. He took a step forward, and I took a step back before I caught myself. "Someone has to uphold the integrity of this show," he said. "The rest of the cast and crew shouldn't have to suffer because the female lead got the role by using means other than talent."

I was taken aback and responded, "I was good out there tonight. In fact, I've been giving my all from the first read-through."

"That's what makes it so sad, London," Timothy said with a shake of his head, as if disappointed in me. "You could have done it the right way."

Tomma chimed in from behind Timothy, "Maybe she could, maybe she couldn't. I'm not saying she's a bad actress, but I've auditioned against her often enough to know this isn't the first role she's earned with her body."

I've had enough of Tomma's accusations. "You should think twice before spreading that kind of vicious rumor. Not only does it show your complete lack of morals, but it also makes you look petty and jealous in the eyes of others."

Tomma's expression darkened as she glared at me. "What are you trying to imply about me?" she snarled. "I won't stand for this kind of accusation."

"I'm simply stating the facts, Tomma. And the fact is, spreading unfounded gossip only serves to harm others and reflects poorly on the speaker. So, think carefully before you open your mouth and start spouting off baseless rumors."

"Is something wrong here?" Spencer's voice stopped the conversation in its tracks.

Timothy tried to play it cool. "We were just talking about how well everything has been going."

Spencer agreed. "Everyone has been performing admirably. It seems American audiences love the story as much as the British."

An awkward silence followed, until Timothy said, "I'm going to change into my street clothes." Tomma followed him without a word, leaving only Spencer and me.

"Will you please tell me what was going on here?" Spencer asked. "And don't tell me everything's fine," he said, taking my hand. "You're upset."

I sighed. "People here think that I slept with you to get my part."

Spencer's expression grew serious. "That's nonsense."

"We know that, and those who know me do too, but everyone else..." I shrugged. "The gossip mill is working overtime, and some cast members are fanning the flames."

"Give me names," Spencer demanded. "Tomorrow will be their last show, and on Monday I'll find replacements."

I shook my head. "You'd have to replace everyone except Vix and Mercedes. Not everyone is openly talking about it, but I know most of the cast is gossiping behind my back."

Spencer figured it out. "Timothy and Tomma are behind it, aren't they?" he asked. "I won't fire them, but I'll talk to them."

"By 'talk' you mean 'threaten,'" I said with a sigh. "No. That'll just make things worse."

Spencer was determined. "I won't stand idly by and watch this happen," he declared. "Let me be your knight in shining armor."

"I appreciate the sentiment," I replied with a smile. "But you know as well as I do that if I run to you every time someone says something mean, it'll look like I can't handle the industry on my own. And with your family watching your every move, you don't need any rumors of nepotism floating around."

Spencer nodded, his brow furrowed in thought. "You make a valid point."

"Thank you for understanding," I said, squeezing his hand.

He looked down at our entwined fingers, a fire in his eyes. "Just promise me one thing - if things ever get to be too much for you to handle, you'll come to me."

"Agreed," I replied after a moment of consideration. "If the situation reaches the point where I would need help, I'll come to you first."

Spencer leaned in, pressing a gentle kiss to my cheek. "Perfect."

I looked up into his eyes, feeling a flutter in my stomach as he gazed back at me with an intensity that took my breath away.

"You know," I whispered, "I'm lucky to have you."

He grinned, that devilish twinkle back in his eyes. "No, my dear, I'm the lucky one."

We both chuckled, the tension from earlier dissipating as we wrapped our arms around each other and shared a comfortable silence. I knew we would face challenges in the future, but with Spencer by my side, I felt like I could take on anything the world threw our way.

THIRTY-THREE

SPENCER

"This week has already sold out, and next week is hot on its heels," Stan informed me with a broad grin as the waiter took our lunch order.

"That's bloody marvelous, mate. I hope the board isn't too concerned about the recent press," I said with a cheeky grin.

"Well, they weren't exactly jumping for joy," Stan chuckled. "But I assured them that the thing between you and London did not affect casting decisions, and that the choice for her in the lead wasn't solely yours."

"Thanks, I suppose," I replied with a smirk. "But I'm not sure that was much of a comfort."

"I know you well enough, you wouldn't let your...er...bits make any important decisions," Stan quipped.

"Thanks for the vote of confidence, old chum," I laughed.

"So, how are things going with London?" Stan asked once the waiter had brought our food and left us to our conversation.

I leaned back in my seat and let out a sigh. "There's been a bit of gossip floating around at work."

"Behind your backs or to your faces?" Stan asked, his eyebrows raised.

"A bit of both, I'm afraid," I shrugged. "But London asked me not to do anything about it."

"That's a tightrope to walk," Stan said, nodding.

"And the worst part is," I added, "I can't even regret it because I would go through worse to have her."

"She's getting rave reviews," Stan said with a grin. "People love her, critics and theatergoers alike. And if she can survive turning down Russ Hayworth, she'll have no trouble weathering this."

"I've been avoiding reviews like the plague," I admitted. "I can handle the bad ones, but I'm not sure I can handle my personal life being dragged into the production commentary."

"Honestly, there has been little since the two of you answered questions outside that restaurant," Stan said with a reassuring nod. "Don't worry about her career. She's got this."

Stan's words were a much-needed shot of confidence, and I felt my anxiety ease. He was right. I had to believe in London, and it was good news that they have written little about the incident since.

The West End might've been England's equivalent to Broadway, but American and English cultures were two different things, no matter what. Stan knew how the New York theater scene worked far better than I did. I could trust him.

Now I could stop worrying about London and focus on something special for Valentine's Day. I knew of romantic places in the city, but I didn't want to take her just to any old random place. I wanted to do something that she would know was just for her. Since I already had plans to meet with Carson a little later today, I intended to ask him for some help in the matter.

With a farewell nod to Stan, I set off toward Carson's studio. It was only a short walk from the restaurant, and as I made my way, my mind was filled with thoughts of London.

However, my good mood was quickly dampened when Carson greeted me with a frosty demeanor unlike any he had shown me before. I trailed behind him as he led me to the back room and gestured for me to take a seat, curious about what had him so frustrated.

"You said you wanted to talk to me about costume designs?"

"Yes," I replied with a cheeky grin. "I've been thinking of sprucing things up a bit for my West End production and wondered if you'd like to get in on the action. After all, you know the lead character like the back of your hand. I'm looking for something slightly different, of course, with different measurements."

"And what makes you think I'd be interested?" he asked, raising a skeptical eyebrow.

"Well, I mean, it's not every day one gets the chance to design costumes for a West End production, now is it?" I chuckled. "And let's not forget the bonus of working with a charming chap like myself."

I waited for him to say something, but he just stared at me, arms still crossed.

Bloody hell.

"Is there a problem, buddy?" I asked, trying to lighten the mood.

"Do you really need to ask?" He leaned forward, his tone accusatory. "Have you any idea the damage your relationship with my sister has caused to her reputation?"

I frowned. "There were a few stories written about us and some comments from her cast mates. I offered to handle the situation at work, but she asked me not to."

"And yet you listened?" Carson's tone was incredulous.

I raised a brow. "You have met your sister, haven't you? Do you honestly think our relationship would survive if I went against her wishes, especially for something that could compromise her professional image?"

"She's not always the best judge of what's best for her," Carson replied, a determined glint in his eye.

"That may be," I said. "But I can't go against her wishes. Besides, she's promised me she'll come to me if things become too difficult."

"And why would she do that?" he asked, with a hint of frustration. "She's the one receiving backlash for sleeping with her boss. Your reputation has barely been impacted."

"I just had lunch with my friend and partner, Stan Longley," I said cheerfully, "and he assured me that the situation is calming down and neither mine nor London's careers will be negatively affected. You know, I'll do everything in my power to protect your sister. I care about her deeply. In fact, I wanted to talk to you about doing something special for her on Valentine's Day."

Carson studied me for a moment before speaking. "I'm still not thrilled about the situation, but I'll give the two of you some time to work things out. And, I suppose, I'll help you come up with a romantic plan for Valentine's Day."

"Thank you, Carson," I said, genuinely grateful. "And I promise to do whatever London wants to keep her safe."

"That'll do for now," Carson said with a resigned sigh. "Now, let's get back to talking about costume designs, and then we'll discuss these romantic plans of yours."

THIRTY-FOUR

LONDON

Last night's relatively calm and quiet production, seeing that people were just giving me sideways looks rather than coming after me, gave me hope things were blowing over.

I'd come in early to work on a specific move I'd had a bit of a problem with last night, and now I was on the stage, walking back and forth, when my foot caught on something, and I turned, crouching down to run my hand over the floor. My fingers quickly found the head of a nail sticking up, and I looked around for something to mark it. Not seeing anything on hand, I went to look for the stage manager to tell him about it.

As I made my way to the backstage area, I nearly ran right into Timothy.

Raising my hands, I stepped back. "Sorry."

"You just don't understand, do you, love?" Timothy spoke with a hint of frustration in his voice.

"What are you on about?" I asked, trying to step around him.

"If you hadn't been so difficult that night when I drove

you home, things would be different for you now," he explained. "You wouldn't be facing this mess with people around here."

My blood began to boil. "Are you saying that because I didn't succumb to your advances, I deserve to be hounded by everyone here?" I said.

"Don't go blaming me, darling," Timothy retorted. "You made your own bed when you got involved with Spencer. You'll have to face the consequences."

I glared at him, my eyes darting to the group of my cast mates who had gathered to watch the argument with eager eyes. I could see the glee in their expressions.

I took a deep breath and tried to calm myself. I didn't want to cause a scene, but I couldn't let Timothy's accusations go unanswered.

"Let's be clear, Timothy," I said firmly. "I did not sleep with Spencer to advance my career or because I wanted to. We fell in love, and I refuse to apologize for that."

He sneered. "Love? Don't make me laugh. You're just using him to get ahead, and you're using this love excuse as a cover."

I felt a surge of anger. How dare he make such assumptions about me and my relationship? I took a step forward, getting into his face.

"You have no right to judge me or my relationship with Spencer. You don't know us or what we have. And for the record, I have been working my butt off for years to get where I am. I don't need anyone to carry me."

Timothy just rolled his eyes. "Whatever you say, London. But when everything comes crashing down, don't come crying to me."

With that, he walked away, leaving me fuming. I took a

deep breath and tried to compose myself, but it was clear that the fight was far from over.

I finally spotted the stage manager, and as I approached him about the nail on the floor, I could see the exhaustion etched on his face. "What now?" he groaned, running a hand through his hair. "I swear, every time I turn around, there's another problem that needs fixing. I don't know how much more of this I can take."

"I'm sorry to add to your workload," I said. "I just wanted to let you know that there's a nail sticking out on the stage floor."

He sighed heavily and nodded. "Yeah, yeah, I'll take care of it. But it's just one more thing on top of all the equipment that's in dire need of repair. We're stretched thin as it is."

I could only nod and offer my understanding, and as I turned to head back to the stage, I overheard one stagehand talking about the ceiling wires that controlled the stage props. They were not running smoothly. My stomach dropped at the thought of something going wrong during a performance and ruin the show, but I pushed the worry away as Darrel, the director, summoned all of us actors to the stage for a briefing.

I took my place in the center, surrounded by my cast mates. Darrel stood at the front, with his back to the empty theater seats. He cleared his throat and spoke.

"Good morning, everyone. I wanted to call this briefing to go over a few things before we begin rehearsals today. Foremost, I want to address the recent rumors about London and Spencer. I know there have been a few stories in the press, but I want to remind everyone that this is a professional setting. I expect everyone to act professionally and not let any personal feelings interfere with our work."

I could feel the weight of the stares from my cast mates, but I lifted my chin and tried to project confidence. Darrel's words were reassuring, but I couldn't shake the feeling that some of my colleagues were still skeptical.

"Let me also say this," Darrel added. "What London and Spencer do in their private lives is none of our business. They have both assured me that this will not affect the show, and I expect everyone to respect that."

I let out a small sigh of relief, grateful for Darrel's understanding.

As I glanced around me, my eyes caught the stagehand, who was now bent over fixing the nail. A glimmer of hope flickered in my mind as I watched him work. Things were being taken care of, and maybe, just maybe, all my problems would be fixed soon too.

With a renewed sense of determination, I made my way to take my spot, ready to focus on my work and not let anything distract me from what was most important. I had a show to put on and a performance to give, and I was going to give it my all.

The rehearsal was going well, and I felt myself getting lost in the world of the play. The lines came naturally, and the movements felt fluid. It was as if all the chaos and drama of the past few days had melted away, leaving only the stage and the performance.

But then, just as the scene was about to end, there was a loud snap, followed by a crash. My heart stopped as I looked up to see one of the backdrops falling from above, the wires that held it up, having given way. The heavy object was hurtling straight towards Timothy standing next to me.

Without thinking, I lunged forward and pushed Timothy out of the way, sending him sprawling to the ground. But as I turned to escape the falling backdrop, I felt a searing pain in my foot. I tried to move, but my foot was pinned to the ground.

The next thing I knew, I was lying on the stage, the pain in my foot pulsing through my body. I could hear voices calling out, but they sounded distant, as if coming from far away. I tried to open my eyes, but they felt heavy, and I couldn't seem to focus.

The last thing I remembered was the sound of someone calling my name, their voice filled with concern and fear. And then everything went dark.

THIRTY-FIVE

SPENCER

I WAS IN THE MIDDLE OF A MEETING WITH A POTENTIAL sponsor when my phone rang. It was Stan. I excused myself and answered the call.

"Spencer, I just heard from Darrel. London had an accident on stage. She's being rushed to the hospital," Stan said, his voice filled with concern.

"What happened? Is she okay?" I asked, my heart racing.

"I'm not sure. The stagehand said it was a backdrop that fell, but he didn't have many details. Mercedes is taking her to the hospital, and I'm heading there now."

"I'll meet you there," I said, already grabbing my coat and rushing out of the meeting.

The cab ride to the hospital felt like it took forever. My mind was racing with thoughts of London and what could have happened. When I finally arrived at the waiting area, I saw Mercedes and Gin sitting together, looking worried.

"How is she?" I asked, my voice trembling.

Gin stood up and gave me a hug. "She's okay, Spencer. They're checking her out now."

I let out a sigh of relief and turned to Mercedes. "Thank you for taking her to the hospital."

"Of course, Spencer. She's my best friend. I had to make sure she was okay," Mercedes said, giving me a small smile.

I paced back and forth in the hospital waiting area, my mind racing with worry, but also anger. How could this have happened? Was the theater not safe?

Finally, Stan arrived, looking frazzled. "How is she?" he asked.

I filled him in on London's status, and my concerns about the state of the theater. "How could a stage prop fall down like that? This is unacceptable," I said, frustration seeping into my voice.

"I know, I know," Stan said, running a hand through his hair. "The Shubert Theatre has needed repairs for a while now, and the stage manager is overloaded. We need to hire more crew and pressure the Shubert Foundation to commit to ongoing repairs."

I nodded in agreement, grateful for Stan's level head. "We'll take care of it. But right now, all I care about is London's well-being."

Just then, a nurse approached us. "Are you here for London McCrae?" she asked.

We all stood up, anxious for news. "Yes, we are," I said.

"She's being discharged now. She's free to go home, but she should rest and take it easy for a week or two," the nurse said.

As the nurse finished her sentence, London appeared from behind her, leaning on crutches and sporting a bandage on her foot. My heart swelled with relief at the sight of her.

"London," I said, rushing over to her. "Are you okay?"

"I'm fine, Spencer. Just a little banged up," she said with a small smile.

Gin and Mercedes stood up to give her a hug, and I helped London to the cab that I had waiting outside. As we made our way to her apartment, I was grateful that she was okay. We chatted about her accident and she told me how fortunate she was that her foot wasn't broken, only sprained.

"I'm just glad you're okay," I said, holding her hand.

"I'm lucky to have you," she replied, squeezing my hand back, leaning her head on my shoulder as she closed her eyes.

Once we arrived at her apartment, I helped her inside and made sure she was comfortable on the couch. I couldn't bear the thought of leaving her side after what had just happened.

"Spencer, I'm okay. You don't have to stay," she said, noticing my worried expression.

"I want to stay," I said firmly. "Just until you're feeling better."

We spent the rest of the evening talking and watching movies, just happy to be in each other's company. As I lay down beside her on the couch, my thoughts turned to how lucky we were to have each other. Nothing else mattered in that moment except our love and the knowledge that we would always be there to support and protect each other.

———

THE TIMING of London's accident meant I had to postpone my Valentine's Day plans for a few days until she was feeling better. But tonight was the night.

At six, I picked up London, keeping the details of the

evening a mystery. Dressed in a sharp, brand-new charcoal gray suit with a matching cap, I was ready for the night ahead.

When London stepped out of the door, her beauty struck me. She was dressed in a strapless, floor-length forest green cocktail dress with a slit that showcased her smooth, toned legs and heels. Her mass of curls flowed down her shoulders, nearly to her waist, and the thought of covering her up for the cold February evening felt almost criminal. She still had to use her crutches, but the ankle was feeling much better. Another week or two, and she would be ready to go back on stage, she told me.

As we approached the entrance to Savoir-faire, London's eyes lit up with excitement. "Seriously?" she asked, and I couldn't help but grin, knowing I had made the right choice. I made a mental note to send her brother a bottle of wine as a thank you for his recommendation.

"Carson said you've always wanted to come here," I told her, offering my hand to help her from the car and tucking it into the crook of my arm as we walked inside.

"How on earth did you manage a reservation? This place is impossible to get into," she asked, a hint of skepticism in her voice.

"Let's just say it pays to be the producer of the hottest show in town," I replied with a cheeky grin. "Remarkable what you can get by offering a pair of front row tickets," I added with a wink.

I gave my name to the hostess, and we followed her over to a table for two near the fireplace. London gazed around the restaurant in awe, and it was impossible not to agree with her. The place was stunning, with chandeliers overhead and rich wood accents everywhere. The round mirror above the fireplace mantel and the tall floor clock against one wall added to the ambiance, making it the perfect setting for a romantic evening.

As we placed our order for the tasting menu with wine pairing, our conversation was infused with a certain je ne sais quoi. We shared tales of our passions and reminisced about our childhoods, discovering new aspects of each other with every passing moment.

"You know, my dear, I've always believed that true love is eternal," I said, taking a sip of my wine.

London's eyes shone bright, and she leaned in closer, captivated. "And what, pray tell, do you define as true love?" she asked, her voice filled with wonder.

"For me, true love is about understanding and embracing each other, imperfections and all," I replied, my gaze never leaving hers.

"How beautifully put," she whispered, her hand resting atop mine.

Lost in the moment, we were briefly interrupted as our server presented us with our second course, seared Atlantic sea scallops with a rosemary smoked yellow tomato coulis and a leek fondue.

"Every time I hear leeks, I think of that movie where they had the leek in a boat and made the play on words," London said with a chuckle.

"I'm not familiar with that one," I replied, intrigued.

"Oh, it's hilarious," she said, laughing. "We'll have to watch it together one day."

As we savored each dish, we bonded over our mutual love of British television, passionately discussing the merits of J. R. R. Tolkien versus C. S. Lewis. But when the topic of work came up, I couldn't help but feel anxious. However, London's account of standing up for herself against Timothy's accusations and Darrel's support in front of everyone brought a sense of comfort and put my worries to rest.

"And what about dessert?" our server asked, whisking away our empty plates.

"Yes, bring it on," I replied, positively bouncing with excitement.

London raised an eyebrow, amused by my boyish enthusiasm for dessert. "Are you truly looking forward to the chocolate souffle that much, or is it something else that has you all excited?" she asked, with a playful glint in her eye.

I gave her a roguish grin. "Can't it be both?"

She chuckled, her eyes sparkling. "Of course."

London gazed out the nearest window, where we could just make out the faint swirl of a light snowfall. "Do you have a specific plan in mind, or are we heading back to the apartment?" she asked.

"I was thinking maybe go to my hotel, if you're up for it, or are you too tired?" I replied, genuinely curious.

"Not at all," she answered truthfully. "I enjoy being with you, no matter where we are. And the suite offers certain amenities," she said with a smile. "Like a jacuzzi and bigger bed."

"I couldn't agree more," I whispered. "I have many plans for us back in my room."

The blush that rose to her cheeks told me she liked the idea, and she reached across the table to take my hand. "Thank you, not just for this romantic evening, but for always being there for me and putting my needs first."

Her fingers tightened around mine for a moment before she leaned back to allow the server to place our dessert in front of us. Heat smoldered in her eyes as she took a bite of the souffle, making a slow, sensual show of licking her fork clean.

I couldn't help but curse under my breath. "You're driving me crazy."

"And I'm loving every minute of it," she said with a wicked wink.

As we indulged in the rich chocolate dessert, the atmosphere between us grew even more charged, our desires simmering just below the surface. And as we finished, and I asked for the check, I could feel the heat building between us, ready to ignite into a blazing passion.

Our car was waiting for us as we left the restaurant, a welcome respite from the frigid air. I was grateful to have dressed up for London, but I couldn't wait to shed as many layers as possible once we were in the privacy of my suite.

As the car pulled up to the hotel, we quickly made our way inside, eager to escape the cold. "Do you want to stop at the bar or go straight to the suite?" I asked.

She shook her head, her eyes blazing with desire. "I can't wait to be in the bedroom with you," she said, her voice filled with longing.

Her beauty took my breath away, and I realized it wasn't the dress that made her so stunning, but the passion and desire in her eyes.

The elevator ride to the tenth floor was a blur, and before I knew it, I was alone with her.

As I turned on the music system, a sultry beat filled the room and London came to me, her gaze locked on mine. She stood tall at the foot of the bed, her presence both commanding and inviting. With a seductive smile, she reached under her dress and slowly slid her panties down her legs, revealing just a glimpse of her thighs. Tossing the delicate lace in my direction, she left me entranced.

I was still a little concerned about her ankle, but she assured me that she was fine, that it was merely a bruise by now. She winked at me as she gracefully climbed onto the bed, giving me a tantalizing display of her swaying figure. I was momentarily spellbound, but as the groovy music in the room changed to a new tune, I undressed, quickly shrugging off my jacket and tossing it onto one chair near the floor-to-ceiling window. People could see us through the glass, which London told me only added to the excitement.

It was time to ignite our passion.

THIRTY-SIX

LONDON

Spencer in a suit was delicious.

Spencer wearing only tight black boxer briefs was downright sinful.

"Unzip your dress," he said as he stood by the side of the bed, his eyes fixed on me, though I knew he was aware people could watch us through the giant windows. He didn't show it, though. He was calm, relaxed, and collected as he waited for me to obey him.

Conscious of the cool silk under my bare ass, I unzipped my dress and waited to see if he'd understood what I intended when I'd removed my panties but not my dress.

"Pull the top down to your waist," he instructed. "Let me see if your bra matches."

He understood.

I smiled, revealing the sheer lace bra that did indeed match my dark green panties. It did, however, have less substance. The material was insubstantial enough that my breasts were seen, nipples visible and tightening.

"You look good enough to eat," he murmured as his gaze ran over me.

I spread my legs as far as my dress allowed. A blatant invitation and one that he quickly accepted. He moved around to the foot of the bed, giving our potential observers a delightful view of his ass.

It was a damn fine ass.

He stretched out between my legs, pulling them over his shoulders as he pushed my dress high enough that he would've exposed my last surprise to all our potential viewers if his broad shoulders hadn't been blocking anything more than glimpses.

"Fuck, babe." He barely kept from saying my name. "What the hell did you do?"

I laughed, the sound turning into a moan as he lightly blew on my now bare skin. My voice was breathless. "A friend suggested it. I thought it sounded fun."

"I've heard it makes the skin extra sensitive." He pressed his lips to my inner thigh. "Shall we find out if that's true?"

Without waiting for an answer, he ran the tip of his tongue up my slit, ghosting over the skin in the faintest touch. A shiver went through me, and it was his turn to chuckle. This time, before he put his mouth on me, he wrapped his hands around my hips to hold me steady.

The first pass of his tongue had my eyes fluttering closed, and I let them stay that way, focusing all my attention on the sensations flowing through me from one focused area. It was nearly overwhelming. Every nerve felt raw, sending jolts strong enough to make me gasp. My entire body jerked when he reached my clit, forcing him to tighten his grip to keep me in place. Three passes of his tongue across the top of that swollen nub, and then his lips closed over it. Only the faintest bit of suction and the already overworked pleasure center of my brain pushed me into orgasm.

I cried out, my hands scrabbling at the sheets as wave after wave of ecstasy rolled over me, Spencer's mouth working my flesh, determined to make it last as long as possible. When he finally relented, my entire body went limp, and my limbs splayed, muscles weak.

My brain was so fuzzy from how quickly I'd come that I didn't even notice he'd moved until his shadow fell over me. He straddled my upper torso. The heat in his eyes took my breath away, and when he hooked his thumbs into the waistband of his underwear, my stomach tightened.

"I'm going to fuck that pretty mouth," he said. "Then I'm going to turn you over and fuck you from behind." He leaned down and lightly kissed my mouth. "I might even play with that tight little asshole of yours."

I shuddered. "Yes, please."

He smirked. "Yes, to what?"

"All of it." I reached up to cup the noticeable bulge he was sporting. "Yes, to all of it."

He pushed down the front of his underwear, freeing an erection that was already long and thick. He situated the waistband under his balls, leaving everything I could want available to my touch.

I put my hands on his thighs as he moved closer, positioning himself so I could take him in my mouth without putting my neck at an uncomfortable angle. The tip of his cock nudged at my lips, and I opened my mouth, darting my tongue out to lick a drop of pre-cum from him. He sucked in a breath; the sound making me smile.

He moved forward, and I opened my mouth wider, letting him slide over my tongue, the taste of him bursting across my taste buds—salt and sweat, a hint of soap, and something uniquely him. I closed my lips around him, but not tight. Not yet. Giving short, shallow thrusts, he worked himself into my mouth, watching my face and judging just how far and deep he could go. My mouth stretched wider to accommodate as much of him as possible, my body struggling against the urge to reject something that threatened to cut off my air.

"Relax, sweetheart." Despite his words, Spencer's voice was strained. "You can take a little more."

I wasn't so sure, but I trusted him and his confidence in me. I shut my eyes and concentrated on taking even breaths through my nose and not tensing. Just when I thought it'd be too much, he began to withdraw, taking his cock almost entirely out of my mouth before pushing forward again. A little faster this time, but not going any deeper. Once he'd found a rhythm, I added suction when he pulled back.

He growled a curse and then demanded, "Look at me."

I opened my eyes and found him staring down at me with a heat that would have made me catch my breath if he hadn't chosen that exact moment to start fucking my mouth again. Taking all of his weight on one hand, his other went to my head, fingers tangling in my hair.

"Deep breath and relax your throat," he instructed. "Take it all for three strokes like a good girl, and then I'll bury myself in your cunt until you come, screaming."

I moaned, pressing my thighs together.

"Tap my leg twice if you need me to stop," he added. "Now, inhale."

I did, the anticipation tightening my stomach. Without hesitating, he smoothly moved past my lips and over my tongue. I dug my nails into his thighs as he went even deeper than before. I could feel myself gagging and fought the sensation.

One.

Two.

On the third, panic flickered in my chest, but then he was moving back, slipping from between my lips..

I gasped, sucking in air as he reached for a condom. Despite my burning lungs and the ache in my jaw, I couldn't look away from where he was rolling the latex over his cock.

Damn.

I could hardly believe I'd fit any of that in my mouth, and my pussy clenched at the thought that all of it would be inside me soon.

"You did brilliantly, love." He winked at me.

"Next time," my voice was rough, "I want you to come in my mouth."

The cocky smile disappeared behind a look of surprise. "Well, damn."

"Not now." It was my turn to wink at him. "You promised to make me scream."

"I always keep my promises." He moved to one side, his body angled. "Turn over and go up on your hands and knees."

I did as told. I assumed Spencer would get in position, but I was wrong. Staying where he was beside me, he slid a hand under my skirt and up the back of my thigh.

"Trust me," he murmured as he pulled aside the fabric, exposing my leg and then one side of my ass.

He leaned down and pressed his lips to my ass cheek in a soft kiss. Then a sharp nip made me yelp. I glared at him over my shoulder, and he just grinned at me.

"Are you going to fuck me, or should I take care of things myself?" I asked.

His eyes darkened as his hand moved back under my dress. "This is mine." With no other warning, he shoved two fingers inside me, making me cry out.

My hands curled in the sheets as he pumped his fingers inside me, all the while moving around to kneel behind me. Only then did he push my dress completely out of the way. With no further teasing, he drove into me with one quick thrust.

I shouted a curse that still couldn't quite express what it felt like to be on the edge of too full. My head fell forward, my hair falling around my face to block the world from my sight. Every other sense was heightened. The taste of him on my tongue. The soft music coming in through the speakers. The mingled scents of the perfume I'd used, Spencer's aftershave, and, of course, our mutual arousal.

And touch. So much touch.

The silk sheets under my palms, knees, and shins.

Strong hands on my hips.

And him inside me. Thick and throbbing. Reaching parts of me that only he had ever been able to get to.

"Fuck, sweetheart," he groaned. "You're perfect."

Unable to help myself, I rocked back against him, making a small sound in the back of my throat. His fingers dug into my flesh, the only warning I received before he pulled back and slammed into me. I cried out at the sharp and almost painful jolt that went through me, but I didn't ask him to stop. I didn't *want* him to stop. I wanted more.

And he gave it to me.

The first time I came with him inside me, it hit so hard and fast that my arms gave out, my scream muffled in the sheets as I fell, face-first, into them. He didn't miss a beat, pounding into me repeatedly, making it impossible for my body to process the pleasure washing over me in waves.

A hand slid up my spine and gripped my shoulder, pulling me upright. He draped his arm over my shoulder and cupped my breast over my bra, holding me to him as he drove up into me. His other hand slid around my waist, fingers slipping between my slick folds to quickly find my swollen clit.

"I should turn you around," Spencer whispered as the hand on my breast plucked at my nipple. "Give these people watching from the other building a bit more of a show. Maybe push down your bra to let them watch me turn this pretty nipple red. Lift your dress to show them how you like your clit rubbed. Spread your legs wider so they can see where my cock is going into your cunt."

I whimpered at his words, my muscles trembling with the need to come again. I danced that edge, the pressure and tension building inside me until it was almost unbearable.

"No," Spencer said. "You're *mine*."

He punctuated the last word with a rough pinch to my nipple and a deep thrust, the combination of the three sending me flying over the edge into oblivion. I felt him speed up, felt his body tense as he went. I heard him growl my name. But all of it was dim, in the recesses of a mind overcome by the most powerful climax I'd ever had.

Afterwards, I barely registered anything, my head still in that pleasant, fuzzy place that came with such intense sex. Spencer seemed amused, and I liked the fondness in the way he looked at me. Neither of us spoke as we showered and climbed into bed, both of us sated enough that our naked skin was comforting rather than arousing.

"Did you enjoy tonight?" he asked as he tucked my body against his.

"I did," I said, turning my head enough to kiss his arm. "Did you?"

"*Bloody* good." After a brief pause, he asked an odd question, "When is your lease up for your apartment?"

Frowning, I turned slightly to look up at him even though my room was dark. "What?"

"I told you I was looking for a place here," he said. "When your lease is up, I'd rather fancy you move in with me."

Maybe I was still riding a post-coital high because my first thought wasn't that we'd only been together for a short while. It was an immediate and resounding, "*Yes*."

We kissed then, and I put other thoughts out of my mind. We'd work through the details at some point, and I'd worry about anything else then. Right now, I just wanted to keep my perfect night and the future I could clearly see in front of me.

With him.

THIRTY-SEVEN
SPENCER

A SHRILL RING PIERCED THROUGH THE SILENCE OF THE room, jolting me awake. For a moment, I was disoriented, until the light from my phone screen illuminated the room and reminded me that London was lying next to me. The phone rang again, and I quickly grabbed it, not wanting to disturb her sleep.

"Hello?" I answered groggily.

"Spencer." It was my mother, and her tone was filled with a strange urgency that immediately set my heart racing.

"What's wrong?" I asked, trying to keep my voice steady. I felt London stir beside me, but I didn't turn to look at her. Instead, I focused on my mother's words.

"It's your father," she said, her voice shaking. "He's gone."

I sat up straight, my heart pounding. "Gone?" I repeated, trying to process what she was saying. 'What do you mean, he's gone?"

"The doctors think it was his heart," she said, her voice

breaking. "We were getting ready for bed, and when I came out of the shower, I found him on the floor."

The lamp beside the bed flickered on, and I turned my head away as my eyes adjusted to the light. My mother continued, "I called 999 and started CPR, but he was already gone."

I felt a wave of pain wash over me, but I pushed it aside and focused on my mother's well-being. "Mum, where are you now?" I asked. "Who's with you?"

"I'm at the hospital," she said, her voice trembling. "Fleur is here with me. Anne is with Gabriella."

I let out a small sigh of relief that she wasn't alone. "Make sure at least one of them stays with you until I get there, okay?" I said, trying to keep my voice steady.

"Get here?" she asked, sounding surprised.

"Yes, I'm coming home," I said firmly. "You don't have to worry about anything. I'll make arrangements."

"Okay," she said, before the sound of some commotion could be heard in the background.

"I have to go now," she said quickly. "You're really coming home?"

"Yes, I'll be there as soon as I can," I assured her, before the call ended.

I sat there in silence, my mind grappling, knowing that my life would never be the same again. The numbness I felt would eventually wear off, but for now, I was grateful for it, as it allowed me to focus on what needed to be done for my family.

"Spencer?" London's soft voice interrupted my thoughts as she placed a comforting hand on my arm. "What happened?"

"My father died," I replied, my voice heavy with a weight I had never felt before.

"Oh, no," she said, wrapping her arms around me in a warm embrace. "I'm so sorry."

"Thank you," I said, grateful for her support.

"What can I do?" she asked, her voice filled with concern.

I appreciated she didn't ask if I was okay, as there was nothing anyone could do to change what had happened. But her presence was soothing, and I leaned into her, grateful for the comfort she provided.

"I have to go back to England," I said, my mind racing with the next steps I needed to take.

"Of course," she said without hesitation. "Do you need me to do anything?"

Before I could think it through, I blurted out, "Come with me." I immediately opened my mouth to retract my offer, but to my surprise, she agreed.

Relief flooded through me, and I closed my eyes. It was a lot to ask of her, especially after her injury, but I didn't have the strength to do this alone. I needed her with me, more than I ever thought possible.

"Thank you," I said, taking a deep breath. "Are you sure you'll be okay with your ankle?" I asked, concerned for her well-being.

London rolled her eyes, reassuring me. "I'll be fine. I can travel. I just can't stand on a stage for hours." She kissed my cheek and asked, "What do we do next?"

I wanted to stay in her embrace and forget about everything else, but I knew plans had to be made. "I have to call Stan," I said, trying to pull myself together. "Make arrangements to leave."

"You're right," she said, getting up from the bed. "I need to make a few calls, too." She hesitated for a moment, her embrace tightening as if she could sense my reluctance to let go. Then she kissed my forehead and got dressed.

I quickly put on my pants and retrieved my phone from my pocket. It took two calls before Stan answered, but his voice was concerned rather than angry, despite the late hour.

"Spencer? Is everything all right?" he asked, his tone filled with worry.

"My father passed away," I replied, the reality of the situation still hitting me.

"My condolences," he said, his words formal, but the sentiment genuine.

"Thank you," I said, feeling a sliver of pain.

"I'm assuming you're calling because you're going home," Stan said.

"I am," I confirmed, glancing at London. "And London's coming with me."

There was a momentary pause before Stan spoke again. "Good idea. Darrel is already preparing Tomma for tomorrow night and the following week. Any idea of how long the two of you will be gone?"

"I don't know," I answered honestly.

"It's not a problem," Stan continued. "Darrel and I can hold down the fort for as long as you need."

"Thanks," I said, grateful for his understanding. "I trust you to handle everything, Stan."

"Is there anything else I can do?" he asked. "Anything you need taken care of before you go?"

"I don't think so," I said, shaking my head even though he couldn't see me.

"What about a flight?" he asked. "Do you need me to arrange anything?"

"No, but thanks," I replied. It occurred to me that the

family jet was in London, but it shouldn't be difficult to get a flight to England flying out today. I glanced over to where London was coming back into the bedroom. "I need to go now."

"Of course," he said. "If you need anything, just call. And again, I'm sorry for your loss."

I thanked him and ended the call. I needed to get dressed, but I sat on the edge of the bed, unmoved, unable to summon the strength to stand. My father was gone, and it left me with a feeling of emptiness.

London placed her hand on my shoulder. "Is everything okay with Stan?"

I nodded. "He'll take care of things."

THIRTY-EIGHT
LONDON

THE WEATHER WAS COLD AND WET WHEN WE DEPARTED
New York City on Monday morning. After a nearly eight-
hour flight, we arrived in London to find it even colder and
just as rainy.

The private plane Spencer had arranged for us had a
sleeping compartment in the back, and we spent a few
hours there, not speaking or trying to sleep. I wasn't sure
what to say, as I had never experienced losing a parent. All I
could do was imagine what I would want from a partner in
a similar situation and hold Spencer.

As we stepped out of the airplane, a fancy car was
waiting for us, and a suited man stood at the back door. He
asked if Spencer wanted to go home, and Spencer replied
he wanted to go wherever his mother was. As we settled
into the luxurious leather seats, Spencer put his arm around
me and pulled me close. I was grateful to be there for him,
offering him comfort in a difficult time. Despite my own
worries about the impact my injury might have on my
career and the uncertainty about the future, my focus was
solely on Spencer. I hugged him tightly and told him I was

there for him, ready to support him in any way he needed. We sat in silence for the entire drive, with Spencer resting his cheek on my head, and I focused all my energy on being there for him in his time of need.

When we finally arrived, the driver opened the door, revealing Spencer's parents' house. Despite the late hour, lights were on, and the front door opened before we reached it. The butler stood at the door with the same stoic expression he had the last time I was here, as if nothing had changed.

Once inside, Gabriella, Spencer's youngest sister, came over to us. She wasn't crying, but I could see the redness in her eyes before she buried her face against Spencer's chest. Spencer wrapped his arms around her, and I stepped back to give them some privacy.

I knew how she felt, as I had lost my brother's best friend, Leo. Being at his funeral felt a lot like this, feeling helpless to ease the pain of those I care about, and hurting more for them than myself.

Gabriella sniffled as she stepped back from Spencer, taking his hand in hers. She finally acknowledged my presence. "London."

"I asked her to come with me," Spencer said in a quiet voice. "Where's Mum?"

An elderly woman's voice echoed from behind us. "Your mother is in the drawing room, waiting for you."

Spencer and Gabriella tensed as the owner of the voice approached us. Her dark blonde hair, streaked with silver, was styled in an elegant knot. Her blue eyes, though they would have been identical to Spencer's if they held any warmth, were cold and distant. She was tall and slender, almost to the point of fragility, yet still carried an air of elegance, even in these trying circumstances.

"Grandmother," Spencer greeted her, kissing her on the cheek.

The woman looked past Spencer, straight at me. "Surely, your company told you we don't tip our drivers for helping with the luggage. It's part of the service," she said in a condescending tone.

It took me a moment to realize that she was addressing me.

"Grandmother, she's not the driver," Spencer interjected, his voice holding a hint of something I couldn't quite identify. "This is London McCrae, my girlfriend. London, meet my grandmother, Opal Johnston York Masters."

"Is that so?" His grandmother approached me, her expression appraising. However, there was something in her eyes that suggested that she hadn't mistaken me for the driver, but rather that it was a test. I wasn't sure if it was for Spencer or for me.

"It's nice to meet you, ma'am. Although I wish it were under better circumstances. Please accept my condolences." I held out my hand.

She looked at my hand for a moment before taking it. As her eyes swept over me, I wished I had changed into something nicer on the plane. I had brought several options for public events and the funeral, but I thought that black dress pants and a light gray sweater would be appropriate for meeting Spencer's family late at night, rather than a dress.

She shook my hand for a few seconds before releasing it and turning away from me in a clear, dismissive gesture. I refused to let it bother me. The woman had just lost her son.

"Gabriella, go wash your face before returning to your mother," she said.

"Yes, Grandmother." Gabriella's response was quiet.

I bit my tongue, keeping my thoughts to myself. Being rude to a stranger was one thing, but to her own grand-daughter? The reprimand seemed unnecessarily harsh, especially given that Gabriella had just lost her father.

But it wasn't my place to interfere. My role here was to support Spencer, not to critique his family.

Spencer reached for my hand, entwining his fingers with mine, and we made our way into the same room where I had met his family the last time we were here.

However, this time, no small children were waiting to greet their favorite uncle, no tense anticipation with wary family members. It was just...grief. Heavy and thick, weighing down the very air.

Spencer's mom sat on the couch with a daughter on either side. As soon as Eloise looked up, Spencer let go of my hand and went to his mother. She let out a small sob and stood, collapsing against him when he opened his arms.

Fleur, Spencer's other sister, coldly questioned my presence. "What are you doing here?"

"I asked her to come," Spencer said, showing his unwavering support for me. "She's here for me."

Fleur's gaze narrowed, but she remained silent as her husband entered the room and sat next to her. I offered Anne a nod, but kept my distance from the family as they huddled around Spencer.

I was so focused on watching him that I missed the whisper of footsteps on the carpet behind me.

"You don't need to be here," Opal said, her voice low.

I looked over at her for a moment before turning my attention back to where Gabriella had joined the rest of the family.

"I don't think Spencer is ready to leave," I said, purposely misunderstanding her intentions.

"He should be surrounded by his family," Opal stated, her voice unwavering. "But you may go to your hotel."

"We're staying at my flat," Spencer interjected, glancing at his grandmother before addressing me. "Look, if you want to go–"

"I'll only go when you do," I said, looking into his eyes. "Unless you'd prefer–"

"I don't," Spencer said, his voice resolute. "Stay."

And so I stayed.

I'D HAD no clue what I was getting into, coming back here with Spencer. I knew his family had money, but I hadn't understood what that would mean for something like this. Not until Spencer and I woke up after a few hours of sleep to head back to the house where the family would receive people who wanted to pay their respects. Or, you know, show off their designer handbags.

I stayed near enough to Spencer to be there if he needed me, but not so close to be in the way. Though I got the impression from most of the family that any place on the entire island would be in the way.

I tried to make the best of it by people-watching, gathering bits and pieces of what I saw to file away for the future, but so much of what I saw drove home the differences between Spencer's family and mine.

And that wasn't all I saw.

Opal stayed in her seat next to Eloise most of the day, but there were a few times Opal made an effort to get up and greet someone who hadn't yet made their way through the insanely long receiving line. Every time, the person she went to talk to was a woman in her twenties with no ring on a very important finger. And every single one was escorted right past me to where Spencer stood beside his mother. I couldn't help but wonder if Opal was collecting potential brides for her grandson. And if so, did I need to practice my curtsey?

His face, of course, remained impassive as he spoke to each of the women. But it was clear to me that Opal was trying to set him up. I couldn't decide which feeling was stronger: disbelief that she would do something like that in the midst of such a solemn occasion or anger that she was putting Spencer in such an awkward position. However, I wouldn't let my emotions show. I would never hurt Spencer that way.

"She's not exactly the epitome of subtlety, my grandmother," Gabriella said, startling me. I hadn't even noticed her leave her spot next to Anne.

"What do you mean?" I asked.

She raised an eyebrow and nodded towards Opal. "My grandmother, trying to arrange something for my brother."

"Yes, I believe she is," I agreed.

"But you haven't felt the need to stake your claim," Gabriella observed.

I shrugged. "I'm not the one keeping Spencer in line."

Gabriella smiled faintly. "May I ask you a question, even though it may be a bit rude?"

My curiosity was piqued. "Sure, go ahead."

"Why did you leave a lead role on Broadway to come to England for a guy you barely know?" she asked, with a touch of curiosity in her voice. "You're not exactly unknown in the theater world, but you're not a household name either. This show must have been important to you."

"Well, to be honest," I said, "I actually injured my foot on stage, so I wouldn't have been able to work for the next two weeks, anyway. But, even if I had been able to perform, I still would have come to England for Spencer. I care about him more than any role I could have played on Broadway."

Gabriella turned to face me then, with a hint of surprise in her eyes. "Splendid answer," she said, nodding in approval.

Stunned by her response, I was momentarily speechless.

"Don't let the rest of the family get to you," Gabriella added with a reassuring smile. "Not even Grandmother. After all, you're here for Spencer, and he needs you more than anyone else right now." She gave me a knowing look before turning to walk away, leaving me standing there, feeling grateful for her support and understanding.

THIRTY-NINE

SPENCER

I FIDDLED WITH MY CUFFLINKS UNTIL LONDON approached me and took my hands in hers. Her touch was enough to steady my nerves, but it wasn't just grief that had me on edge. The reality of what this loss meant for me beyond the grieving process had become clearer in the past two days, and I didn't have the strength to deal with it on top of everything else.

"One breath at a time," London said, kissing my knuckles. "That's how we'll get through this. Just focus on taking the next breath."

I nodded, grateful for her words. "Thank you," I said.

"Is there anything else we need to do before we leave?" she asked.

"I don't think so," I replied, looking around my bedroom. It felt strange being here, even though I hadn't been gone for long and I had returned to my flat twice since going to New York. Perhaps it was the fact that I had been looking at places in New York that made me feel like something was off.

"I have your keys, wallet, and phone in my purse,"

London said, releasing my hands. "We don't want to ruin the line of your suit."

"Grandmother would have my head if I did," I agreed.

"Was there anything you needed to take for your mother or sisters, or the kids?"

"No, I think I have everything," I said, and we made it halfway to the door before I realized I had forgotten something. "Bugger, my eulogy. Where did I put it?"

"I have it," London said, taking one of my hands and squeezing it. "You gave it to me to hold so you wouldn't forget it."

"Right, of course. Thank you, darling," I said. "You're always so on top of things. It's no wonder I can't keep up."

The ride to St. George in the East was spent mostly reviewing the itinerary given to me by Grandmother the day before. The funeral was to be a typical Church of England service, held at the same church where all our family's weddings and funerals had taken place since Grandmother and Grandfather's marriage.

"The church is beautiful," London said as we came to a stop in front of the building.

"I've always thought so," I said absentmindedly, checking my phone. "Mom and Gabriella will be here shortly."

"Do you want to wait for them?" she asked.

"No, Grandmother is already here, and I think the car behind us is Fleur and the family. Grandmother will already be annoyed that I wasn't the first one here," I replied.

The driver opened London's door, but she took a moment to reach over and squeeze my hand. "Whatever you need from me today, just let me know. Even if it means distracting your grandmother," she said.

The corners of my mouth twitched. Not quite a smile, but enough for London to smile back. She allowed the driver to help her out, then stepped aside to wait for me. I took a deep breath and stepped out into the chilly February air, taking London's hand to ground me.

We walked towards Grandmother and the vicar, waiting by the door, each step taking effort. Behind me, I could hear the kids getting out of their car.

"Why are we at church on a Thursday?" Matthew asked.

"It's Grandfather's funeral," Harrison whispered loudly.

"I want down," Jane demanded in her typical loud three-year-old voice.

"Not now, love, we don't want you to get dirty," Parker said.

"Hush now," Fleur said sharply. "You three need to behave. You're representing the York family today, and you want to make Grandfather proud, don't you?"

My chest tightened at Fleur's words, reminding me of the many times Grandmother had said similar things to me. The York family name, making them proud. I could see all of that on Grandmother's face as London and I climbed the steps.

"My deepest condolences for your loss, Lord York," the vicar said.

"Thank you," I replied automatically.

I felt London stiffen beside me, and it took me a moment to realize what had caused her reaction.

With everything going on, I'd forgotten that London was unaware of my family's nobility. My father, and his father before him, had held the title of Baron, and now I held it too.

"Spencer, you'll be standing between Vicar Warfield and me," Grandmother instructed. "We'll greet everyone as they arrive."

I nodded, following the itinerary she'd provided. I was to remain with her while my mother and sisters went ahead into the church to take their seats and receive the attendees. Grandmother had meticulously planned every aspect of the service, including where each person would be and when. I'd been prepared to argue for my mother to stand with Grandmother and me, but she'd reassured me that she preferred to be inside to greet people. I couldn't blame her for wanting to keep her distance from Grandmother, who seemed to treat my father's death as if she was the only person allowed to grieve.

"There's no need for you to wait outside in the cold," Grandmother said to London in a polite but chilly tone. "There are plenty of seats available inside."

London looked at me. "Do you want me to wait for your mother?"

I squeezed her hand, grateful for her understanding of what was most important. "Go on in," I said. "Thank you."

After kissing my cheek, she squeezed my hand and went inside alone. I watched her go, wishing I could have asked her to stand by my side, but I needed to show strength, not just for my family, but also because of my title. To do that, I had to stand alone.

"Make sure she's seated in an appropriate place," Grandmother said quietly to Fleur.

"She'll be sitting next to me," I said firmly.

Fleur scowled. "She's not family."

"I don't care," I replied.

"Not here," Grandmother warned through a clenched smile.

I nodded, knowing that I would take care of London's seating arrangements when I went inside.

———

IT TOOK hours before Grandmother spoke to me again. "I cannot believe you brought that woman to your father's funeral," she said.

"She's my girlfriend," I replied coolly.

"And this is your first public function as the new baron. She's inappropriate."

I took a slow breath and greeted the Wembley family with a properly somber expression. After they moved on, I addressed Grandmother's comment.

"London isn't just some random woman I picked up off the street," I said.

"She's an actress," Grandmother said, the single word dripping with snobbery.

"She's also the daughter of Patrick McCrae, the multi-billionaire who owns MIRI," I added, choosing to ignore the slight against the career path I'd chosen.

"So, she's not just American, she's Scottish," Grandmother sniffed.

When Lord and Lady Fitzpatrick approached, Grandmother swallowed any further insults she might have levied at the Scottish people. Lady Fitzpatrick was a baroness in her own right, and while her husband might have been three generations removed from his Scottish roots, they wore the surname with pride. It had been quite the scandal, or so I'd heard.

After the Fitzpatricks came a Count and Countess, along with their twenty-something daughter. It was no surprise that Grandmother made a point of introducing the young woman to me. I waited until the trio was out of earshot before speaking.

"Don't you think that's a little inappropriate?" I said, keeping my voice low. "Practically throwing a woman at me at my father's funeral, and not to mention that I already have a girlfriend."

Grandmother gave me a stern look. "You're the baron now. The time for your selfish indulgences has come to an end. You have duties."

"I know," I snapped. "I know my duties, and I'll do what I must. Just give me today to grieve for my father."

Something about my tone must have gotten through to Grandmother, or perhaps she finally realized that I had emotions regarding my father's death. Whatever it was, she simply nodded and turned her attention to the next group of people approaching us.

Grateful for the reprieve, I couldn't stop the realization from bouncing around in my head, knowing what Grandmother meant. I'd have to send London back to New York while I stayed here.

AFTER THE FUNERAL and everything that followed, by the time London and I returned to my flat, all I wanted was to forget the entire day. When she asked what she could do to help, that's what I said. "Make me forget."

And then, suddenly, my thoughts were consumed by her. Her scent. The sight of her above me, riding me. The feel of her pussy squeezing my cock. The ecstasy that turned the world white.

"Did it work?" London asked as she rolled over to grab her phone.

"Yes, thank you," I replied, crossing my arms behind my head. "You're amazing, you know that?"

"I aim to please," she said in a playful tone. After a moment of silence, she added, "I was thinking maybe we should stay longer. I won't be able to perform on stage for at least another week."

I turned to face her as she put her phone down. "Are you sure? I don't want to be a burden to you," I said.

"I'm positive," she replied. "I'm not taking a vacation, after all. I want to be here for you."

I hugged her closer to me and whispered in her ear, "You have no idea how grateful I am to have you here. Your presence makes everything better."

We lay there quietly for a few moments, basking in the afterglow of our shared moment.

I let out a contented sigh, thinking that I didn't care what my grandmother demanded. London was not leaving, and I wanted her to stay with me for as long as possible.

"You know, Spencer," London said, turning to face me with a mischievous glint in her eye. "I think you might be developing a bit of a dependency on me. What will you do when I finally have to leave?"

"Oh, I'll just have to follow you to the ends of the earth," I replied with a cheeky grin. "I'll forever be your biggest fan, cheering you on from the front row at every performance."

London laughed and leaned in for a kiss. "Well, in that case, I better make sure I put on a good show," she said, a playful smile on her lips.

FORTY

LONDON

"Tomma Ackman is a breath of fresh air, a perfect fit for a unique new vision," read the review. "After just one week of performances, Tomma Ackman has stepped into the lead role previously held by London McCrae, proving that McCrae wasn't the sole reason for the show's success. Understudy Tomma Ackman shines in the lead role."

I had read the reviews until I had them memorized, and then I read the new ones. I read, I stewed, and I worried. But I didn't say a word about it to anyone. How could I burden Spencer with my concerns about work when he was going through so much already? All he needed to know was that the show was still shining without us there.

Yesterday, with nothing to do but wait, I used the time to reach out to my family and tell them I was considering staying longer. I half expected them to discourage me, but they encouraged me to follow my heart. Carson and Maggie seemed a little extra concerned about my well-being, which made me suspect they had read the reviews too, but I appreciated them not bringing it up. I could have talked to them about it if I wanted to, but I didn't want to sound petty and jealous.

I didn't want Tomma to fail in the role, of course, as that could ruin the entire production, but I also didn't want her to receive all the rave reviews I was seeing everywhere. If she was that good, would I even be able to come back? It was all so overwhelming.

Spencer informed me that he had to fulfill an obligation of his father's and wanted me to accompany him. I initially assumed it would be some legal matter related to the will or estate.

But I was wrong.

It was a Garden Party at Buckingham Palace.

Luckily, I'd brought a refined and elegant sheath dress in the perfect shade of cream to match my skin tone. One of Carson's designs. The dress had long lace sleeves and a hem that reached mid-calf, along with matching shoes and a handbag. I took some time to style my hair to match the fanciest hat I'd ever owned, and I was confident that not even Spencer's grandmother could have found fault with my appearance.

When I entered the main room of Spencer's flat, he was sitting on the couch, focused on his phone. For a moment, I thought he might be reading the reviews about Tomma, but I was relieved when he looked up and said, "Our car will be here in a minute." He stood up and offered me his arm, saying, "You look lovely." I thanked him and complimented his suit, and we left for the party.

Being on the "wrong" side of the road always threw me off, so it took me a moment to realize we had arrived. The driver opened the door, and Spencer got out first, then offered me his hand to help me from the car. I tried not to stare as we walked towards Buckingham Palace. I had seen castles in Scotland, but there was something unique about a palace where royalty still lived.

We arrived a little early, which seemed to be the norm rather than the "fashionably late" trend. This allowed us to follow the crowd as they made their way into the back gardens. Despite it being February, the gardens were still a breathtaking sight.

The space was massive, with a perfectly manicured lawn, a large pond in the distance, and garden beds waiting for spring to arrive. The trees were bare, but I always found beauty in the starkness of nature.

We followed the path to where several large canopies had been set up. As I continued, I noticed that there were heaters, raising the temperature to a comfortable level for outdoor events. They were designed so cleverly that they blended seamlessly into the surroundings.

"Baron Spencer York! Trenton Hemmingford from The Daily Telegraph. May I have a moment of your time?"

I expected Spencer to decline and move on, but he surprised me by saying, "Yes, of course."

"First, let me offer my heartfelt condolences on your loss," Trenton said.

Spencer stiffened, but he maintained his polite and false smile. "Thank you."

"As I'm sure you're aware, there have been rumors about this young lady and her relationship to you," Trenton said, flashing a set of white teeth. "We know her as London McCrae, the lead in your American production. May I ask why she's here with you?"

"London is my girlfriend," Spencer said calmly. "She's here to support me during this difficult time."

"And how are you finding London, London?" Trenton's eyes twinkled as if he had made a clever comment.

"It's lovely," I replied truthfully.

"How long will you be staying?" Trenton asked, looking back and forth between Spencer and me. "I'm sure you're eager to get back on stage."

"Nothing is set in stone at the moment," Spencer answered, and Trenton nodded.

After we finished answering more questions, Spencer said, "I'll be talking to a few reporters, but you don't have to say anything if you don't want to."

"Thank you," I said, squeezing his arm. "I'm fine."

He nodded, then turned his attention to an elderly couple who I recognized from the funeral.

"London, I'd like to introduce you to Lord and Lady Fitzpatrick," Spencer said, inclining his head to each. "Sir, Madam, this is London McCrae, my girlfriend."

"Lovely to meet you," Lady Fitzpatrick said warmly.

"Likewise," I replied.

The trio began chatting about something related to Lady Fitzpatrick being a baroness, but I couldn't keep up with the unfamiliar terms. They weren't intentionally excluding me from the conversation, but I hated feeling like a third wheel.

When we moved on, another reporter from The Independent approached us, and I was feeling silly standing at Spencer's side, smiling and looking pretty, unable to contribute to the conversation. But I reminded myself that I was here for Spencer, not for myself.

Growing up wealthy and having a Scottish father, I thought Spencer and I wouldn't have much separating us. I didn't know he would inherit a title, but even if I had, I didn't think it would have hit me until now. Few Americans can understand what it means to be part of the English nobility.

And Spencer fit in perfectly. I now realized that he was born for this to be a part of this world. And it was clear from the way he carried himself and spoke all day.

"I must say, I'm a bit surprised your grandmother didn't accompany you today," the Earl of Pembroke said. "She was a regular attendee at events with your father."

"Yesterday was quite exhausting for my grandmother and mother," Spencer replied, politely sidestepping the earl's inquiry.

Before the earl could pursue the matter further, our attention was drawn to a couple who approached us.

"Spencer," I whispered, "is that...?"

"Yes, it is," Spencer whispered back. "And if you look over there, you'll see His Majesty, the King of England."

As I watched the King speak to a couple of women, I was in disbelief. I knew it would amaze my friends when I told them about this. I committed everything to memory, knowing they would want a detailed account when I returned.

By the end of the day, I was mentally exhausted.

"What do you say we take a trip?" Spencer suggested suddenly. "Go to my family's country estate, just the two of us?"

I felt an immense relief at the possibility of us getting away from all the scrutiny. "That sounds perfect."

"Excellent. We'll leave first thing in the morning."

FORTY-ONE
SPENCER

Nestled on nearly 100 acres in Oxfordshire, the country estate had been in my family for generations and had undergone modernization over the years. With an 11-bedroom main house and two four-bedroom cottages, it could comfortably accommodate the entire family when necessary. But for now, London and I had it to ourselves, along with the staff, as the estate could not run without them, especially since it was left empty for long periods of time. I made a call after the garden party the day before to ensure everything was ready for our arrival.

"It's a beautiful day," London said as I turned onto the long drive. "Do you think we can take a walk around the grounds? You said it's a lot of property, right?" I reached over and took her hand, interlocking our fingers. "Yes, that sounds great. I'd love to show you everything. Some of my fondest memories from my childhood are here. My parents would bring my sisters and me here to escape the city."

As we approached the bend, I glanced at London, eager to see her reaction when she saw the house for the first time. She lit up with excitement. "Wow, just...wow," she said.

The staff was waiting for us and as soon as we pulled up in front of the house, a few people stepped forward and lined up at the steps. "Okay, that's a little weird," London said quietly. "Grandmother trained them well," I replied wryly. "Let's go make introductions."

I couldn't quite read the expression on London's face, but I suspected it was a mix of disbelief and amazement at the formality of my family's staff, something she might not have expected.

"Everyone, this is my girlfriend, London McCrae," I said, looking at each person in line as I introduced them. Carlyle Wilkes was our estate manager, a ginger man in his late forties, who was the third generation of his family to work here. Next to him was Thera Stanwood, the household manager, with her dark, silver-streaked hair pulled back and her steel-gray eyes as hard and unreadable as ever. Tava Groves was the head housekeeper and cook when needed, an attractive woman in her late forties who had been with the family for over a decade. Sophie Krupin, with her copper-colored waves, was another member of the housekeeping staff. The lean young man with golden blond hair was Webster Pond, the new lead groom, hired by my father. And last, Neville Redgrave, a red-haired man I knew from the nearby town when we were kids, was now the head groundskeeper.

"I'll do my best to remember everyone's names," London said with a smile. "It's nice to meet you all."

Thera raised an eyebrow just a fraction, but I didn't address it. Instead, I made a polite request. "Thera, if you could see that our belongings are taken to my room, London and I would like to take a walk around the grounds. Tava, please prepare afternoon tea and something for us to warm up later before you leave for the day."

"Yes, Sir," Tava said, nodding.

"Yes, m'lord," Thera said, bowing her head as well.

I smiled. "Thank you all." I took London's hand and led her down the path that would take us around the property. "Besides the three living spaces we have—"

London burst into laughter, cutting me off.

"What's so funny?" I asked, amused rather than annoyed.

"You just referred to that mansion as a 'living space,'" she said, gesturing behind us. "I mean, really?"

I chuckled. "What would you suggest I call it?"

She thought for a moment and then shook her head. "No, you're right. There's really no word that fits. Living spaces, it is then. Continue."

I paused, searching for my place again.

"The glass structure attached to the main living space is the pool," I said, glancing at her with a small smile. "It's heated, if you want to take a swim later."

"And that over there?" she asked, pointing to a glass building a few yards down the path.

"That's the greenhouse," I said. "My mother loves plants and flowers, so my father built that for her as a first anniversary gift. It contains all of her favorites."

"That's so sweet," London said, squeezing my hand in understanding. She knew that the mention of my father was still a sensitive topic for me.

"Down there are the stables," I continued. "A few of my cousins keep their competition horses here, but there are several that we can ride. I believe there are eight horses available for general use, if you're interested."

"I'm not much of a rider," London said, "but I'll have to let my sister Rose know. She loves animals. She has a ranch in Colorado."

I was about to suggest that Rose would be welcome to visit us at the estate any time, but I remembered the limitations of my family's expectations. If I were to accept my father's title and become the head of the York family, I would have to leave New York behind.

I had thought that I would make this choice, but the more I learned about the life my grandmother had planned for me, the more I realized I couldn't. Not because I was unable to handle the responsibilities, but because I couldn't bear to lose London. If there was a way to have both, I would take it, but as long as I had to choose between them, I would choose her.

That's why I had wanted her to attend the garden party with me yesterday and why I wanted to show her the estate today. Once I made it known that I wouldn't be staying in England and marrying someone appropriate, I wasn't sure if I would still have access to all of this.

"I say, I'm feeling a bit peckish," I blurted. "Shall we see if Tava has laid out tea?"

London chuckled and shook her head.

"What did I do now?"

"Did you know you sound more English the longer you're here?" she asked with a smile. "I mean, you had a bit of an accent in New York, but now you're talking about 'tea' and being 'peckish.'"

I raised an eyebrow. "Is that so?"

She stretched up and planted a kiss on my cheek. "I think it's charming."

"Charming." I sighed, feigning a dramatic tone. "Just what every chap wants to hear."

"How about handsome? Irresistible? Dashing? Riveting?"

"Riveting?" I chuckled. "I'm not sure that's an improvement over charming."

As we made our way back to the main house, I felt some of the weight of my grief lifting. My father might not have had the chance to get to know London, and I didn't know if he would have ever overcome my grandmother's objections, but I like to think he would have wanted me to be happy, and London made me happy.

HER BODY SHUDDERED UNDER ME, my name spilling from her lips as she came. The sound of it, the feel of her pussy tightening around my cock, and the look of sheer bliss on her face pushed me over the edge. White-hot pleasure washed over me, pulling me under until I couldn't even think.

A few minutes—or maybe hours—later, I found myself lying on my back, staring at the ceiling, listening to London's breathing slow down. The day had been good all around, ending with a bloody excellent finale. The estate was as beautiful as I remembered, and the staff was as competent as ever.

However, a nagging voice in my head whispered that something had been amiss with the staff. They had been stiff, even by British standards. I understood it would take time for everyone to get used to me being the Baron, but I had not considered the practical implications of my new position. The last time I was here, I was just another York child, no more special than any of my siblings. Now, I was in charge, the one responsible for signing their paychecks.

I looked over at London as she let out a sigh. "Is something wrong?" I asked.

"I was hoping I could distract you from overthinking," she said.

I put my arm around her and pulled her close, kissing her temple. "You did, love. My mind is just especially active."

"Try to get some sleep," she said, her fingers tracing patterns across my chest.

"I will," I replied, finding it difficult to turn off my brain. But as I focused on the feeling of London in my arms and the sound of her breathing, I gradually grew drowsy and finally fell into a peaceful sleep.

I didn't stir until morning, having slept deeply without a single dream. London was already up and getting dressed, her hair damp from her morning shower.

"Good morning," she greeted me with a smile. "How are you feeling?"

"Better," I said truthfully. "I haven't slept that well in a while."

"I told Tava we would like brunch instead of breakfast since it's almost noon," London said. "And I was thinking I'd like to check out the greenhouse today. Do you think your mother would be okay with that?"

"Of course," I said with a smile. "She'd love for you to enjoy anything you'd like."

I suggested she should go down to the back garden and enjoy the morning air while I got ready. A little over half an hour later, I made my way downstairs to join her. As I stepped outside, I saw her standing near the hollyhocks, but she wasn't alone. Neville was speaking to her, and his posture was stiff.

I hurried over to them, waiting until I was within earshot before speaking.

"There you are, love," I said, relief clear on London's face.

Between the relief on her face and the way Neville stiffened at my arrival, I could tell that I had interrupted something unpleasant. I reined in my temper and went straight to London, giving her a light kiss before addressing Neville.

"Is there a problem?" I asked, my tone firm.

Neville's blue eyes held a level of dislike that I hadn't seen from him before. "Not at all, Lord York," he said, his tone stiff.

"London?" I looked at her, seeing her hesitation. "If something happened, please tell me."

"It was just a misunderstanding," she said.

"Neville." I used the same tone I would use with cast members who were reluctant to tell me something.

"She asked for a key to the greenhouse," he said.

"And?" I raised an eyebrow, waiting for more information.

"Forgive me, but only York family members and certain staff members may have keys to any of the buildings," Neville said, his tone bordering on disrespectful.

"It's not a big deal," London said quietly. "You can give Spencer the keys, and we can go look at the greenhouse after we eat. Everything is fine."

"I don't need you defending me," Neville muttered, glaring at London.

"What was that?" I asked, my tone sharpening.

"Spencer," London grabbed my arm, trying to calm me down.

Neville stuck out his chin defiantly. "I said I don't need some slag speaking for me, allowing me to do my job."

My hand clenched into a fist, and I took a step forward, ready to teach Neville a lesson. But London's tight grip on my arm made me stop and reconsider my actions. Though it would feel good to shut Neville up with a punch, I needed to handle this situation in a more tactful manner.

"You're fired," I said, my voice cold and final.

Neville stared at me as if he couldn't believe what he was hearing. "What?"

"Let me be clear," I said, squaring off against him. "I'm not firing you for refusing to give London a key to the greenhouse. You're being fired for unprofessional behavior, specifically, calling my girlfriend a derogatory name."

"You can't fire me," Neville said. "Lady Opal–"

"Is not your employer," I interrupted. "I am. You have thirty minutes to vacate the premises. If you can't do that in a professional manner, I'll have you escorted off my property, and Carlyle will pack up your things."

For a moment, I thought Neville might take a swing at me, but then he swore and stormed off.

"I'm so sorry about that, love." I turned to London and wrapped my arms around her.

"I didn't mean to cause any problems," she said.

"It's not your fault," I said, shaking my head. "I noticed yesterday that everyone was a bit stiff. Has anyone else said anything?"

"No," she said, but something in her tone made me pull back and look at her.

"London, please be truthful," I said.

She shrugged. "No one's been as rude as Neville, but I feel they don't approve of me."

I sighed. "I'm sorry. I wanted us to have a pleasant time here together. But we can go back to the city first thing. We'll have a few days to just enjoy each other's company."

"Maybe we can do something else," London said, a smile lighting up her face. "What do you think about visiting my family's estate in Scotland? Maybe we could meet some of my extended family?"

I smiled at London's suggestion, feeling grateful for her ability to turn a difficult situation into something positive. "I think that's a great idea," I said, holding her hand. "We can leave tomorrow and spend a few days up there. Maybe it will be just what we need."

London smiled back at me, and for a moment, all the stress and tension of the past few days melted away.

FORTY-TWO
LONDON

"I'LL SAY IT AGAIN BECAUSE IT DESERVES REPEATING: it's a castle."

Spencer's statement made me laugh, just as much today as it did yesterday evening when we first arrived. One benefit of being able to charter a private plane at a moment's notice was that instead of spending nearly an entire day driving from London to Fife, we'd flown most of the way.

"Aye, it is," I teased, mimicking my father's accent.

"I thought you said your father's family was from Edinburgh," Spencer said, turning to me. "I meant to ask that yesterday when we left the city, but I was a little taken aback by the, um...well, castle."

"They are," I said, taking his hand. "My great-grandfather wanted a place in Edinburgh as well. The house he purchased there is where my father and his siblings grew up. When their father passed, each of them inherited a portion of this estate and the one in Edinburgh. My father's sister, Janet, wanted to raise her family in Edinburgh, so she bought out her siblings' shares. Eidheann Castle still belongs to all of them, though. We get along well enough that it's never been a problem sharing."

"Eidheann Castle," Spencer repeated the name, enunciating it carefully.

"Ivy," I said, pointing at the ivy covering nearly a third of the stone. "Eidheann is Gaelic for ivy."

"And what about where we're staying?" Spencer gestured to the house behind us.

"Cluaran Cottage," I said. "Thistle."

"And that one?" Spencer pointed to the other guest house.

"Craobh Cottage," I explained. "Tree."

"Tree House?" Spencer asked.

I shrugged. "My great-grandfather had a fondness for plants."

"Is that where the staff live?"

"The estate manager lives in the gatehouse," I said, gesturing to the large iron gates at the entrance of the drive. "The head housekeeper has an apartment above the garage, and any other staff who live on site are in the Summer House," I indicated the tall building further back on the property. "I know little about who lives there now. It's been a couple of years since I've been here."

"This is...impressive," Spencer said, shaking his head. "You said your family had money, and I've heard of MIRI, so I thought I had an understanding. I never imagined this."

"This isn't mine," I said, clarifying my earlier statement. "Technically, we kids will inherit my father's share of the estate someday, but we don't claim ownership. The McCrae family, whether by blood, marriage, or adoption, owns it together, and it's always been that way."

"And everyone is okay with that?" Spencer asked, sounding impressed.

"As far as I know," I replied, pausing to think. "We see this estate as our family history and roots, and we wouldn't want any disputes to prevent future generations from enjoying it. That's more important to us than individual ownership."

"I'm thinking the castle is not the most remarkable thing about the McCraes," Spencer commented. "I can't imagine my siblings, let alone cousins, being so cooperative."

"Maybe that's the difference between us Scots and you Sassenachs," I teased, using the Scottish term for non-Scots.

Spencer chuckled. "Did you seriously just call me that?"

"I thought it would make you laugh," I said, kissing his cheek. "Come on, I want to give you a tour of the house. It's big for just the two of us, but I still want to show you around."

The way Spencer's family and staff treated me had been bothering me more than I'd let on, but it also made me excited to show off the house.

"This is my favorite room," I said, leading him into the library. "When my great-grandfather bought Eidheann, this was one of the reception rooms, but my great-grandmother loved to read, so they converted it into a library. The original library was much smaller and next to the study on the first floor."

Spencer let out a low whistle as he entered the room. I followed, feeling proud as I looked around. The library had high ceilings, with a beautiful chandelier in the center casting light on the floor-to-ceiling bookshelves lining every wall. Each wall had a rolling ladder, allowing even the top shelves to be accessed.

"This isn't mine," I said to Spencer. "Technically, we'll inherit my dad's portion one day, but it's always been understood that it belongs to the McCrae family, whether that's blood, married in, or adopted. No petty squabbles to keep anyone from sharing it with future generations."

I ended the tour in the tower bedroom, where I'd always loved to sleep as a kid.

As we came down the stairs, my cousins Carr and Konnor arrived. I hugged Carr, who'd gotten a haircut, and greeted Konnor. I introduced Spencer to them and the O'Malley twins, who were also a year older than me.

As I chatted with my cousins, I observed Spencer's interactions with them. I had felt that he was trying to show me that his life in England was more important than our relationship, but now I wasn't so sure. He had fired someone for being disrespectful to me and offered to take me away from his cold staff. He seemed eager to get to know my cousins and seemed to want them to like him, which felt more like someone who wanted to build a relationship, not end it.

Spencer impressed my cousins. They asked him questions, and he answered them with ease. They all had things to do, so before sunset, we said our goodbyes and promised to see each other soon.

Back in the kitchen, Spencer hugged me from behind and whispered, "That was fun."

I agreed. "I'm glad you enjoyed yourself."

Spencer placed a kiss on my neck and asked, "Do you know what else I'd enjoy?"

"I have a good idea," I said, turning to face him.

"What are the chances of someone walking in on us?" he asked, his hand sliding under my shirt.

"Slim to none," I replied, grateful that I had told Mrs. Chisolm that I'd clean up.

The hand not currently making its way up my torso

pushed its way past the waistband of my jeans. Even as a finger ghosted over my clit, he cupped my breast, squeezing lightly before beginning to tease my hardening nipple through my bra. Closing my eyes, I gave myself over to sensation and pushed all thoughts of propriety away.

"After I make you come on my fingers," his voice was low in my ear, "I'm going to put you up here on display and eat you out until you scream."

"Fuck." A shudder went through me.

"Then I want you on your knees, right here, sucking me off." His fingers pressed harder against my clit. "Every time you're in this kitchen, I want you to remember how I tasted."

My fingers gripped the edge of the counter until my knuckles turned white.

"After that, we're going to make some memories in our cottage, too." He scraped his teeth along the back of my neck. "I have such plans for you."

His words, as much as he was doing with his hands, sent me flying over the edge. His arms tightened around me, keeping me upright when my knees gave out. The feel of his body pressed against my back, the hard length of him impossible to ignore, grounded me, bringing me back to myself.

He nipped my earlobe and then whispered, "Ready for another go round?"

I'D TOLD him I was ready, but in the hours that passed from when he asked the question, I'd learned that when it came to sex with Spencer, *ready* was a relative term. Despite all the amazing sex we'd had together, I hadn't been prepared for tonight. Maybe I was right. This was one last hurrah before he sent me on my way, or maybe he had so much pressure built up inside him that he'd finally needed to release it. No matter the reason, I'd lost count of the times I'd come, and my legs still felt like jello as I made my way to the bathroom.

Spencer had fallen asleep as soon as we finished, and I lay there for a while, half-awake, before mustering the energy to get up. The call of nature was the only reason I got out of bed. Once I was done, I started searching the bathroom cabinet for toilet paper and suddenly stopped.

The box in front of me didn't contain toilet paper, but tampons. My mother always made sure the staff kept all the bathrooms stocked in case someone had an emergency and didn't want to drive to the nearest store in the middle of the night. I didn't need them, but my mind did the math, anyway. I should have finished my period around the time we left New York, but I hadn't even started. With everything going on, I'd lost track of time, but now the realization hit me hard.

I was late. Really late, and I never deviated more than a day from my cycle, especially since I started taking the pill.

Shit.

I tried to calm myself down. It must be stress, right? I was on the pill and we always used a condom.

But then I remembered the night during previews when we'd made up after a fight. I'd told Spencer we were safe because I was on the pill. And yesterday morning, I thought the count of my pills was a little off, as if I'd missed taking them once or twice.

Double shit.

I wasn't feeling sick, but my mother had told us that she

didn't feel sick at all with her pregnancies, so lack of morning sickness didn't give me any answers.

It could just be stress. I decided to wait. We planned to return to London tomorrow evening, so I would slip out to the store as soon as Spencer was occupied and get a pregnancy test. I didn't know anything for certain, and I didn't want to panic when there were other explanations.

Panic? No.

Quietly freak out for a couple of minutes alone in the bathroom? Definitely.

FORTY-THREE
LONDON

Spencer's busy schedule once we returned to London made it easy for me to get my hands on a pregnancy test. But talking myself into actually using it was a different story.

Part of me clung to the idea that if I didn't take the test, I could pretend being pregnant wasn't a possibility. But after an hour of internal debate, I took the test.

The results confirmed what I already knew deep down: I was pregnant.

I expected to panic. To call my mom or a sibling. To call my friends and ask for advice. But I just stared at the tests.

A knock on the door made me jump.

"Miss McCrae?" an unfamiliar female voice called out. "It's Mrs. Redwine, the housekeeper."

I realized I had forgotten about her scheduled visit on Wednesdays and Saturdays. "Just a minute," I responded.

I quickly disposed of the pregnancy tests in the trash, washed my face, and opened the door with a smile for the dark-haired Mrs. Redwine.

"Good morning," I greeted her. "I didn't hear you come in."

"Do you need me to come back later?" she asked.

I shook my head. "No, I'm actually going to take a walk."

"Very good, mam," Mrs. Redwine replied.

I grabbed my coat and purse and headed to the elevator. Fresh air might help me clear my thoughts. Although I felt calm, I knew it wouldn't last long, and I needed to figure out how to tell Spencer about the latest development.

As I walked the streets of the city, I wasn't paying attention to my surroundings. The weather had turned cold again, a last-ditch effort of winter to keep spring from coming, and I pulled my coat more tightly around me. I could've ducked into one of the many shops I passed, but I didn't want to talk to anyone, even someone just wanting to ask if I needed any help.

By the time I returned to the flat, I had a plan in mind. I intended to talk to Spencer about my return to New York and inform him of my pregnancy in the same conversation. To make it a special evening, I decided to prepare a nice dinner for when Spencer got home.

As I was making my way into the room, I realized that there was a guest sitting on the couch.

"Oh! Hi." I said.

Opal raised an eyebrow but didn't say anything.

"Um, Spencer isn't here right now," I said.

"I know that," Opal said, standing up and eyeing me disapprovingly. "In fact, I know many things."

My mind immediately raced to the pregnancy, but I told myself it wasn't possible for Opal to know. I had only just found out myself and no one could have guessed. And the pregnancy tests were in the trash.

But then Opal said, "I know, for instance, that there are two positive pregnancy tests in the bag of garbage that Mrs. Redwine took out."

It shocked me to see Opal smirk at me.

"Oh, yes, Mrs. Redwine looks out for my interests regarding my grandson," Opal continued. "I asked her to keep an extra close eye on you, and it seems my caution has paid off."

I realized that this would not be a pleasant conversation.

"I know your kind," Opal said, her tone scathing. "As soon as you feel a man like Spencer slipping through your fingers, your first thought is to trap him with a baby."

I was taken aback by her accusations. I had never considered what Spencer's family would think of my pregnancy, but I certainly didn't expect any of them to accuse me of trying to force Spencer into anything.

Anger quickly overtook my surprise, but I kept my temper in check. I reminded myself that Opal had just lost a son and that no one was at their best during mourning.

"This pregnancy was not intentional," I said calmly. "And I am not giving Spencer any ultimatums or asking him for anything, but I will not hide it from him either."

"How much?" she asked.

I hoped she wasn't saying what I thought she was saying. "I'm sorry. What do you mean?"

"How much to make this go away?" Opal's eyes narrowed. "From the moment I learned of you, I knew it would come to this, eventually. We've just arrived at this point sooner than I expected."

"You knew you would try to bribe me." I made it a statement, not a question.

"I knew there was a possibility that he would want to keep you as his mistress after he married a proper bride, and that you might need some...incentive to return to your home." Her eyes flickered to my stomach. "If he allows you to keep the child, make no mistake, he will not acknowledge it as his heir."

For the first time since finding out I was pregnant, I felt sick. "He doesn't have to allow me to do anything. It's my choice."

"He can't force you," she agreed. "But there are ways to convince someone to do what's right."

"Excuse me if I don't take advice on 'what's right' from someone who's trying to pay off their grandson's pregnant girlfriend," I said through gritted teeth, my hold on my temper slipping with each word that came out of her mouth.

"Let's speak plainly," she said.

I had trouble thinking of something that could be plainer than what she'd already said.

"My grandson has known from childhood that he would one day take his father's place as baron. He knows his duties, and anything that has caught his fancy in the past has only been a mere distraction," said Opal, her eyes as cold as her voice. "That includes you, Miss McCrae."

Her words stung, but I could still picture the relief on Spencer's face when I said I'd stay longer. I could still feel the way he clung to my hand and the effort he made to get to know my cousins. Those were all proof that he didn't see me the same way his grandmother did, weren't they?

"Spencer is kind," Opal continued. "Perhaps too kind. We all know you will never fit into his life, not now. His place is here, with his family. His future is with a woman of impeccable breeding and character, not with some American actress who uses her feminine wiles to acquire her parts."

I was still trying to process the insult about my "impeccable breeding and character" when I registered the implications of the phrase "feminine wiles." "What is that supposed to mean?" I asked.

"Sex," Opal said bluntly. "I'm speaking of your reputation as someone who will do whatever it takes to get what you want. I have no doubt your past success inspired you to seduce my grandson."

"What are you talking about?" I asked, feeling a sinking feeling in my stomach.

"I hired a private investigator in New York City," she said, her eyes shining with triumph. "He met with a few people who had interesting things to say about you, specifically Jerry Niyaz and Russ Heyworth."

"And what, exactly, did they have to say about me?" I asked.

"Enough for me to demand a paternity test if you choose to continue the pregnancy and name Spencer as the father," she said.

I opened my mouth to defend myself, but Opal continued speaking.

"Know this. If you persist in this, the York name will not be the only one dragged through the mud. I will instruct my investigator to delve deeper into you and your family. I know you took Spencer to a sex club, and I'm sure that's just the tip of the iceberg."

Panic washed over me as I realized the damage Opal could inflict upon Spencer and me if she dug deeper into Show & Tell.

But Opal wasn't finished yet. "I won't stop with just you. I'll target the entire McCrae clan. Your fashion designer brother and his girlfriend, who's a member of a cult. Your musician sister, who's recently stirred up a scandal. I'll uncover every hidden thing, every hint of impropriety, and I'll make sure it makes front-page news."

All the fight left me. I couldn't keep pretending that everything was going to work out, even if Spencer wanted it to. If I had been the only one at risk, I might have used my considerable resources to push back. I knew that Maggie and Carson would have told me they could protect themselves, but they had already been through so much. And I doubted Opal would stop at just my siblings in New York. There were kids to consider, not just adults.

My own child.

I couldn't risk the amount of stress that fighting Opal would bring. My baby had to come first, before everyone else, including Spencer. If I tried to force myself into a place where I didn't belong, I would end up hurting everyone I cared about.

"I'll pack my things." I walked away without looking back at Opal's expression. She had gotten what she wanted. I couldn't bear to see her gloating about it. I just needed to be gone.

FORTY-FOUR
SPENCER

Thoughts of London and a good bottle of wine were the only things that kept me going through a long day. It was later than I expected when I finally headed home. I sent texts to London throughout the day, letting her know I would be delayed, but received no response. I wondered if she was mad, but considering her previous support, it was more likely that she had simply misplaced her phone or forgotten to charge it. I decided to buy her some flowers as a token of apology and thanks for everything she had done.

When I entered my flat, the silence struck me. London always had some background noise, whether it was music or the TV, but I heard nothing as I closed the door behind me. The only light came from a lamp, making me wonder if she had gone to bed early.

Suddenly, I noticed someone sitting on the couch. "I was beginning to wonder if you would come back tonight," she said.

"Grandmother? Where is London?" I asked, a feeling of unease settling in my stomach.

"I've made arrangements with two moving companies

that have openings this weekend," she said, standing up. "If you want to keep this flat for personal reasons, just mark the items you want to take with you, and they will leave the rest."

"I'm moving?" I asked, trying to get an answer about London, but knowing that if I pushed, my grandmother would simply dig in her heels and refuse to give me any information.

"A baron does not live in a flat when he has a perfectly suitable home," she said, using the same exasperated tone she used when I was a child and wanted to play with my friends instead of going over accounts with my father.

"That suitable home already has residents," I replied, trying to control my impatience.

"Neither of those residents is currently a baroness," she countered.

It was on the tip of my tongue to remind her that she was no longer a baroness and hadn't been for quite some time, but I needed her information.

"I have no intention of living with my mother and sister or evicting them from their home," I said firmly.

Grandmother's eyes narrowed. "You swore to fulfill your duties."

"And I will," I replied, "but on my own terms."

Ignoring my words, she continued, "There will be an event next Saturday evening to officially mark the transfer of the title. My top five choices for a bride will be in attendance."

I had had enough. "Where is London?"

A scowl appeared on Grandmother's face, but she quickly regained her composure. "That woman will no longer interfere in family affairs."

"Excuse me?"

"I've taken care of it," she said dismissively. "You don't need to worry about it."

"Bloody hell, I don't!"

Her eyes widened. "Watch your language, young man. You will not speak to me in that manner."

"Where. Is. London?"

Grandmother let out a long-suffering sigh and sat back down on the couch. "I suppose you won't let this go until you know everything, will you?"

"Just answer the damn question."

For the first time in my life, I saw Grandmother taken aback, whether by my language or my persistence. I wasn't sure. Either way, she now realized that things were coming to a head between us..

"This morning, I received a phone call from Mrs. Redwine," she began.

"My housekeeper? Why is my housekeeper talking to you?"

Grandmother raised an eyebrow. "Did you forget I recommended her?"

My grandmother had planted a spy in my house. "We'll come back to that, but for now, tell me where London is."

"Miss McCrae intended to deceive you," Grandmother said firmly. "She planned to tell you she was pregnant and trap you into marriage."

I couldn't believe what I was hearing. "What? That's crazy."

"She knew you would feel obligated to marry her in order to legitimize your child. Then all she had to do was wait until she had a ring on her finger, and then tell you she had miscarried. You are too honorable to divorce her after such a loss."

I shook my head. "No. London wouldn't do that."

"Women like her will do anything to get what they want," Grandmother said. "That's why I knew I had to intervene when Mrs. Redwine called me."

I frowned. I'd forgotten about the phone call. "So, my girlfriend suddenly confided in a complete stranger, revealing her entire plan, and then my housekeeper called you to tell you?"

Grandmother gave me an annoyed look. "Sarcasm doesn't become you."

"It really doesn't," I countered. "Your story makes little sense. Try again."

"Mrs. Redwine called me because she found two positive pregnancy tests in the bathroom trash bin."

"Pregnancy tests?"

Grandmother's eyes flickered. "I assume they were part of London's plan. She probably had some pregnant person take the tests and intended to show them to you as proof."

That was illogical. "Some pregnant person? The only people she knows here are family members."

Grandmother stood and brushed off her clothes. "I suppose she found some random stranger then. Some people will do anything for money."

She was lying.

I was sure of it.

My grandmother was lying.

"I need you to tell me the truth," I demanded. "No more lies."

Grandmother tried to hold my gaze, but I was relentless.

"Even if she's pregnant, the baby might not be yours," she said, confirming my worst fears.

"Where is she?" I asked, barely able to keep my voice steady. "You said you 'took care of things.' What did you do?"

Grandmother lifted her chin. "I merely told her the truth. She has no place in your life now. She packed a few things and left without telling me where she was going."

I felt a coldness spread through me as I went to my bedroom. All of London's things were gone. Her clothes, her luggage, even her purse. A quick check of the bathroom showed that all of her personal items were missing, too.

I dug out my phone, grateful that I had Konner's number, London's cousin. Her brother, Xander, was still in Brazil with his football team, so she wouldn't have gone to him. If she hadn't already left for New York, she would have reached out to her cousins. That was where I had to start. And if I had to, I would go anywhere to find her.

My grandmother was about to learn that she had exhausted all my patience and goodwill. I was done with the games and the politics. London and our child were all that mattered to me now.

FORTY-FIVE
LONDON

Exhausted and emotionally drained, I should have been able to sleep on the long flight back to the States, but my mind was too active to allow it. Instead, I was plagued by a stream of disconnected thoughts, like I should eat something, but I had no appetite, and I should have worn more comfortable shoes.

Despite being lucky enough to secure a flight straight away, I couldn't even summon the energy to feel grateful. Instead, I simply sat in my seat and stared blankly at the in-flight movies. It wasn't until the announcement came we were approaching our destination that I finally started thinking about what would happen next.

During a layover in Boston, I sent a text to my parents, telling them I was coming to San Ramon and asking them to pick me up. I didn't give them any details, and because I told them I would be back in the air soon, they didn't ask. Now that the plane was about to land, I had to decide what I would tell them, starting with why I was in California instead of New York.

As soon as I stepped out of the airport, I saw my

parents' car, and before I could take a few steps, my father was there, trying to conceal his concern.

"Hi there, honey."

"Hi, Da." I swallowed hard, fighting the urge to cry.

He hugged me, and I pressed my face against his chest, taking comfort in his familiar scent. I couldn't linger long, but I allowed myself a few precious moments before stepping back.

"Let me take your bags, and you go say hello to your mom."

I nodded and got into the back seat of the car, leaning forward to kiss my mother's cheek.

"Hello, sweetheart." She turned to look at me. "It's good to see you."

I could see the questions in her eyes, but she didn't ask them. This was yet another reason I loved my parents; they always gave me the space and time I needed to work things out.

I waited until we were out of the airport traffic before asking, "Da, have you heard of a Raynard York in England? A baron?"

Da thought for a minute before answering, "No, I don't think so." He glanced in the rearview mirror. "Isn't York your boyfriend's last name?"

My stomach tightened at his words. "Raynard was Spencer's father."

"Your boyfriend is a baron?" Mom asked, her voice sharp.

"It was a surprise to me too," I said. "I didn't find out until the funeral service. Spencer inherited the title."

"He lied to you?" Mom's voice was stern.

"He didn't lie about it, but he didn't mention it either." I shook my head. "He warned me that his family was particular, but even if he had been more specific, I never would have guessed."

I sighed, knowing there was no easy way to say what I needed to say. I rubbed my forehead as my parents waited for me to find the words.

"Spencer has responsibilities in England, duties to his family. He has a place there, not here," I said, bracing myself for the revelation that would make this more than just a breakup. "And I'm pregnant."

For several seconds, neither of my parents reacted. Then Mom partially turned towards me, her eyes filled with various emotions. "Are you okay?"

I nodded, unable to speak just yet.

"What did he say?" Da asked, anger clear in his voice. "What did Spencer York say when you told him?"

"I haven't," I said.

Mom's eyebrows shot up. "You didn't tell him?"

My guilt made me defensive, even though I didn't hear a hint of judgment in her tone. "I just found out this morning."

"Sweetie, I know you," Mom said. "You don't run away just because something's unpleasant or hard. What made you come here before even talking to him? Did he hurt you?"

"No," I blurted. "Never."

"Then what happened?"

"It was his grandmother," I said with a sigh. "Opal York Masters or something like that."

"Opal Masters?" Da glanced back at me. "That's a name I know."

"Really?" I was surprised.

"I never met the woman personally," Da continued, "but she's had a few interactions with your Aunt May. From what I remember, unpleasant would be a kind word for Opal Masters."

"She's a bitch," I blurted out before I could stop myself. "Sorry, Mom, but it's the truth."

"What did she say to you?" Mom's voice was sharp.

"Just what I already knew," I said. "That I don't belong there."

"That wasn't all, was it?" Mom asked.

I told them everything. The words came pouring out: the hurtful things Opal said, the threats she made, and my insecurities about whether Spencer would want the baby.

"I don't know what I'm going to do," I admitted. "But I can't figure things out when I have to worry about Spencer's grandmother stabbing me in the back."

"If we turn around, I'm sure I can get a flight to England," Mom said. "I'll go have a talk with this Opal."

"And end up getting arrested for assault?" Da said. "I think not."

I laughed, relieved to see the lightheartedness in my parents' expressions.

"I'm not planning on staying long," I said. "But I need to clear my head and figure out a plan."

"Whatever you need, lass," Da said. "We're here for you."

And that's why I came home. No matter how crazy my world became, I knew my family would always be there for me. The Yorks might not have been able to depend on each other, but the McCraes could, regardless of their last name.

FORTY-SIX
SPENCER

I TRIED TO SLEEP DURING THE FLIGHT, BUT MY MIND wouldn't allow it. The adrenaline that had driven me to leave England had worn off, leaving me emotionally and physically exhausted. I spent the entire flight running through different scenarios in my head, imagining the conversations I would have with London. Apologizing for my grandmother's behavior, trying to express my feelings about her pregnancy and her decision to leave without telling me.

Although finding out she was pregnant was a shock to me, the thought of having a baby with her filled me with excitement. I wanted to have that life, to tell her that our child and she were more important to me than anything else, including my title and my grandmother's opinions.

But the fact that she left without even a text or a word to me cut me deep. I wanted to place the blame on her, be angry that she didn't trust me enough to come to me, but I knew it wasn't her fault. I hadn't prepared her for what my family was like or what their expectations of me were. And

I hadn't told her that I was figuring out how to give it all up for her.

Thanks to the time difference, I arrived in New York at almost the same time I'd departed from England. I snatched my bag and headed straight to a waiting taxi. I told the driver to take me to London's place, as I tried to hold back my curiosity and refrained from asking him if he had recently picked up a strawberry blonde. As we navigated through the busy morning traffic, I leaned back in my seat, taking a deep breath and preparing myself for what was to come.

I twisted my cap in my hands, trying to calm my nerves when I spotted London's street. I already had my wallet out, eager to pay the driver as soon as we came to a stop. I quickly exited the taxi without a second thought, not even bothering to ask the driver to wait for me.

The doorman at the building remembered me and allowed me into the lobby, but that was where my luck ran out, as he informed me that he hadn't seen London. While it was possible that she had come in without him noticing, I didn't think that was likely. Nevertheless, I went up to her apartment and knocked on the door, but there was no answer.

Frustrated, I retraced my steps back to the lobby, regretting my hasty decision to dismiss the taxi.

I was at a loss as to my next move.

The enormity of New York City made finding London seem like a formidable challenge. Although London had friends in the city, I didn't believe she would seek them out, particularly not Mercedes. The possibility of her staying in a hotel crossed my mind, but I deemed it unlikely.

Thus, my only recourse was to try and locate one of her

siblings. I resolved to start with Maggie, as I sought to avoid any confrontations with Carson if I could avoid it.

With no cabs in sight, I did what I should have done upon my arrival and ordered a private car service for the day. Within ten minutes, a black town car pulled up to the curb in front of me. Upon entering the back seat, I swiftly retrieved Maggie and Drake's address. The traffic was manageable, and when I arrived at my destination, the solemn expression on Drake's face when he opened the door showed he was fully aware of my purpose for being there.

Maggie fixed me with a stern gaze as I stepped into the apartment, so I threw my hands up in surrender. "I just need to speak with her," I explained.

"Why?" Maggie asked, arms crossed.

I didn't want to just blurt out news about the baby to her family, so I asked, "What did she tell you?"

Maggie raised an eyebrow. "I know enough that I need a compelling reason to give you her location."

"I don't know what you've heard, but my grandmother doesn't speak for me," I said. "Please, I need to talk to London face-to-face."

Maggie let out a sigh. "Listen, I hope you showing up here means you're really into London, but if you're not ready to fully commit, it's best you head back to England."

"I'm not leaving her unless she asks me to," I replied.

Maggie's expression relaxed a bit. "Good."

The tension in my chest dissipated as I realized she was going to help me.

"London's back home in California," Maggie informed me. "She went straight to our parents. She only called me because I'm watching over her place while she's away."

I hadn't even considered that option. The thought that I

had hurt her so much that she had fled to the opposite coast was devastating.

"I'll give Mom a heads up that you're coming," Maggie offered. "Cause trust me, you won't get past her and Dad otherwise."

"Thanks," I said, grateful for her help.

Maggie gave a nod as she rummaged through a drawer for a pen and paper. She focused on her writing as she spoke to me again. "Just so you know, if you hurt my little sister, I'll make sure you regret it. Are we clear?"

"Crystal clear," I responded, taking the paper from her. "I promise, Maggie, I'll do everything in my power to make things right."

"I hope it'll be enough," she said, looking up at me.

I met her gaze. "Me too."

FORTY-SEVEN

LONDON

Comfy purple hedgehog pajamas? Check.

Gran's homemade quilt? Check.

A quart of mint chocolate chip ice cream? Check.

A bun in the oven? I placed my hand on my still-flat belly. Yes, check.

My phone buzzed and my heart raced with nerves as I picked it up. I was relieved to see that it wasn't Spencer, but I still felt a pang of disappointment. I had to remind myself that I was the one who had left without a word, so I had no right to be upset that he wasn't trying to reach out.

The message was from Mercedes.

"Hey, just checking in to see if you've figured out when you're coming back. Tomma is driving me up the wall, claiming she should've been the lead from the get-go. She keeps saying that you only got the role because you were sleeping with the producer, but I told her good luck going on stage with a black eye."

I couldn't help but chuckle. I had been pondering work, but in a hazy sort of manner. I needed to process the fact that I was pregnant and deal with the situation with Spencer before I could decide about the show.

I had set myself a schedule: wallow today, sort out the baby and dad stuff tomorrow, have a plan for work by Saturday night.

I didn't share all of this with Mercedes, however.

"A few things have come up, but I'm aiming to be back in New York by the weekend. As for the show, I'm not sure what's going to happen. And before you ask, no, Spencer's not being a jerk. Thanks for having my back, but please don't do anything illegal. I don't think Gin and Rocio could scrape together enough cash for bail."

I hit send and turned my attention back to the TV. A few minutes later, my phone rang again.

It was still Mercedes. "Why does it feel like you're keeping something from me?"

I rubbed my forehead as I pondered my potential responses. I didn't want to lie to her, but I couldn't spill the beans, not when I hadn't even talked to Spencer yet.

"Because I am, but I can't go into detail right now. I promise to fill you in as soon as I can."

Her reply was quick. "Are you okay?"

If she had asked if I was good, I might have struggled to be truthful. But her choice of words allowed me to respond with complete honesty.

"I am," I answered. "Promise."

Mercedes sent another message, "If you need me, I'm here." I smiled as I replied, "I know. Thanks a lot. Have a good night."

"You too," she responded.

I set down my phone and picked up a spoonful of ice cream and chocolate syrup.

"Hey, sweetie," Mom entered the den. "How are you doing?"

I swallowed and managed a decent smile. "I'm okay, Mom."

"Good enough to take a break from watching Fear Thy Neighbor?" she asked.

"I'm done with that," I said. "I'm watching Buried in the Backyard now."

"London," Mom said, with a sigh.

"I probably should put the ice cream back before it melts," I said.

"Think you might progress to regular clothes sometime soon?" Mom asked as she led the way out of the den.

"Not as long as I have..." I trailed off when I saw Spencer, disheveled and standing in the middle of the living room. "Spencer."

"Hi," he said, giving me a soft, tired smile. He glanced at Mom and said, "Thank you, Mrs. McCrae, for letting me speak with London."

"If she says you go, then you go," Mom said, pointing at him. "Understand?"

"Yes, ma'am," Spencer replied sincerely.

"Your dad and I will be in the kitchen if you need us," Mom said to me.

I nodded, waiting until she left before gesturing towards the lounge. "Have a seat."

"You're not immediately throwing me out, so I'm hoping that's a good sign," he said, sitting on the couch. He twisted his ever-present cap in his hands, betraying his nervousness.

"I'm not mad at you," I said, settling at the other end of the couch. I couldn't take my eyes off of him, still in disbelief that he was actually here.

He looked exhausted, with dark circles under his eyes and pale skin. The thought that he might have slept as little as I had over the past few days made my heart ache for causing him so much stress.

"That's good to hear," he said, reaching for my hand. He moved cautiously, giving me the opportunity to pull away if I wasn't comfortable with him touching me. I allowed him to take my hand and felt my heart give a hesitant thump in my chest.

"Your grandmother filled you in on everything about my...?"

"She did," he said, clasping my hand tightly.

For a moment, I was overwhelmed with panic, but then a small smile appeared on his lips.

"You're pregnant."

I took a deep breath, preparing myself for him to be upset with me for causing this situation. "I was on the pill, but with all the stress, I missed a dose or two."

"It's all right," he said, his eyes showing that he meant it. The knot of tension in my shoulders relaxed a bit.

"Really?"

He nodded. "I'm shocked, especially about how I found out, but I'm not mad."

Guilt consumed me. "I'm so sorry you had to find out like that. I should have called and told you, but I was just..."

"We both have a lot on our minds," he interrupted. "But that's not what's important now."

"I know," I said, avoiding his gaze. "Your grandmother made sure I was aware of what's important."

He placed his hand on my cheek, gently guiding my face to meet his. "You matter. Our baby matters."

I raised an eyebrow. "What will your grandmother say about that?"

"I don't care," he said, his gaze intense. "I choose you."

Those three words caught me off guard, leaving me speechless. "What?"

He leaned in and brushed his lips across mine. "I. Choose. You."

His lips were soft and gentle as they met mine, and I felt the world fade away. But as much as I wanted to stay in this moment forever, I pulled away from him, taking a deep breath to steady my nerves.

"What about your grandmother's expectations and responsibilities to your family and title?" I asked.

Spencer shook his head. "My grandmother's views are outdated. She still thinks that the most important thing for my sisters to do for our family is to marry and have children."

"She wasn't too thrilled about the idea of you having kids," I added. "Her key problem seems to be with me."

His expression became serious. "I get the feeling she didn't tell me the complete story."

"She probably didn't mention that she told me the best I could hope for from you was an apartment and to be treated as your mistress. You'd only acknowledge our child in private, and if I made any demands, she would ruin my reputation and go after my family."

"Fucking hell," he swore, raking his fingers through his hair. "Just when I thought the grandmother couldn't surprise me anymore, she goes and does something like this."

"I don't agree with her approach," I said, "but I think she just wants what's best for your family."

"She wants what *she* thinks is best for the family," Spencer replied, anger clear in his voice. "She's always trying to control all of us and make sure we uphold the York name and title." He practically spat the last word.

"Could you lose your title if you don't marry someone of the same rank?" I asked, trying to hide my nervousness.

"I'm not sure," Spencer replied. "But even if I did, it wouldn't matter. I won't let my grandmother dictate who I choose to be with. I'll give up the title if I have to."

"I don't want to cause any trouble between you and your family," I said.

"You're my family now," Spencer said, his gaze intense. "I love you and have known it for a while. I should've told you sooner. Even if you weren't pregnant, I would choose you." He squeezed my hand reassuringly.

I could only think of one response to his words. "Come with me," I said, offering him my hand. "Let me show you my room."

FORTY-EIGHT
SPENCER

"Come with me."

Those three words had my heart racing. I took London's hand, and a rush of heat went through me at her touch. She led us up the staircase, past two doors on the left, and stopped at the third.

Having seen London's bedroom in her New York apartment, I immediately recognized her style. The poster of "The Phantom of the Opera" on the wall was a dead giveaway.

"I'm sorry I didn't tell you before I left," she said quietly. "You deserved to hear it from me, not from your grandmother."

"After how she treated you, I don't blame you for running away," I said. "I was so angry when I heard what she said to you. I don't think I've ever been that furious at someone."

"I didn't leave because your grandmother was mean," London said, with a small smile playing around her lips.

"I'm a little confused then," I admitted.

"I was overwhelmed," London explained. "So many big

things happened within a short time, and everything your grandmother said was just the icing on the cake. It was too much. I needed space and time to think, but I couldn't do that in England. I needed to be somewhere familiar."

"Do you still need time?" I asked, trying not to assume anything. "I didn't say all that to pressure you into anything."

London smiled and shook her head. "You came for me," she said, moving closer and putting her hands on my chest. "You chose me."

"I did," I said, placing my hands on her hips. I loved the way her gentle curves felt under my touch. "I always will."

"I know we still have things to figure out," she said, "but that's just practicalities. I don't need more time to know what I want."

"And what is that?" I asked, giving her hips a gentle squeeze. "I need to know we're on the same page."

She stood on her tiptoes and lightly kissed my lips. "I choose you too."

That was all I needed to take her mouth in a passionate kiss. She leaned into me, parting her lips, and a warm wave of desire rushed through me. As I savored the taste of mint and chocolate on her tongue, I groaned, lifting her off the ground. Her legs wrapped around my waist as I deepened the kiss. I couldn't believe how much I had missed her, and it felt like an eternity since I had held her in my arms.

I walked us over to the bed and set her on the edge as I sank to my knees. Without taking my mouth from hers, I slid my fingers under the waistband of her adorable—and ridiculous—hedgehog pajama bottoms and tugged at them. She made a surprised sound but lifted her hips to allow me to pull off her pants. She took care of the top, leaving her in a pair of plain cotton knickers.

Her skin was hot as I ran my hands up her sides and around to cup her small, firm breasts. She moaned into my mouth as I flicked my thumbs back and forth across her nipples. They hardened under my touch, and I was filled with the sudden urge to have them in my mouth.

But not yet.

I pulled her to the edge of the bed and finally broke our kiss. I saw the dazed look on her face before I pulled off her lilac-colored underwear and dropped them on the floor. I didn't wait for her to regain her senses before I buried my face between her legs, licking right along her slit.

She let out a squeal that quickly became muffled. A glance up as I ran my tongue between her folds showed that she'd put her hand over her mouth. Smart. I intended to make her come, and the last thing we needed was her parents bursting in while I was doing it.

Increasing suction on her clit, I curled my fingers inside her core, carefully rubbing the tips against her top wall until I found what I was looking for. Her entire body jerked, and then, a moment later, she cried out, back arching off the bed as she climaxed.

Easing my fingers out of her, I stood, stripping off my clothes. By the time I finished, London had pushed herself onto the middle of the bed and looked up at me, only a thin ring of brandy-colored iris showing around wide pupils. I took a step toward the bed and stopped.

"What's wrong?" she asked.

"Condom," I said, reaching for my pants.

"I don't think I can get any more pregnant," she laughed.

The reality of the situation hit me then, and I sat down on the edge of the bed. "You're going to have a baby. We're going to have a baby."

She laughed again, this time a softer sound, and she wrapped her arms around me. "Yes, we are."

I looked at her. "Are you okay? Physically, I mean. I never even thought to ask if you're feeling up to it."

London kissed my cheek. "If I didn't feel like having sex, I would have said something. I feel fine. Either I'm one of those women who doesn't get morning sickness, or it hasn't hit me yet."

"Are you sure?" I asked. "I don't want you to do anything that could hurt the baby or-"

"Spencer." London reached down and wrapped her fingers around my flagging cock. Two firm strokes had me up and ready to go again, my stomach tightening in anticipation. "I need you inside me. Please."

That was all I needed to hear. In one quick move, I had her on her back, legs perfectly spread to let me settle between them. I paused one more moment, tucking a curl behind her ear.

"I love you."

She reached up and curled her hand around the back of my neck. "I love you, too."

As she pulled my head down for a kiss, I surged forward, filling her with one thrust. I drove deep, never taking my mouth from hers, even as she lifted her hips to meet me. We moved together as if we'd done this a million times, but it still felt as exciting as the first. The way we fit, how her body responded to mine. As we both found our pleasure together, one word echoed through my mind.

Love.

FORTY-NINE
LONDON

I must have fallen asleep after Spencer and I had sex, because the next thing I knew, I was waking up at eight-thirty to the smell of bacon.

I rubbed the sleep from my eyes as I made my way downstairs. The sight that greeted me was unexpected. Spencer stood at the stove, flipping bacon in a pan while chatting with my parents. They were all laughing and having a good time, and it felt like they had been friends for years.

"Good morning," I said, walking into the kitchen.

"Good morning, love," Spencer said, smiling at me. "I hope you're hungry. I made breakfast."

"I am," I said, smiling back at him. "And it smells amazing."

"It does," my mom added. "Spencer has been telling us about his life in England and how he's been trying to modernize his family's approach to things. He's quite the interesting young man."

"We're happy to hear that he's serious about you and

the baby," my dad said, nodding in agreement. "We want what's best for you."

I sat down at the table and took a deep breath, grateful for their support. It was a surreal moment, but I was ready to face whatever came next.

We spent the day in San Ramon making some important decisions, including flying back to New York the next day. Spencer had wanted me to take all the time I needed, but now my foot was completely healed, I was eager to get back on stage. By flying in on a Saturday, I'd have Sunday and Monday to adjust before Tuesday's performance.

We arrived in New York via a private plane in the afternoon and headed straight to my apartment. After settling in, we had a few calls to make when the doorbell rang.

"Hold on, Maggie," I said, taking my phone off my ear. "I think that might be someone at the door."

I walked over and hit the intercom button. "Hello?"

"Miss McCrae," the doorman's voice came through, sounding annoyed. "I have two women down here that want to speak with you."

"Not with her," a sharp female voice chimed in, not as clear but still recognizable. "I need to speak with my grandson."

It was Spencer's grandmother.

I sighed and hit the intercom button again. "Let them up," I said with resignation.

"Is someone here?" Spencer asked, coming out of the kitchen.

"Your grandmother," I replied.

Spencer's eyebrows raised. "Bloody hell."

"I'm not sure why we're surprised," I said with a sigh. "She's not exactly the type to let things go when they don't go her way."

"No," Spencer agreed. "She's not."

When I opened the door a minute later, however, Opal wasn't alone.

"Mum?" Spencer said, surprised.

Eloise's face was pale and drawn, with dark circles under her eyes more pronounced than the last time I saw her. She opened her mouth to speak, but Opal beat her to it.

"I see your manners are every bit as lacking as I would expect from a Scottish American," Opal sniffed.

I managed a tight smile. "Won't you both come in?"

"How did you know where London lives?" Spencer asked as his mother and grandmother entered the apartment.

"I'm guessing her private investigator had the information, and was probably watching, waiting to see if you would show up here," I replied.

"You have someone watching her?" Spencer's voice was quiet, but I could sense the irritation in it.

"I protect my family, Spencer," Opal declared. "Something you would do well to remember. Your mother and I have come here for that very reason." She looked around my apartment with obvious distaste.

"Before you start telling me what you think I need to do, I have a few things to say," Spencer said, taking my hand. "You already know that London and I are having a baby..."

Eloise's jaw dropped. "A baby?"

"You didn't tell her?" Spencer looked at his grandmother with surprise.

"You knew?" Eloise looked hurt.

"Don't be dramatic, Eloise," Opal said dismissively. "I only knew what she told me, and Americans have only a passing acquaintance with the truth."

Spencer stepped in. "That's enough. I won't tolerate you speaking about the woman I love like that."

My stomach flipped as I heard Spencer's words. He had told me that he loved me before, but there was something powerful about him saying it so confidently in front of his grandmother.

"Love?" Opal made a disdainful sound. "You have a duty to your family."

"I do," Spencer agreed. "London and the baby are my family."

Opal's lips thinned. "Well, your flat will do for now, I suppose. Once we move you out—"

"My flat?" Spencer's grip on my hand tightened. "She's not going to be my mistress. Soon, I'll ask her to be my wife."

My heart skipped a beat...or ten.

"It will be a proper proposal, I swear," he promised me softly.

"I'll hold you to that," I replied, feeling overwhelmed by his commitment.

"Enough!" Opal interrupted, her voice sharp. "I've had enough of this nonsense. You will do as I say."

"No, Grandmother," Spencer replied firmly. "I won't."

Opal took a step toward us, her expression determined. "Then you will no longer be a part of our family. Do you understand? I will disinherit you. Take everything from you."

Spencer stood his ground. "The fact that you think money and a title mean so much that I would leave the woman I love and our child shows that you never really knew me."

The pain in Spencer's voice cut through me. I couldn't understand a family behaving this way. No matter what my siblings or I did, we knew our parents would always have our backs.

"I'm not only talking about money," Opal continued. "You'll be disowned."

"No, he won't." Eloise's words were quiet but held a powerful impact.

"Pardon me?" Opal seemed shocked and offended.

"I will not disown my son for following his heart," Eloise spoke firmly, still looking tired but with newfound strength. "He will always be my son, and his family will always be my family."

"I'll have you cut off as well," Opal threatened. "I'll take everything."

"You may have convinced my late husband to give you the final say over money connected to the barony, but Raynard understood you better than you knew," Eloise said, coming over to stand next to Spencer. "Each of the children has an independent inheritance over which you have no control. And so do I."

"Do you truly think that you'll be able to survive on such a pittance? You both have spent your entire lives with wealth at your fingertips. Mark my words, once you're forced to limit yourselves, you'll take whatever terms I set," Opal said, her cool composure cracking as she became flushed.

"I think you've underestimated us," Spencer said confidently.

"I'll fight you in court for what my son left you," Opal threatened. "And you won't have the money to fight back."

"But I do," I interjected, catching their attention.

"You don't need to-" Spencer started, but I cut him off.

"If I'm your family, then you're mine," I stated, looking

into Spencer's eyes. "And I won't let anyone try to come between us."

Opal shook her head. "You have no idea what-"

"London's a multi-millionaire," Spencer informed.

Eloise and Opal both looked stunned as they gazed at me.

I shrugged nonchalantly. "I have a trust fund. I don't overspend, and I make excellent investments."

I had a bit more than Spencer was aware of, but I felt that disclosure might be too much for Opal to believe.

And right now, there was only one thing I wanted from that woman. "Now, this is my home, and you've said what you came to say," I said firmly. "If you don't plan to be a part of this family, it's time for you to leave."

No one had ever spoken to Opal like this before, judging by the expressions on everyone's faces.

"Excuse me?" Opal finally managed to say.

"It's time for you to go, Er, um...or *sod off,* as you English like to say." I plastered a sugar-sweet smile on my face. "In case you don't leave, I'll call building security and have them call the police. I won't hesitate to have you removed for trespassing and will make sure the press gets pictures, too."

Eloise made a sound that could've been a laugh, a cough, or just a general noise of surprise.

"And one more thing." I let go of Spencer's hand and took a step towards Opal. "If you come after my family or anyone I love, I'll use every penny and connection I have to make sure you regret it. Trust me, you don't want to know the extent of my reach." I gestured toward the exit. "Now, the door is over there."

Opal glared at me for a moment longer, as if trying to come up with a retort, but she finally spun on her heels and left the apartment without another word. As her footsteps faded away down the hall, I let out a deep breath that I didn't even realize I was holding. My hands were shaking with adrenaline, and my heart was pounding so hard that I could hear it in my ears. Despite feeling victorious, I couldn't shake the unease that came with standing up to someone like Opal.

FIFTY

SPENCER

GRANDMOTHER HAD WALKED OUT WITHOUT ANOTHER word, leaving my mother and I both shocked. When London turned to us, her cheeks were pink, but I wasn't sure if it was from embarrassment or the fading anger.

"What?" London asked.

I raised an eyebrow. "I've never seen my grandmother listen to anyone. Ever."

London shrugged. "I think I caught her off guard, that's all."

"You should be proud," my mother said. "You handled yourself beautifully."

"Thanks," London said, glancing at me with a questioning look.

I didn't have an answer for her, but I was still in awe of how she stood up to my grandmother.

"I'm sorry, London." My mom's voice was sincere. "I should have been better. I owe you an apology. Both of you."

"Mom, you don't have to—" I started.

"I do, Spencer," she interrupted. "I should have respected your choices. All of them."

She turned back to London. "From the moment I met you, I should have told you that my son was lucky to have you in his life. You're an exceptional young woman and I'm honored to have you in my family."

London smiled, her eyes bright with what I suspected were tears. "Thank you."

Mom looked at me. "Have you two decided where you'll be living?"

I looked at London, and when she nodded, I said, "Here. I believe we're planning on living here in New York."

My mum surprised me with a smile. "I've always wanted to spend some time in the Big Apple," she said.

"Really?" I raised an eyebrow.

"A change of scenery might do me some good," she continued. "I'll fly back home to sort things out with your sisters, then find a place to rent here. I want to be here for the arrival of my grandchild, after all."

London hugged her. "It'll be great to have you here with my mom being so far away," she said. "How about you staying for dinner tonight? Let's get to know each other better."

"I'd love that," my mum replied, her eyes shining.

As I placed the order for dinner, I couldn't help but feel grateful for the turn of events. Just a few hours ago, I was worried about the future of my relationship with London. Now, it seemed like everything was falling into place.

NEXT DAY, I walked into the crowded restaurant, scanning the room for Stan. He had asked me to meet him for lunch so I could get caught up on the current state of the musical. I spotted him and made my way over.

"Hey Spencer," Stan greeted me, standing up for a hug. "Glad you could make it on a Sunday. What's up?"

I took a seat across from him at our usual booth in the deli's corner. The aroma of pastrami and corned beef filled the air, making my stomach grumble.

"So, Tomma's done a good job filling in for London, right?" I asked, taking a bite of my sandwich.

Stan nodded, still chewing. "Yeah, she's gotten excellent reviews. But, to be honest, I'm glad London's back. Tomma got a little too big for her britches, spreading rumors."

I raised an eyebrow. "What kind of rumors?"

"I don't really know," Stan said with a shrug. "But Tomma's been causing a lot of tension backstage. The chemistry between Timothy and Tomma was great, but it doesn't hold a candle to the chemistry he had with London. Though, to be fair, that faded towards the end, right before London got hurt."

I felt a pang of guilt in my chest. I knew I was partly to blame for the tension between London and Timothy.

I sighed. "Well, I'll talk to Timothy. Make sure he knows that just because London and I are a couple now, it doesn't mean she can't act in a love scene with him on stage."

Stan chuckled. "I think he'll appreciate that."

"I'll make it right," I said, determined. "London and Timothy are both talented actors, and I won't let anything I've caused stand in the way of the show's success."

Stan clapped me on the back. "That's what I like to

hear, my friend. Let's make this show a hit musical that'll run on Broadway for decades."

I took a sip of my beer and grinned. "You got it. Let's do this."

FIFTY-ONE
LONDON

Tuesday was my first night back in the theater after my accident almost three weeks ago, and I was eager to get back on stage. I arrived early to go over my lines and choreography, but as I rehearsed a couple of dance moves on stage, I felt rusty. Afterwards, as I made my way to my dressing room, my nerves kicked in.

I settled into my chair to go over my script once again, when I heard a knock on the door. Tomma strolled in without waiting for an invitation, carrying a smirk on her face. I barely looked up from my script, but her next words caught my attention.

"London, dear," she said, her voice dripping with sarcasm. "You really should practice more. That was pathetic what you just did out there."

I stood up, my anger rising. It was clear she was in my dressing room just to get under my skin before the show.

"What are you doing, Tomma? Spreading more false rumors? I'm tired of hearing all the lies you've been telling everyone, including my best friend Mercedes."

Tomma chuckled. "London, dear, you always appear so

innocent. Don't even try to deny it. You want to make us think you got this lead role because of your talent? Ha! It's because you're sleeping with the producer. I know the truth, and let me tell you, tonight will be your last performance. So go ahead and sleep with whoever you want. I have things in motion, and soon no one will want to work with you."

With that, Tomma sauntered out of my dressing room, leaving me feeling shaken and unsure.

Fuck Tomma. She had been spreading false rumors about me for weeks, trying to sabotage my career from the first time she saw me.

As I drew a deep breath, I tried to calm myself, but Tomma's plan to ruin my career lingered in the back of my mind. Just then, Spencer walked in, his warm smile lighting up the room as he approached me.

"Good luck tonight, my love," Spencer said, giving me a warm hug and a sweet kiss. "I just know you're going to kill it out there."

I smiled, grateful for his support. "Thanks, honey. Let's hope so."

"And, hey," he continued, a twinkle in his eye. "After the show, I've got a little surprise planned for us. Something spicy, just for you."

His words made me feel better, and I couldn't help but smile. Despite my nerves, I was excited about the show and for what Spencer had in store for us later. Not wanting to cause any friction right before the show, I kept Tomma's visit to myself. I wouldn't let her words get to me and ruin my performance. I was determined to put on a great show, no matter what Tomma said or did.

Spencer left me alone to finish getting ready, and fifteen minutes later, when I made my way to the stage, I paused and pushed all thoughts of Tomma out of my mind. The lights were bright; the audience was buzzing with excitement, and I was ready. I was going to prove Tomma wrong and show her I was a talented actress who had earned my place in the spotlight.

Just then, Timothy stopped me. He looked upset and I could tell something was bothering him.

"Tomma just walked into my dressing room wearing nothing but a robe," he said, his voice shaking with anger. "She dropped the robe and offered me that if I told Darrel that I wanted her as my co-star instead of you, she would return the favor in a big way."

I wasn't surprised. With Tomma, I should have suspected something like that.

"She's lost her mind," he said. "I don't need her to get laid. And to be honest, I always preferred doing the scenes with you, not Tomma. And, hey! I never got to thank you for saving my sorry ass that day. That was a close call. Glad to see you're okay again."

With Timothy's words ringing in my ears, I took the stage, determined to give the performance of my life. Tomma's lies and manipulation had only made me more committed to prove her wrong.

I sang and acted with all my heart, giving it my all on stage, feeling a sense of pride and accomplishment, despite not knowing the impact of my performance and if Tomma's plan to ruin my career will be thwarted. But this was all I could do.

FIFTY-TWO
SPENCER

The theater was packed, the energy palpable as London and Timothy took the stage for the last duet of the show. I sat on the edge of my seat, my eyes fixed on London as she belted out the lyrics, her voice soaring through the auditorium. Timothy joined in, their voices melding together in perfect harmony. The audience erupted into applause as the song ended, and I found myself on my feet, cheering with the rest of the crowd.

But as the last notes died away, I still felt a pang of discontent shoot through me as London and Timothy shared a passionate kiss. "Stop it, Spencer. It is just acting," I told myself.

Shaking off my apprehension, I made my way backstage to congratulate everybody. As I approached Timothy, he beamed at me, his eyes shining with excitement. "We did it, Spencer! That was amazing, wasn't it?"

I smiled, pushing aside the jealousy that still lingered in my heart. "It was incredible. You two were really something up there. If I didn't know better, I would almost believe it wasn't an act."

Timothy's smile faltered a bit as he looked at me. "Are you okay with everything, Spencer? I mean, with the love scenes and all?"

I took a deep breath, trying to steady my emotions. "Of course, man. It's just acting. I know that."

Timothy nodded, looking relieved. "Good. I didn't want to cause any problems between you and London."

I shrugged. "No problems, Timothy. You just focus on the show, and let me worry about my own feelings."

Timothy's grin widened. "Thanks, man. I appreciate it. Listen, I need to talk to you about something."

I braced myself, wondering what was coming. Timothy's expression turned serious as he told me about Tomma's advances towards him. My blood boiled. It was clear that Tomma was still trying to push London away, so she could take the spotlight. For too long, she was getting away with it.

As soon as the conversation was over, I stormed off to find Darrel. No one messes with my friends, and especially not my girlfriend. I needed to take action, and fast.

I marched straight to Darrel's office, my heart pounding with a fierce determination.

"Darrel, we have a problem," I declared. "Tomma's been causing trouble."

He raised an eyebrow. "What kind of trouble?"

I didn't mince words as I told him about her inappropriate behavior towards Timothy.

We quickly agreed that it was time to let her go, and I volunteered to be the one to deliver the news. I needed to put an end to her scheming once and for all.

I made my way to Tomma's dressing room, my heart pounding with a mix of anger and determination. I knocked sharply on the door, and Tomma answered with a smirk on her face.

"What do you want, Spencer?" she sneered.

I cut to the chase. "Tomma, it's time for you to go. Your behavior towards Timothy earlier was completely inappropriate, and it's not something we tolerate on this show."

Tomma's face twisted into a sensual smile. "I see. Only producers get an exception. So, what's it going to take to make this all go away?"

I felt my stomach churn at the implication. "I want nothing from you, Tomma. You need to leave the theater immediately."

Tomma's expression hardened. "Fine. But if you ever change your mind, you know where to find me."

I felt a surge of anger at Tomma's words. "I will never change my mind, Tomma. What you did was wrong, and it's not something I take lightly."

Tomma chuckled, her voice dripping with venom. "Oh, you're such a hypocrite, Spencer. You're just trying to protect your little girlfriend."

I felt my fists clenching at my sides. "Watch your mouth, Tomma. You have no idea what you're talking about."

Tomma fired back. "Oh, I think I do. You're just like all the other Broadway big shots. You think you can do whatever you want, and nobody will call you out on it."

I stood my ground, refusing to let her intimidate me. "I'm not like that. And neither is anyone else on this show besides you. We're all here to create something special, not to indulge in petty drama."

Tomma rolled her eyes. "Sure, Spencer. Whatever you say. It's your loss."

As I watched her leave, I felt a sense of relief mixed with a lingering anger. I knew I had made the right decision.

FIFTY-THREE
LONDON

Last fall, my friends and I had pizza and beer at my place while we watched the Tonys. Tonight, Gin and Rocio were watching on television as Spencer and I, along with Mercedes and the rest of the cast, attended the live show.

Six nominations. Best Musical, Best Book of a Musical, best lead actor in a musical for Timothy, best costume design, best set design, and best lead actress in a musical.

Yeah, I was nominated for a Tony.

Even as Spencer held out a hand to help me out of the limo, I could barely believe it. Hell, the entire last year felt like a dream.

I'd picked up the week after we'd returned to New York and managed not to miss another day until two weeks ago, when I finally hit the point where even creative costuming couldn't hide the fact that I was pregnant. I was one of those women who didn't really 'pop' until later because I'd barely been showing through my whole pregnancy, and then it was like I woke up one morning and, bam, there it was.

Not for the first time, I was grateful my brother was a

fashion designer. Carson had outdone himself this time, designing something that he could make quick alterations to this morning, so it fit perfectly for the show tonight.

Still, I couldn't help looking at Mercedes in her gorgeous deep blue dress and five-inch heels and thinking that no matter how good my brother was, I still looked like a beached whale compared to the other 'beautiful people' here.

"You're blazing smashing," Spencer said in my ear.

"What?"

He smiled at me and kissed my temple. "I know what you're thinking, luv, and you're just as beautiful as your friend."

"You're biased," I pointed out. "We live together, and you're partly responsible for my appearance tonight."

He chuckled. "I suppose you're right."

"At least your son isn't tap dancing on my bladder today," I said, putting a hand on my belly.

"London," Timothy was suddenly in front of us. "They want pictures of us together."

"Of course." I took his arm and let him lead me to where several members of the press were waiting. "You look nice tonight."

"So do you." He smiled, the expression once again easy with me.

Oddly enough, I had Tomma to thank for Timothy and me finding our chemistry again. Without her to cause drama, Timothy and I had quickly found back to the sparks from the early days.

"I hear Lily is doing well," I said to Timothy as we posed for pictures. Lily was my new understudy, taking over my part until after my delivery.

"She is," he said. "Not as good as you, but headed in

that direction with a little more polish." He glanced at me. "How are you and Spencer doing?"

I couldn't stop what I knew to be a wholly besotted smile. "We're great."

"Remind me, when are you due?"

"October sixteenth," I said. "Less than a month."

"Well, you look good." Timothy offered me his arm again and took me back to where Spencer was waiting. They nodded at each other before Timothy excused himself and returned to his date, a preschool teacher from Queens who looked a little overwhelmed by the attention.

I made a mental note to have a word with her at some point this evening to help ease her nerves. She seemed like a sweet woman, and Timothy, despite his arrogance, was a decent man. She might even temper that bit of him.

Spencer and I made our way past the press, stopping every so often to answer a question or pose for a picture. By the time we reached our seats, my feet were killing me, and I was more than ready to sit down.

"Are you all right?" Spencer asked, concern on his face. "We can leave. I'm sure everyone will understand."

I shook my head. "I'll just slip my shoes off and hope I remember to put them back on when the show wins Best Musical."

"I'm sure everyone will forgive you if you forget when you win Best Actress."

I laughed as I took off my shoes and tucked my feet under the seat in front of me. "We all know Bebe Neuwirth is going to win tonight. And she deserves it."

"Maybe," Spencer said. "But you're wicked good too."

I reached over and took his hand, smiling as everyone settled around us. The music played, and excitement chased away my discomfort. I was here at the Tonys, sitting behind Aaron Tveit, about to watch the opening number.

Then, before I knew it, Myles Frost and Rob McClure were announcing the nominees in my category, and Spencer had my hand gripped tight in his, waiting for the inevitable moment.

"And the winner is...London McCrae!"

For two heartbeats, I couldn't react. My brain refused to process what I heard because it couldn't be real. Then the crowd's applause broke through, and there, underneath it, was Spencer's voice, telling me that he was proud of me.

And to put on my shoes.

I clung to his arm as he helped me up and to the stage, not releasing him when I reached the stairs. With a smile, he got me the rest of the way, then stood aside to let me step up to accept the award. A moment later, I was at the microphone.

"Um, wow. This is...this is...." I shook my head. "Sorry. Usually, when I'm on stage, someone else has already written the words for me to say."

I heard laughter from in front of me, but the familiar sound of Spencer's chuckle grounded me and allowed me to gather myself enough to continue speaking.

"First, I have to say what an honor it is to be nominated with such an amazing group of women. I know people say all the time that they didn't expect to win, but I really didn't. I need to thank my parents, who always believed in me, and my siblings, who know why I don't list you all by name. Thank you to my friends, as well as the cast and crew. And, of course, thank you to Spencer." I looked at him and held up the award. "This is the second-best thing this show has brought to me. The best is you. I love you."

My throat closed with all the emotion flooding through me, but that was okay. I'd finished my speech.

By the night's end, I felt like I was walking on clouds. Besides my win, we also won Best Musical. Mercedes was practically giddy. Our phones had been blowing up with congratulations all night, but it wasn't until Spencer and I got back into the limo that I even looked at it.

"Mum says Gin's going out to get some more champagne," Spencer said. "They want to make sure we have enough for the toast when we get to the party." He glanced at me. "Sorry, sparkling cider for you, luv."

As the car pulled into traffic, Spencer turned toward me, setting his phone on the seat behind him. "Before we arrive, I'm hoping we can have a moment to talk."

I put my phone aside, curious. "Of course."

He smiled as he took something out of his pocket. "I promised that it'd be a proper proposal when I did this."

My breath caught in my throat as I realized what he was holding.

"London McCrae, you're the love of my life and the mother of my child. I want to spend the rest of my life with you. Will you marry me?"

I nodded, unable to speak for a moment. "Yes," I finally managed to say. "Yes, I'll marry you!"

I didn't even look at the ring as he slid it onto my finger. All I cared about was that I was going to marry the man I loved.

FIFTY-FOUR
SPENCER

I still couldn't quite believe it. My son was nearly two months old, and even now, there were times I found myself looking at him and wondering how lucky I was. A lovely fiancée, an award-winning show on Broadway, and a healthy child.

A loud wail came from where the priest was dripping water on my son's head, making everyone chuckle. Even the more serious members of my family.

Well, the most serious ones here, anyway. One particularly prominent and angry family member was *not* here.

I hadn't spoken to Grandmother since she left London's apartment that day. Through my siblings, I knew she'd been furious that I'd kept the barony and even more so when her barrister couldn't find any way to take it from me. I hadn't even bothered trying to take legal action regarding the money connected to the barony, which pissed her off even more.

Alexander stopped crying as soon as they handed him over to London, his little face still red from the effort. Mum cooed at him, making little noises. He had her wrapped around his little finger.

"Are we done yet?" Jane asked, her voice easily carrying through St. Mary's.

A chuckle ran through our observers, and Fleur's cheeks flushed. Parker reached over and picked up his daughter, answering her in tones too hushed for anyone to make out.

I'd been a tad surprised Fleur had come around once Mum assured her that London wasn't after our money. I doubted my oldest sister and I would ever be close, but I had to admit that choosing me over Grandmother meant something to me. She'd told Mum that our father's death had made her rethink her family's importance to her.

Less than thirty minutes later, London, Alexander, and I walked into the hall we rented for today's dinner. The caterers had everything prepared and ready to go by the time we arrived, and I made a mental note to talk to London about confirming them for our wedding in the spring. Everything smelled blinding fantastic.

It didn't take long for everyone to settle at their tables, and as quick as Bob's your uncle, I thanked them all for coming. I wasn't the only one who was hungry. London took care of feeding Spencer while I went to the food and made a plate for both of us.

"I see my nephew has London's fondness for the spotlight," Carson said as he came up behind me.

I chuckled. "Considering how much applause he heard while London was pregnant, it's not surprising."

"I got a call on Friday from one of your theater friends," Carson continued. "They want me to create designs for their entire cast. Twelve of them."

"Will you do it?"

He shrugged. "I asked for the weekend to think about it.

I never saw myself as a costume designer, but I enjoyed doing the work for you."

We talked for a few more minutes as we finished filling our plates and then went our separate ways. I hadn't gone far before another of my soon-to-be brothers-in-law stopped me.

"I heard that you're coming to San Ramon for Christmas." The man standing before me had blue eyes and a scar through his right eyebrow. This McCrae brother was Alec, the one who ran MIRI out of Seattle.

"We are," I said. "Any advice?"

"Don't bring alcohol," he said. "Brody always brings his newest whisky and Theresa makes the best eggnog. You'll end up the butt of jokes."

"Chocolate or fruit cake then?" I asked.

"Does anyone actually eat fruitcake?" Alec laughed. "Chocolate. Canna go wrong with an assortment."

"Thanks," I said. "Now, I need to leg it over to your sister before she murders me. There'll be no Christmas chocolate if I'm dead."

He laughed again, and I moved around him to put a plate in front of London.

"Are my brothers harassing you?" she asked. "I've told them to behave themselves."

I shook my head. "They've all been lovely."

"Just wait until Christmas when they're *all* together," she warned. "They feed off each other."

"Speaking of feeding." I gestured to her plate. "Bon appétit."

"If you keep feeding me like this, I'll never fit into my wedding dress," she warned me.

"Your brother made same-day alterations to the dress you wore to the Tonys," I reminded her.

She glared at me but dug into the food I'd brought her while I bounced my son the way he liked. It was strange how content I was right now. Living in New York with a fiancée and a baby was *not* what I'd pictured for my life, but I wouldn't want it any other way.

"You're thinking awfully hard about something," London said.

"Do you realize you auditioned for me one year ago today?" I asked.

She looked startled, then thought for a moment before laughing. "No, I didn't. Wow." She shook her head. "You know, if you would've told me, after I finished that first awful audition, that I'd be sitting here like this in a year's time, I would've said you were crazy ...or bonkers as you Brits would say."

She leaned in, tickled the baby's cheek, and spoke to him in that tone meant for babies, "Bonkers...yes, you'll have to learn what your daddy means with all his British words, yes you will."

"I rather fancy my British way of saying things." I chuckled, brushed a finger across my son's plump cheek, then leaned over and gave London a light kiss. "But I wouldn't have it any other way."

"Me either." She held out her hands for our son, and I passed him over.

I paused for a moment to be thankful for everything. I wasn't naïve enough to think that everything would always be smooth sailing for the rest of our lives, but I would get through it because I had all I ever needed and more right here.

THE END

OFFICE ROMANCES BY M. S. PARKER

Printed in Dunstable, United Kingdom

65569802R00208